ONE DAY I'LL FLY AWAY

NICK EVETTS

UKBookPublishing.com

Copyright © Nick Evetts, 2023

The moral right of this author has been asserted.

All rights reserved.

All characters and events in this publication, other than those clearly in the public domain, are fictitious and any resemblance to real persons, living or dead, is purely coincidental.

No part of this publication may be reproduced, stored in a retrieval system, or transmitted, in any form or by any means, without the prior permission in writing of the publisher, nor be otherwise circulated in any form of binding or cover other than that in which it is published and without a similar condition including this condition being imposed on the subsequent purchaser.

Cover design by H.A. Dudley

Editing, typesetting and publishing by UK Book Publishing

www.ukbookpublishing.com

ISBN: 978-1-916572-50-8

ONE DAY I'LL FLY AWAY

*This is for my children Jacob, Hannah, and Harriet,
who are now, and always have been, my pride*

CHAPTER ONE

Dire Straits' Romeo and Juliet was playing barely audibly on the sound system as he pushed open the scruffy and scuff-marked wooden door and ambled into the small quayside pub.

The small estuary town that he knew and loved so well was much quieter than he had ever seen or remembered it. Mid-May and the place appeared to be only slowly emerging from its winter slumbers. He had been able to find a slot for the car with ease in the usually congested town car park, and standing and stretching after so long hunched over the steering wheel, he decided that a quick drink was required, if for no better reason than to clear his head, shake his befuddled mind into some kind of rational thought.

It was the typical small pub lounge that he had expected. Bars in the middle of the day always wore that unkempt and uncared for look, dowdy and gloomy, like an ageing courtesan who looked mysterious and glamourous in the soft lights of the evening, but in the harsh light of morning just looked old and unkempt. The midday lack of customers showed up the dust and grime in the almost empty space like the evening never did.

A handful of lunchtime drinkers were sitting disconsolately at small dark wooden tables, one or two were leaning against the bar. At a table against the far window a young couple gazed lovingly into each other's eyes, oblivious to their surroundings. He envied them immediately their absorption – nothing was going to enter their world save themselves. In the darkest corner a gaming machine winked and clucked its presence but went unheeded.

A shaft of sharp spring sunlight penetrated the gloom, angling across the room like a white bar, signalling that the rain, which had persisted all morning, had now moved on, and sunlight was streaming from between the rain clouds. The dust motes that swam within its beam swirled and danced in the draught.

He sighed and shuffled up to the bar, scanning the brightly lit optics along the shelf as he did so. What would it be? Gin, Scotch, a Jack Daniels, Vodka? 'No, come on, mate,' he said to himself, 'that's not a good idea.'

He was depressed and not a little confused. Should he go on with this? He did not know. His eyes ached and so did his back; he had been driving for hours. The endless motorway relentlessly heading south, the inane chatter from the succession of radio DJs, the noise of the car, the roar of the tyres, and the constant drone of the other traffic. He was fatigued and knew it. He needed a drink and to sit down. He must think.

CHAPTER ONE

The young barmaid had a pleasant face, framed as it was by a bob of peroxide blonde hair. Her smile he knew was a professional tool, but it seemed almost genuine, and he returned it as he felt in his pocket for money.

"What can I get you, my lovely?"

"A beer please. What do you have?"

She indicated three or four garish plastic badges atop the taps and recommended one.

"OK," he said, "that's fine."

Placing a frothing plastic glass in front of him, she named the price, and he handed over the change absently. He needed fresh air, he felt claustrophobic. 'It's gloomy in here' – he could hear his wife say it as clear as if she were standing next to him. Irritation and guilt flared side by side and he shoved the thought aside.

"Can I take this outside?"

"Surely." She nodded. "It's in plastic anyway. I thought you might want to do that." She could have been pretty with a little effort, her smile again seemed genuine.

"Thanks," he said, and picking up his beer walked out through the door into the sunlight that now seemed too bright, forcing him to squint. The call and squawk of the seagulls was loud and raucous out here, and the sounds of outboard engines on the water grated on his nerves. Somewhere in the distance children were laughing and shouting.

He needed to make some decisions. God, he was tired, dispirited, sad. He wasn't himself at all, he knew that for a fact. He needed quiet time. There was only one free bench right near to the edge of the quay, so he sat wearily down and gazed at the sluggish estuary water that lapped the wall ten feet below. 'Had he done the right thing?'

What else could he do? 'You could have stayed and grown a pair, David.' He could hear his dear old dad saying it. How long had his father been dead? God knew. He was too tired to work it out. He really missed the old man's sage, well-meaning advice. He missed a lot of things.

He rubbed his eyes irritably, and absently reached for his beer, lifting it to his lips.

"Oogh what the hell?"

The complaint was loud and directed at no one. The taste of the hell's brew he had been sold was revolting. Flat and lifeless with a vague hint of dishwater – he just stopped himself from spitting it out but swallowed quickly and peered owlishly at the brown swirling liquid through the clear plastic glass.

"Bloody awful, isn't it?" The female voice was light and unaccented, friendly. He looked around and noticed for the first time a young woman sitting on the quay a few feet away, leaning against a bollard, her jeaned legs dangling over the water.

He grunted a friendly assent and forced himself to smile. "Bloody awful." His response was one of those unrehearsed automatic replies one utters without thinking. Banal, unconvincing.

"They sell three beers in these parts and two of them are absolutely disgusting." She laughed, a light carefree

CHAPTER ONE

sound, and he copied her without thought. She was pretty, he noticed: curly, unruly dark brown hair, shoulder length, framing a small aquiline, fine-featured face. A hint of freckles browsed across her nose. The white chunky jumper she was wearing reflected the sunlight onto her face, and its size emphasized her petite body.

He glanced away before she noticed he was looking, and ruefully remembered a good-natured quote from one of his old friends from a million years ago. 'They always know you're looking, mate. Bastards.' He smiled despite himself at the memory.

"Which one do you recommend then?" A banal conversation about local beers? Really? Was that what he needed?

She named the brand and turned away to gaze once more over the water. A small ferry boat carrying perhaps half a dozen tourists nudged busily up to the wall and disgorged its passengers. The boatman looked around and seeing that no one was waiting to jump aboard, tied up his small craft and loped off down the road for a sandwich.

Well, if she did not want to continue the conversation that was OK, he wasn't going to push it, he needed quiet. He needed to think things through. After an interval she turned to look at him once more. "Tourist?" she mouthed. "I haven't seen you around before."

He shook his head a little disconcerted at this direct question from a stranger. "No." He took another swig of the beer before he remembered not to, and with a grimace put down the plastic glass. "I've only just arrived actually. Been on the road for hours. Thought to have a beer even though I never drink at this time of the day, well not for a long time." The old cynical voice inside his head said, 'Dave, shut the hell up for Christ's sake.'

Whatever question she was tempted to ask she refrained and just nodded instead, waiting for him to continue, but he didn't. She sipped her own drink, and he noticed that her fingernails were painted black with just one painted a green. Why do women do that? He thought. He'd noticed the trend a lot recently. Was it some fashion statement he'd missed? He was getting past it and with a small flare of irritation pushed the thoughts of age aside.

The door of the pub swung open behind him as a man in overalls came out. The music had changed, and he caught a bar or two of Adele singing 'Set fire to the rain'. They had been to see her in concert in London. How long ago was that? He couldn't remember. Had he done the right thing? Again, he asked himself the same question, and again shied away from answering. He realised she was speaking to him once more. She had half turned around to lean against the bollard so that she could address him without craning her head. He noticed she had just a hint of lipstick on and the barest brush of eyeshadow. Just enough makeup to accentuate her prettiness, but not enough to appear as if she were trying. The ghost of a smile crossed his face as he realised that he had noticed all these things without conscious thought. 'You're still not over the hill yet, mate,'

CHAPTER ONE

he realised. She was talking again, and he had not heard.

"Sorry," he mouthed. "What did you say?"

She smiled at his apology and shook her head. "That's OK. I asked if you had a fag?"

"No," he said. "Don't smoke." He realised that this sounded a little unfriendly so added, "Anyway I thought young people were all against that type of thing."

"What type of thing?"

"Well, you know, smoking, meat eating, and so on. Following the ways of the greenies, and what's her name? Greta something."

"Oh please," she groaned. "I like smoking, right. Not many, just now and again, and I like a drink as well. It's all about moderation, isn't it?" She smiled at him; her face open, uncomplicated.

He nodded absently. "I suppose you're right." Feeling he should save face a little he added somewhat lamely, "I do have the occasional cigar."

"Have you got one with you now?" The small breeze moved her hair away from her face and he noticed that her eyes were green. Again, he was irritated by the things he registered without wanting to.

"One small one," he said. "Time was when I smoked expensive cigars but that was long ago when the world was young."

She laughed at his choice of phrase. "Oh yes," she chuckled. "When there was a lot of horse-drawn traffic around and you had to hail a Hansom cab as you went home."

She had a sense of humour, this young stranger, and ruefully he realised that she was correct. One of his old mates lectured him constantly about always referring to himself as old. But it was how he felt, he couldn't help that, but a man wasn't old in his early forties was he?

They exchanged a few more inconsequential pleasantries as total strangers do. After a while he began to feel a little better, a little less anxious. Perhaps it was the fresh air and the sunshine, or perhaps it was talking to this good-looking young woman with her frank, friendly gaze. He levered himself up off the bench. "Look, I'm off to get a proper drink to get rid of the taste of this crap. When I get back, I'll share a cigar with you." He almost hoped in a way that she would take offence at his brisk tone and bugger off. He wanted to be by himself, to think, to rest. "My name's Dave by the way." Inanely he held out his hand.

She looked up and shook it briefly, amused at the formality. "I'm Helen. Hi."

Without looking back, he strode over to the swing door of the pub and shouldered his way inside. It was Ed Sheeran playing now, droning on about his bed sheets smelling like someone.

Standing at the bar he gazed at his reflection in the mirrors that backed the upturned bottles of spirit on the shelves. A haggard, pale, worn face peered back at him from between the Scotch, gin and vodka. His old work shirt looked crumpled, and his tie was at half-mast and awry. He had noticed some months ago that his dark blond hair

CHAPTER ONE

was getting streaks of grey in it as though he had run ash-covered fingers through it. 'Bloody hell, mate,' he said to himself, 'you look washed up.'

Outside she rose and sat on one end of the bench in case someone else should claim it. She was bored, and a bit down this morning. It was her day off and she had nothing to do, and no one to do it with. Six months ago, she would have relished such a day, but not now.

What was she doing talking to this guy? Was she flirting? No, definitely not, she considered, not her style at all. Idly she gazed across the estuary at the small, jumbled village on the other side of the water. Picture book in its setting, the steep fields behind it, glowing emerald in the sharp sunlight. She breathed in the slight ozone smell on the breeze. Raising one knee, she clasped her hands around it and thought about the rest of the day. She used to like being alone, sought it, but that was then. She felt old and lonely today. She was thirty next month. Thirty wasn't old, was it? Of course not. Irritated with herself she released her leg and reaching into the back pocket of her jeans brought out her mobile phone to check for messages. Nothing as usual. You'd think at least her mom would have called or texted or something. She hadn't heard from her in over a week. True that they had bickered and sniped at each other during their last conversation, but nothing out of the ordinary in that. 'Dad sends his love,' her mom had told her. 'Can't he tell me himself?' had been her caustic reply met with the familiar tetch of annoyance from the other end of the phone. There had been further conversation but about what she could not remember. Anyway, that was some days ago now, and nothing since. She replaced the phone into her pocket and stifled a yawn.

Where had that guy gone? Had he disappeared to find a better drink somewhere else? He looked all in. Dowdy clothes, pale, drawn face.

His movements were jerky as if he was having to think about what he said, or how to move his arms and legs. She should have just sat quietly and enjoyed her own drink – why had she spoken at all, would she never learn?

A hand appeared over her shoulder holding a small plastic glass of vodka. "Thought I'd get you another of those whilst I was there, I noticed you were almost empty. I guessed vodka, but it's just occurred to me it could be gin."

He slumped down next to her and took a large swig of what appeared to be an enormous scotch. "That's better."

She stammered her thanks. "It was gin, but vodka's fine, thank you."

She sipped delicately, feeling the warmth of the drink make its way down her throat. A large fishing trawler was crawling past them in mid-channel, heading upriver, coming in from the sea; a swarm of seagulls hovered around its stern, littering its wake, hoping for scraps to be thrown overboard. An expensive looking yacht was motoring the other way; three or four young men all dressed alike in matching blue and grey waterproofs were busy around the deck readying the boat for the sail ahead.

CHAPTER ONE

"So," he said, "are you a local? You don't seem to have the accent."

She gave a half laugh. "No. Much as I like this place, I'm not sure I could live here. I have a six-month contract with the local council cataloguing all the hundreds of items in the small-town museum." Why on earth had she volunteered that information to a total stranger, she wondered, irritated with herself.

He turned his head to look at her; this close he could detect the faint aroma of the subtle perfume she was wearing. "Really? Don't you have to be, well you know, qualified to do something like that? How do you know what you are looking at?" He sipped his drink again.

He seemed to have difficulty concentrating, she thought. His movements were still jerky, his eyes restless.

"I am qualified, you cheeky bugger." She smiled to dilute the rebuke. "Courtesy of a degree in archaeology hard earned years ago."

"Oh, I see," he stammered. Why had he assumed that she worked in a supermarket or something similar? He realised he had pre-judged her, a trait he always abhorred in other people. "Sorry." He smiled. "No offence intended."

His smile was infectious, and she returned it without thought. "It's OK, it's my day off so slouching around in an old jumper and jeans is what I like to do." She pulled at the neck of her sweater. "When I'm working, I'm a bit more formal."

He nodded amiably and they chatted on about nothing for some minutes. Non-committal, informal. Easy. She had obviously taken the state of his clothes, he thought, and been too polite to mention it. After a while conversation faltered and finished with her mouthing the usual stale phrases that people use when they cannot think of anything else to say.

"What a lovely day."

He nodded and gazed out at the water, knowing what would come next, and it did.

She turned towards him, leaning her elbow on the back of the bench. "And you? You did not answer me, what are you doing here, you look a bit out of place if you don't mind me saying. This bench, this quayside, not exactly the place to be wearing suit trousers, a shirt and a tie, is it? If you worked in the local estate agents or something I would have noticed you about in these last months."

He was unsure how to answer. This was a total stranger, after all. He shuffled his feet awkwardly and then made the decision to be honest.

"Fuck it!" he said as he decided to tell the truth. "I've run away." His half laugh was embarrassment.

She coloured under her light tan. "Oh God, I'm so sorry, I didn't mean to pry."

He chuckled despite himself. 'Of course you did,' he thought, but just smiled.

She leaned slightly forward, a playful glint in her eyes. "So, what do you mean, run away? From whom, from what?"

He shook his head just slightly. "Listen, Helen, don't ever get married, don't have kids, and don't ever be forty-two." He looked away towards the estuary mouth where the

CHAPTER ONE

river collided with the sea and gave a small cough to hide his discomfort. He had already said more than he intended.

"Look," she said, realising he was not going to say anything further, "I didn't mean to be rude. It's none of my business."

He held up his hand and smiled. "It's OK, not your fault, it's no big secret."

He needed to collect his thoughts before he said more.

"So, you're forty-two then?" she said lamely.

He gave a small, harsh laugh. "Brilliant, Sherlock, it's easy to see you're intelligent." It was said without malice. "No wonder you have a good job." Why on earth did he say that? He did not know this good-looking girl. This was just pub chat, wasn't it?

She took a small sip of the vodka and smiled. He was nice, this stranger. No great looker but nice, had a good sense of humour and friendly eyes, although they looked tired. Not the hard calculating arrogant eyes of many of her male contemporaries.

He was smiling at her. "Sorry again," he said, embarrassed at his mild reprimand. "Yep," he began. "Forty-two, no prospects, no money, and now no family."

Did she detect sorrow in that voice or just resignation? "What do you mean, no family?"

He took a deep breath and looked straight at her. "I told you I've run away. Bailed out like the coward I am, just left. I got up this morning, made the wife a coffee, looked in on the kids' bedrooms to check they were OK, had a coffee myself." He paused for a sip of scotch, but the words were coming faster now; he needed to tell his story to someone, anyone. "Got dressed as usual in one of my two work suits, backed the car off the drive, but when I got to the main road just… turned the wrong way and came down here." He shrugged. "So here I am four hours and two hundred miles later." His hand, she noticed, was trembling slightly as he rubbed his eyes. "I have the car, and about one hundred and fifty quid in my pocket – I went to the cashpoint before I left my hometown, how's that for calculating?" He looked down at his drink. "And I have a large scotch."

She hoped this was not going to get embarrassing – this guy, nice or not, was obviously carrying a lot of baggage. Did she want to get involved? She knew her nosiness and empathy had gotten her into trouble with guys in the past, but this man was not what she was used to. Despite herself, she had to carry on talking; it was irresistible.

"You'll go back," she said breezily. "Probably later today when you have calmed down. We all have more control over our lives than we imagine."

He snorted derisively. "Yeah sure. I've heard it all before, usually spouted by young people who believe all this crap they hear from idiots on the TV. Amateur philosophers. 'All you've got to do is want something badly enough and you can have it, right'?" His laugh was harsh. "Wrong, so wrong." He was getting warmed up now, old rancour at the injustice of the world tainting his voice. "That and other crap like 'The harder you work the luckier you get'. Heard

CHAPTER ONE

that one? Absolute rubbish. All I've ever found is the harder you work the more tired you get. Now *that* is the truth, young lady, believe it."

He knew he should stop there but now he had voiced his shaky catechism he had more to add. "To mis-quote a line from some old film 'you're never going to get what you want in life, that's just a wish list to make it seem like there's more to life than the shit we got stuck with'." He stopped abruptly, appalled at his own lack of control. He grinned sheepishly, took another sip of scotch, and looked away.

She swigged back what remained of her drink and prepared to leave. This was getting too heavy. It was her day off, for Christ's sake. Her tone was brisk. "That sounds really cynical; I'm sorry, but it does."

His head jerked around to look at her as if he had forgotten she was there. "My wife always tells me that," he said. "'You're so cynical, so judgemental all of the time'. I can hear her saying it now."

A battered scruffy van pulled up behind them, delivering to the pub, and an old man in a baker's striped apron and straw boater jumped out and opened the back doors. "Morning Helen! How are you today, my lovely?" he called.

"I'm fine, thank you," she mouthed back and laughed a light carefree sound.

"Not working today?" He was getting a large basket of something from the back of his van. He had the calm assurance of someone who knows his place in the world and is comfortable with it. He waved at an old woman crossing in front of his vehicle and she waved back.

"No," called Helen. "Day off, things to do, people to see." She giggled.

He laughed and waving a cheery hand disappeared through the pub door.

"You're well known, it seems," smiled David, glad of a change of subject and seizing on it.

"Yeah," she said. "A small cottage comes with the contract, it's down there near the water." She pointed vaguely up the estuary. "It's small and run down, but it suits me."

He wanted to stay away from his own problems so hurried on. "So what's your story, why here?"

It was her turn to shrug. "Why not here? It beats a single bedsit in Reading and a benefits cheque. A degree doesn't guarantee the wonderful life they promise you, does it, and a summer living here appealed to me, rather than working at a fast food takeaway. No friends here, of course, but back home they're all married now with young kids anyway." Her voice faltered.

"And you're not?" The question hung in the air. He was appalled at his audacity. Why had he said that? It was none of his business, for Christ's sake. She would now tell him to bugger off, he knew it. But she did not. Doubt flitted across her face. Did she want to share old hurts with this stranger, she thought. Oh, what the hell.

"Married and divorced within eighteen months," she said. "Seems his idea about marriage vows and mine didn't

CHAPTER ONE

match. Keeping only to each other didn't compute with him. My parents wanted me to move back in with them afterwards but sod that. Three years away at university and then three years with a home of my own – there was no way I was going back to live with them." A sudden thought occurred to her. "Hey we were going to share a cigar, weren't we?"

He realised she wanted to end this line of conversation quickly, and he agreed with her. He pulled the battered small cheroot in question out of the top pocket of his shirt. He lit it, and after taking a long drag passed it to her. He felt urbane and dangerous sharing a smoke with a pretty girl he hardly knew.

The sun had come out properly now and was quite warm on his shoulders. The clouds had melted away and the few that were left were drifting slowly over the horizon. A light breeze had arisen, and several small sailing dinghies from the outward-bound school were zig-zagging their way upstream, teenage voices calling to each other as they made a race of it. It was a pleasant scene, and one could drift away into lethargy just watching.

Suddenly he remembered where he was and what he should be doing instead of loafing on a bench talking to a pretty, young stranger.

"Keep it," he said suddenly, pointing at the cigar. "I've got to go." He stood up jerkily and peered around him, seeking inspiration. She looked surprised at this complete change of subject.

"That was sudden," she said. Why was it she felt comfortable enough to say that to this guy?

"I've just realised I've got to find somewhere to sleep, and I could do with buying another shirt." Talking to this girl had dulled his senses a little or was it the large scotch? He could have sat here all day thinking of nothing in particular, and talking about trivia. But he couldn't, he knew that. He must make some plans, some kind of order. What the hell had he done?

Her face hardened unexpectedly. "Oh please," she snarled. "Really? Really?"

Genuinely puzzled, he could only manage: "Pardon me?" Where the hell had he put his car keys? He was rummaging in his pockets. He felt a flare of panic as he realised, he did not have his mobile either, then remembered he had thrown it out of the car window onto the hard shoulder of the motorway as he passed Exeter.

"Do you honestly think I would fall for that?" She affected a southern American accent: "Why sure, mister, you can come and stay at my place. A warm bed, good food and all the sex you can handle. Jesus, give me a break." She took a long drag on the cigar and blew out a stream of smoke which carried away on the breeze.

His mouth sagged open in surprise. What was she talking about? A middle-aged couple passing arm in arm had heard her outburst and peered suspiciously at him as they walked on. He was stunned into a sharp reply.

CHAPTER ONE

"What on earth are you talking about. If you think for one moment..."

She held up her hand to stay his outburst, realising too late that she had misjudged him. "Sorry," she said. "Sorry, but it's been tried before."

He was not placated; his face was pale with anger. "Not by me it hasn't." He turned away abruptly and ambled across the road. "See you," he called over his shoulder.

She had been wrong, and she knew it, he seemed a nice man, something she was not really used to, and she had probably misconstrued his comment; it would not be the first time. She was not as streetwise as she liked to think. Quick, what could she say to put it right.

"If you really can't find anywhere by tonight," she called after his disappearing back, "my cottage is down there." Ridiculously, because he was not looking, she pointed. "It has a purple door." She was not sure if he had heard as he turned around a corner of the pub and disappeared.

"Brilliant, Helen," she mouthed to herself. "Put your foot in it again with your big mouth, babe." She took a last hopeful sip from her already empty glass and sighed ruminatively. What could she do to fill her time this afternoon?

***

Pam decided that she would stop for a coffee soon. Her back was aching, and she felt as if her backside had gone to sleep during the length of time she had been sitting on this bloody dining room chair. Hunched over the laptop on the dining room table in front of her and with the bloody phone headpiece clamped across her head, she felt like some latter day Quasimodo. She had been promoting and trying to sell kitchen gadgets for three hours now and had only sold one item which she calculated would bring in about £3.50 in commission.

The kids had been difficult this morning and they had all left for the short drive to school ten minutes late. The rain had soaked her sandaled feet before she had gone a few yards from the car – where the hell were her boots? – and little Petey kept complaining his knee hurt. Darcy kept up her non-stop chatter about her teddy bear collection and she realised that she had not put a juice bottle into the little girl's knapsack. How was it that some women arrived at the school gates looking as if they had just stepped out of a hairdresser? Perfectly dressed, clean, tidy, obviously in control, with kids looking the same? Perhaps it was her? Perhaps she was a complete fuck-up as a mom? She was always resentful when, their job done for the day, or at least until they had to collect their kids again mid-afternoon, they felt perfectly entitled to stand around for a gossip before heading home for their first coffee. Her resentment flared again as she thought about it now, but the problem was that once in a million years when she had the chance to stand with them, they were all annoyingly pleasant. There were no Mrs Bouquets amongst them droning on about their latest new car or where they had booked their latest

CHAPTER ONE

holiday. They were just, well, pleasant. Intelligent women in the main who had their lives under control and were happy with who they were.

She stood up and stretched, realising she needed the loo. Why was it, she reflected as she plugged in the kettle, that life was so random with its gifts?

How come some people struggled all their lives whilst others seemed to drift through it all in some sort of serene pre-planned existence where stress and anxiety, rush, and fatigue were something they had heard of but never experienced.

As she spooned something rich and dark into her mug she laughed at her own grouchiness and forced herself to acknowledge that although she was feeling sorry for herself at this moment, there were millions of people worse off than Dave and herself. They had a roof over their heads, albeit work needed to be done on this ageing house to stop it degenerating further. They had food on the table although she did wish that occasionally they had spare money for something 'Finger licking good', or something with a 'filled crust' – but what the hell, they didn't go hungry. Her 'work at home' job as a kitchen utensil telephone salesgirl was helping to keep the wolf from the door and she did not have to spend half of the money she would earn from a full-time job on someone to take and collect the kids from school. But there was little room for any luxuries. Never had been.

She noticed Dave's wrapped sandwiches on the kitchen side and realised that once again he had forgotten to pick them up as he rushed out of the door before the kids were even awake. With a tetch of irritation she put them in the fridge. Oh well they would do for tomorrow.

The coffee was good, hot and invigorating and she felt it lift her mood slightly as she sauntered into the lounge for a quick sit down. Cupping her hands around the mug, she sat back and let the oversoft lounge chair ease her aching back. From the kitchen radio which she had turned on whilst waiting for the kettle she could hear some sanctimonious DJ sympathizing with a caller who was moaning about the university fees she was having to pay for one of her sons. "Oh dear," he was prating, "I feel so sorry for you." Here he stopped to give a huge theatrical sympathetic sigh. "Anyway, my darling, let George Michael soothe your troubles" and his voice promptly disappeared as George crooned on about a different corner.

Idly she peered out of the window. The rain was still falling heavily and had obviously set in for the day. She would change from her damp skirt into her jeans before this afternoon's school run.

Her mobile beeped to signal an incoming call. Where the hell had she left it? With a sigh she realised it was on the dining room table and levered herself reluctantly out of the chair's embrace and moved towards it.

"Hello."

"Hi Pam. It's Roger here."

Oh God it was oily Roger, Dave's boss, and someone she disliked intensely for his well ... oiliness. There was

CHAPTER ONE

no other way of putting it. Even his voice with its mock mid-counties accent and his habit of saying 'yeah' after every sentence irritated her immensely. But on the very few occasions when she had anything to do with him, she had to mask her dislike for the sake of Dave's job.

"Hi Roger." She did not offer more but waited for the reason for his call.

"Sorry to bother you, Pam, but is Dave there?"

"Dave?" she said. "No of course he isn't, he's with you, isn't he?"

There was a small, embarrassed laugh at the other end of the line. "Well that's just it, no he isn't. He didn't turn up at the office this morning and I've had to designate a junior member of staff to look after his desk. He hadn't phoned in, so I thought to give him a call, find out what the crack is."

She sat down once again on her dining room chair and peered at the mobile as if it would give her an explanation.

"Roger, I haven't spoken to him since he got out of bed this morning." She remembered with a slight thrill that just before he climbed out from beneath the warm duvet, he had been very free with his hands, and she had wished it was not a workday. "But I heard him leave at the usual time. Heard the car pull off the drive as usual. What the hell?"

"So, he left for work? Oh, dear oh dear. No problems at home are there?"

She felt a flare of annoyance. Roger had not been above making the odd lewd suggestion to her in an undertone when she had attended the rare office 'do'.

"No not at all," she countered. "Leave this with me, Roger." She was tired of him already and wanted him gone.

"Look if I can be of any help, you only" … She cut him off in mid-sentence and slammed the mobile on to the table. In the kitchen the DJ was now placating another irate listener.

Where the hell had he gone? He had no dentist or doctor's appointment, and he would have told her anyway. Another woman? Nah, not Dave, not in a million years. Despite this, a small worm of unease wriggled inside her stomach.

She retrieved her mobile and quickly pressed speed dial for his number. The metallic automatic voice informed her that 'this phone may be turned off'. Sighing hugely, she tried again with the same result. It was only then that she noticed the little flashing image in the corner of the screen advising she had a text message. When had that gone off? Must have been when she had grabbed a quick shower before taking the kids, and she had not seen it until now.

She pressed 'read'.

'Sorry Love, I know this is a cowardly thing, but I can't do this anymore. I've had enough, I'm no good to you. You all deserve better. I'm not going to do anything stupid, I just need some time, or a way out. All my love to you and the kids. Take care of yourself. Dave'.

She stared at the bald words on the screen stupidly. 'What the fuck,' she mouthed. 'What, what?' It was unusual

CHAPTER ONE

for her to swear out loud, especially the 'F' word. It was a sign of her shock and confusion.

Stabbing at the screen she dialled his number once again. Once more, the metallic voice informed her 'this phone may be turned off'.

She threw the phone to the floor, balled her fists and screamed in impotent anger and dismay. "You bastard," she screamed. "You bloody bloody cowardly bastard."

From the kitchen as if on cue the DJ's mellifluous tones purred 'now let's sail away with Rod Stewart for a few minutes. Go on, sit down, have that cuppa you've been promising yourself".

She could not remember what she did next or how long she had been sitting on the sofa staring out of the window before she became aware again. Shock does strange things to the mind in turmoil and glancing at the wall clock she realised she had lost an hour somewhere. As if to convince herself it was not some nightmare that she had imagined, she opened the texts on her mobile once more and stared stupidly at the message. 'What on earth was he thinking? Where was he going?'

She shook her head to clear it and went to the sideboard to pour herself a large vodka. She was not a great drinker but 'Christ' she needed one. There were a couple of half empty bottles left over from Christmas. Neither her, nor Dave, were home drinkers. Swigging down the clear liquid she gasped as it burned a trail down through her body. Her eyes watered and then became tears. She sobbed and took another large swig, then cried some more. She noticed her tears were falling in huge drips onto the carpet, and angrily wiped her hand across her eyes.

"This can't be happening," she said out loud. "Tell me it's a joke, Dave." She pictured his face as she said the words and incongruously, he was laughing his old familiar laugh. How long had it been since she had seen him laugh like that when something really amused him? Not for a great while, she realised, and fell to sobbing again. Her tears were from anguish and anger, and frustration. She did not know which to feel first.

Her mobile buzzed loudly, making her start. Perhaps this was him: she pressed the loudspeaker button and answered.

"Dave?"

"No, love, it's me" the sharp, concerned voice of her mother. "Are you OK you sound a bit nasal?"

Pan sighed with disappointment. "No, Mom, I'm fine, just a bit of a cold coming, I think." There was no way she was telling her mother anything just yet. She needed to pull herself together and think.

What the hell do I do now? she thought, but then realised her mother was speaking again and she had not heard.

"Sorry, Mom, I dropped the phone, what did you say?"

Her mother gave a tetch of irritation and said more slowly as if talking to a child: "I said if you are feeling poorly do you want me to collect the kids from school? I can give them tea and bring them over later if you like. Give you an hour's peace."

CHAPTER ONE

"Yes, please, Mom. That would be great." She was not really sure what she wanted, but a little time to think was a good idea. She hurried on, anxious not to become involved in a banal domestic conversation about family matters. "Look, Mom, I'm not being rude but someone else is trying to get through and it might be work. Can I see you later?"

Her mother just had time to say "Of course, dear" before Pam cut her off and tossed the phone down on to the chair.

She paced into the kitchen and threw a few drops of water on to her face. The DJ burbled on oblivious to the crisis in her life and she found it somehow comforting. Standing at the sink she peered out of the window noticing that the rain had turned to a steady drizzle. Idly she watched a raindrop dribble down the window, and then her vision blurred with tears again.

"Oh God, Dave," she whispered. "What the fucking hell?"

***

Much later that day and two hundred miles to the south, in a drab little estuary side cottage a small fire burned in a stone grate casting a warm glow across the tiny lounge that was just big enough for a few items of furniture and the sofa and the single matching chair.

The flowery pattern of their covering had seen better days and here and there a frayed little hole had appeared through long use. A front door of panelled wood rattled slightly in the wind as the worsening weather swept in from the west. Through the open door that led to the kitchen opposite, small domestic sounds could be heard as a meal was prepared. The clink of crockery and a kettle boiling sounded above the drone of a microwave. In the tiny lounge the mellifluous choral sounds of a Thomas Tallis aria crooned from the small stereo unit that was perched atop the cupboard in the corner, next to the framed black and white photo of a middle-aged couple grinning self-consciously at a camera long ago. It was a homely scene and as Helen sidled into the room from her kitchen, she took pleasure in the homely ambience and gratefully sank down on to the small sofa. Automatically her arm reached out and she turned on the small lamp that stood atop the tiny side table. She noticed for the hundredth time the small hole in one arm of the chair covering and once again made a mental note to buy some throws to cover the suite.

She was clutching a rapidly cooling coffee mug and forced herself to take another sip. She really must stop making cups of coffee that she did not finish. Why was her mind so restless?

She took conscious pleasure from the measured soaring voices that filled the room and mentally congratulated herself on her eclectic tastes in music as she grew older. She could at any moment switch from the rantings of Stormzy, to the searing vocals of Robert Plant, or to the cultured renderings of Mozart or Sibelius, it really depended on her mood. For the moment Tomas Tallis was perfect and she took time to acknowledge that she was listening to notes

CHAPTER ONE

and phrases that first formed in the mind of a man whose brain had been dust for five hundred years.

A gust of heavy rain rattled the casement window next to the door, and she thought she should really draw the heavy curtain soon to block out both the dark night and the draught. The weather was unseasonably rough for this time of year and although she knew that Cornwall boasted a more moderate climate than much of the country further north or 'up country' as the locals called it, it was still chilly this evening. The takeaway lasagne that she had put into the oven in the tiny kitchen would not be ready for some minutes yet, so she took another sip of her coffee and settled back further into the sofa.

Her mother had still not telephoned, and it was going to become a 'thing' between them as to who called whom first. She had seen this scenario develop in the past and she was determined this time that it would not be she who folded and telephoned. She was sitting alone in a small if cosy cottage on the edge of a tiny Cornish estuary village, whilst most of her old friends were probably running around preparing evening meals for kids and husbands or driving home from busy careers to continue their busy lives possibly with a night out, or a visit to the theatre. What the hell was she doing here? Ruefully she realised she may have taken the odd wrong turn in the past. Getting married to Nigel was most certainly one of them, but it had seemed so right at the time. Hadn't it? What did she want out of life back then? Exactly what she thought all her contemporaries had, a good job, a loving partner, a blossoming career, perhaps a family a little further down the line. Isn't that what they had all hoped and planned for whilst living in awful damp and crumbling digs at university?

She levered her legs up onto the couch and forced herself to shrug off such thoughts. 'Stop feeling sorry for yourself, Helen,' she said out aloud. 'Just think about tomorrow. We'll put it all right then.' She laughed at the absurdity of speaking aloud to herself and took another large sip of coffee.

It was good even though it was now lukewarm. Her taste for expensive coffee was one of the few luxuries she allowed herself, even whilst at Uni.

Suddenly she remembered, some of the great nights out back then with her best friend Audrey and smiled broadly as a snippet of Audrey's 'Maid of Honour' speech at her wedding had drawn laughter and applause from the audience. "Helen and I used to go to lots of great parties and many times we were the only two there."

She chuckled again. She must ring Audrey. She was still in the States working as a sports instructor as far as she knew, but she must have her number somewhere. She would look tomorrow.

Was that a tap at the door? Amidst the muted boom of the wind, and the heavy rain against the window she could not be sure.

Ludicrously she craned her head around to look at the door as if it would provide an answer. No, she decided, it was just the wind.

CHAPTER ONE

She wondered what that chap she had met earlier today outside the pub had done. Was he even now on his way back north to his wife and kids? She suspected so. He was a lame duck if ever she had seen one and she was well out of it. But he had had nice eyes, she acknowledged. The corners of them creased when he smiled as if he had laughed a lot in the past. 'Oh, please, Helen,' her inner voice said again, 'you really are getting desperate.' Impatiently she tipped back her mug, emptying the last cold dregs of her coffee and stood to move back into the kitchen.

It was then that a knock came again at the door, louder, more insistent this time. There was definitely someone outside. Should she answer it? It was her natural wariness that made her hesitate. She was a woman alone, and for all her breezy confidence in front of her peers she was increasingly aware of her vulnerability.

Slowly she moved over to the door and stood irresolutely facing it. Another slight shudder shook it as a gust of wind brushed it outside.

"Hello." She had spoken before she really meant to. There was no answer. "Hello," she repeated.

A muffled male voice was dimly heard. "Hi, look I'm really sorry, but you told me where you live and well, look, I've nowhere else to go."

It was that guy she realised. The chap from the pub. Deciding she was being pathetic, she pulled back the bolt and opened the door a few inches. He looked like a drowned rat. It was him, but he had changed his clothes somehow in the last few hours. Faded jeans that had definitely seen better days, and a black zip up fleece that almost hid the work shirt. No tie now. He was drenched, his hair plastered to his head, and he appeared to be shivering.

"Oh hi," she managed. "It's you."

He tried to grin but somehow it did not work and made him look as if he had grimaced in pain.

"Look," he said, "I'm really sorry about this and annoyed with myself as well. I've tried everywhere, literally everywhere but there seems to be no room at the inn as they say. I even went to grab a kip in the car, but a copper banged on my window and told me I couldn't sleep in the car park." He rubbed one hand across his eyes and forehead to wipe away the rain. "You shouted after me today, telling me where you lived. Don't know if you meant it, but I'm that cold and tired I had to take a chance." He put both of his hands into his fleece pockets and peered up and down the road as if an answer might be out there in the darkness.

What should she do? Every ounce of common sense was screaming at her not to let him in, not to be such a fool.

"Well, I…" she began.

"Look," he interrupted. "If you can just give me a cup of tea and a chance to dry off, I'll be away and out of your hair." He could see that she was unsure, but Christ he was cold. "I'm not an axe murderer or a pervert, I promise." He held up his hand as if to swear an oath.

Despite herself she smiled. "OK," she said, and stepped back from the door. "Come on in, you look like a drowned

CHAPTER ONE

rat." He stepped past her and stood irresolutely in front of the fire, dripping water on to the rug, and steaming slightly.

Re-bolting the door, she moved past him to the kitchen. "I thought later after you'd gone that you might find it difficult. It's regatta week next week and all the B&Bs, pubs and hotels have been booked up for months."

He looked at her as if he had difficulty understanding what she was saying, but then peered down at the fire as he held his hands up to it. "Oh regatta," he said, "I wondered." He was having trouble focusing on her voice as every molecule of his being was screaming to sit down and close his eyes. He had never been so tired or felt so alone and desolate.

She came back into the room and pointed at the single armchair. "Sit down, you look all in. I see you found a change of clothes. Bloody good job in this weather."

He almost collapsed into the welcoming chair and stretched out his legs. "Yeah," he said, speaking slowly as if he was having to concentrate. "Dog walking clothes that I always keep in the boot." He gazed at his wet jeans and, as if the thought had just occurred to him, unzipped his fleece. "Wish my wellies had been in there as well." He gave a small chuckle. "Typical of me to forget the necessities."

"Tea or coffee?" she said abruptly, attempting to hide her concern.

Again, he seemed to have trouble understanding what she had said and had to think for some seconds. "Coffee please. However it comes, as long as it's hot. That's very nice of you." As she moved back into the kitchen, he allowed himself the luxury of leaning back in the chair.

Quickly she turned off the boiling kettle and poured two cups of rich dark coffee. Then as an afterthought she placed the cups on her small plastic tray and reached down a packet of shortbread biscuits from the cabinet to go with them. She fussed over the tray for a few minutes.

"I wasn't sure you'd heard me," she began as she walked back into the lounge, "and I'm sorry if I was a bit of a cow as you left, it's a failing of mine." She looked down at him and stopped in her tracks, still holding the tray. He was fast asleep and dead to the world. His hands hanging limply either side of the chair, his chest under his shirt rising and falling slowly with the depth of his exhausted sleep. She stood for some moments gazing down at him, this total stranger, obviously in some turmoil and distress, who was now fast asleep in her lounge.

She was still unsure of what to do. Did she need a lame duck in her life at this moment? Didn't she have enough problems of her own?

With a sigh she returned the tray to the kitchen side and leaning against the sink sipped her own coffee whilst she considered. No, she decided, he was not an axe murderer or a pervert, just someone in need of a shelter for the night! Well, she could do that, couldn't she? Yes! She decided she could.

She disappeared briefly up the steep rickety stairs that led from the kitchen to the upper floor and returned almost immediately with a blanket. She moved silently into the

CHAPTER ONE

lounge and draped it over his prone form.

Standing back, she surveyed her handiwork: it would do. "There you go, mate," she said in a low voice. "You've had yourself a bit of a day, haven't you, and that's the best I can do for you, I'm afraid."

With a last look around the room she reached down and turned off the table lamp, leaving the room bathed only in the warm glow from the fire. Turning off the stereo, she moved into the kitchen and tramped up the stairs to bed. Making sure to lock her bedroom door.

As she slipped into bed, she heard the microwave ping as it turned itself off in the kitchen below her.

CHAPTER TWO

She thought the flight from Corfu had been awful. There had been a lot of turbulence, which she always hated, and despite repeated assurances from the attentive and polite but over made-up air hostess, she sat gripping the arms of her seat for at least two hours.

The in-flight coffee was only lukewarm, and she hated those polystyrene cups, and the little capsules of milk that accompanied it. The young couple in the seats in front of her barely had control of their little son who persisted, despite her coldest stare, to raise himself up and peer over his headrest at her, and to top it all one of her 'hold up' stockings constantly slid remorselessly down her left thigh. She had adjusted it once surreptitiously but glancing up noticed the male passenger with the bald head the other side of the gangway watching with a frank amused and lascivious stare. Her glare had ensured that he quickly looked down at his magazine, but she was reluctant to go through the whole process again. Why on earth had she chosen to travel in a skirt and not jeans?

CHAPTER TWO

All in all, Maggie had been very glad indeed to feel the slight jolt as the protesting tyres touched down on the Gatwick runway. Why did people stand as the plane was still taxiing to its dock and proceed to open baggage cupboards above your head and shove their groins or backsides into your face as if it was a race to dash off the plane as soon as the doors were open? Were they being pursued by a gunman? Or late for a very important date as the Mad Hatter had sung? Who knew, but it was extremely annoying.

Her current 'boyfriend' had proved to be an irritating disappointment – why did people still call each other boyfriend and girlfriend when they were in their mid-forties? She didn't know and didn't care. The phone call from her oldest friend, Pam obviously distraught and in some distress, had been the excuse she had been looking for to cut the holiday short and inform Darren, she did not think it would work, that it was her and not him, and perhaps they should call it a day. 'Men,' she thought as she was jostled and barged in the queue for the checkout. 'Bloody men, why do we put ourselves through it? Why?' She knew why, because she liked sex, and companionship, and for some reason the husband, kids, and roses around the door had passed her by. She had not been bothered one jot when she was younger but now there were times when she wondered with some dismay if she was destined to spend her later years alone. It was probably too late for kids now, but there might be Mr Right out there somewhere, she would just have to keep kissing frogs until she found her Prince. She yelped as the old lady behind her ran her wheeled bag into her heel.

"I'm so sorry, my dear," soothed the old lady, who didn't seem sorry at all, but anxious and intent to push past Maggie and get one metre nearer the checkout desk.

Biting back an angry response, Maggie just glared and peered down at the ladder in her stocking that had opened above her heel. "Fucking hell," she breathed, "Pammy you'd better appreciate this."

An hour and a half later the taxi was dropping her onto the pavement outside Pam's house. It was almost dark now and the lights behind the drawn yellow curtains were pulsing a pleasing glow across the small front lawn and untidy flower beds. She rang the doorbell and almost immediately the door was opened by a careworn, almost haggard Pam.

"Maggie," she said and hugged her friend fiercely. "Come on in, let me have that bag. How was your journey? You look great." All of this in a rush and she realised her old friend was acting. "Mom's just about to leave, she's just finished putting the kids to bed, go through to the lounge." Her mom was here, that was why there was the false 'bonhomie' mused Maggie.

She had just managed to say "OK" and call "Hi Mrs Davis" to Pam's mom before she was almost shoved into the small lounge. She peered around at the jumble of toys, and children's books that were strewn across the floor and, laying her coat across the arm of the sofa, started to tidy up a little.

CHAPTER TWO

She could hear Pam's goodbyes with her mother, and Mrs Davis saying, "Now don't forget, just call if you need anything, I'm only ten minutes away." Then the door banged, and she was gone.

Pam came in and hugged Maggie again. "Oh, Mags, I'm so glad you came. Sit down, never mind the mess. I am so sorry if I've buggered up your dirty fortnight away."

"You haven't buggered up anything," reassured Maggie. "We'd reached the stage where it was going rapidly downhill anyway, I was glad to come."

Maggie rose and disappeared into the kitchen. "I'll get us a drink. Is white wine OK?"

Maggie laughed. "Do you have to ask?"

Pam came back into the room, two wine glasses clutched in one hand and a bottle in the other. "I've had this chilling in the fridge since this morning. I don't intend to put it back. Right?"

"Absolutely," nodded Maggie, falling into an armchair. "Let's have at it, I'm parched."

Half an hour passed during which both women became slightly drunk, but the talk became more honest. Pam had told Maggie everything she knew which wasn't much more than she'd told her over the phone, but more detailed. Close up, Maggie could see the pain her old friend was in; she was hanging in there and trying probably for the kids to hold it together. There were dark shadows under her eyes, her hair was a mess, and she had a careworn, ragged look about her. Maggie was tempted to launch a withering verbal attack on Dave and men in general, but she realised that this was not what was required, and in any case, Dave was a decent bloke. She'd known him almost since Pam and he had started dating. Worked hard, looked after Pam, was great with his kids. Running off with some floozy was certainly not his style, so where had he gone? None of this made sense.

"So, you've heard nothing from him at all?" queried Maggie. With almost half a bottle of wine down her neck she was feeling decidedly chilled and was leaning far back into the comfortable lounge chair. Her voice was only slightly slurred.

"No not a bloody thing," said Pam. "Not a fucking word. It's been almost two weeks now. I went to the police but when I showed them the text message, they said it was obviously domestic and nothing to do with them."

"Well, I can see their point," said Maggie. "What about the car?"

Pam laughed. "What, trace his car? What do they say on TV 'Put out an all-points bulletin', don't think that's possible, Mags."

Despite themselves both women laughed. Rising, Pam moved to the kitchen. "I've another bottle somewhere here, may as well open that, let's get pissed."

"I'm all for that," called Maggie chuckling. "Bring it on."

As she settled herself back on the sofa having replenished both of their glasses, Pam said, "I've had that arsehole Roger on the phone half a dozen times asking where Dave is. I'm not sure he believes me when I tell him yet again, I don't know. He's such a wanker."

CHAPTER TWO

"Roger?" queried Maggie. "Oh you mean Dave's boss. Well to be fair, Pammy, you can't blame him, he's got an office to run."

Pam took a long sip of her drink. "Yes, I suppose you're right, but he's still a wanker." Both women laughed. "I'm so glad you're here, Mags," said Pam, "just talking about it with an old mate makes it seem a bit better."

"Your mom and dad know, I assume?" said Maggie.

"Ooh yes," Pam replied. "Dad was apoplectic, Mom stunned. They've calmed down a bit now. I'm not sure if they make things better or worse." She sipped again ruminatively. "I'm being unfair, they've been brilliant the last two weeks, I don't know what I would have done without them. The kids would have gone hungry, that's for sure, cooking meals in the first few days was not high on my agenda."

"No, I can imagine." Maggie rummaged in her handbag. "Mind if I smoke, Pammy?"

"No, go ahead," said Pam, not really pleased about the idea, but what the hell, her friend had cut short a holiday and flown a long way to be with her in her hour of need.

"So how was Darren then?" she queried as Maggie withdrew a lighter from her bag and with practised ease lit her cigarette. Darren was the latest in a long line of the so-called 'boyfriends' of her mate and would probably last no longer than all the others, but you never knew.

Maggie took a long drag and exhaled a jet of smoke before answering: "Bit of a disaster really. Same old story, you fancy someone, and he is a looker, but then once you've had sex and seen each other naked, you realise you have nothing in common really and don't have much if anything to talk about. Not his fault, poor bugger." She laughed aloud at a memory. "Second night there we decided it would be a bit of an adventure to, you know, do it on the beach in the sand dunes after it got dark. We felt really daring. Anyway, as we got down to it lying in the sand and were …well loosening each other's clothes, I suddenly realised there was something in my knickers and it wasn't his hand."

"What?" chortled Pam. "What was it?"

"Well, I didn't know, I just screamed and scrambled up, banging his nose with my elbow as I did. Around the dunes comes one of the hotel security guards with a torch and sees me, my sundress up around my waist, hands down my knickers and Darren sitting holding his nose which is pouring with blood."

For the first time in many a day, Pam burst out laughing out loud. "Oh my God, Mags, what happened?"

"Took a bit of embarrassed explaining I can tell you," said Maggie, smiling at the recollection and taking another sip of wine, "but it all got sorted in the end. Darren was mollified but it didn't help that every time I looked at his swollen nose in the next few days I chuckled. I think we were on a downward slope after that."

Amidst the laughter a thought occurred to Pam "So what was it, you know, in your pants?"

"Some sort of tiny crab I think," snorted Maggie. "I didn't look that close, as you can imagine with the guard shining his torch full on me, I wasn't going to root around for long in my underwear. But whatever it was it dropped out and scuttled off anyway. That's the last time I try anything like that on a beach – from now on I'm strictly a bed girl."

They both laughed and Pam felt herself relaxing, despite herself. This is what old friends were for, to put everything in perspective. To highlight the absurd in life and find humour in it.

Leaning forward, Maggie picked up Pam's mobile from the coffee table and once more gazed at the text message, the bald statements, stark in their bleakness. "And there was no warning about this, Pammie? No depression, no dramatics?"

"No," said Pam, shaking her head. "Nothing at all, he was just, well... Dave."

"Have you been getting on OK; I mean you know, no rows or especial problems?"

"No nothing. Well... Money problems, but everyone has those. God knows all our married life has been money problems, but you live with it, don't you."

"Yeah, tell me about it. Sex?" queried Maggie, feeling a bit guilty at such a question even to an old friend.

Pam chuckled. "Not enough, for a long time now. It's the way life develops as you get older, isn't it, high days and holidays mostly. I'm not a raging nympho and he's not a frustrated stud, but we still have our moments. We all like a shag, don't we?"

Maggie nodded noncommittally wondering how people did without regular sex but keeping her own counsel. "And you're sure there's not another woman?" she said. "No late nights out with the boys? No extra baths? No new aftershave or trendy clothes?"

"Nah," said Pam. "Nothing like that, this is Dave." She took a long sip of her wine. "That's what makes it all so unbelievable. You live with someone for twelve years, wash their socks and their underpants, think you know them inside out and one day you get up, take the kids to school and then find a message like that on your phone." She sniffed and gave her eyes a quick annoyed wipe with her hands. "It only seems five minutes ago we were 'bright young things' listening to Oasis, or Pulp, remember 'Common People'? When did everything get so serious, Mags? When I first met Dave at that club, I thought he was so cool coz he was into 'The Beastie Boys' – remember them?" They both smiled reliving their teenage years.

Maggie took another sip of her wine. "And, old friend of mine, it was not so long before that we were both running home from school to watch 'Stig of the dump' or 'Super Gran'." They both laughed at the shared memories of early life, in the days when it was all knee socks, and hitching your school skirt up to make it shorter and stealing your mom's lipstick.

Then gradually the mood passed, and Pam stood up. "Mags, I'm so tired. I think I'm going up; do you mind? You've got the back bedroom; well box room really, is that OK?"

CHAPTER TWO

"Yeah fine," said Maggie looking at the half full bottle of wine and realising with regret that the drinking session was over. "You don't want me to sleep with you?"

"What!" laughed Pam. "Margaret Rogers, what are you suggesting?"

Maggie snorted and laughed herself. "Don't be an arse. I just thought, well, you know, a double bed can be a lonely place at a time like this."

Pam picked up her phone from the coffee table and automatically checked it for messages. Nothing. "No, I'm fine thanks." Suddenly she needed reassurance. She leaned down and gripped Maggie's arm. "Do you think I'll ever hear from him again, Mags? This isn't the end, is it?"

Maggie stood and hugged her friend. "No, Pam, of course not," she soothed, although overall she was not really sure. "It'll sort itself out, you'll see. You just hang in there." She gave an extra hug and then released Pam and turned to pick up her handbag. "Listen, if you don't hear from him soon, I'll find the bugger myself and give him a real good kick in the bollocks."

Pam smiled again. "I bet you would as well."

"Too bloody right, Pammie," laughed Maggie. "He's upset my bestest mate and that's a no-no."

Laughing together as old friends do, they climbed the stairs.

***

The drizzle of earlier in the day had cleared and the sun now shone down from a clear azure sky. It was not that hot yet this early in the season, but the fine weather always tempted people out and the quayside was busy with tourists. Children screamed with excitement, almost but not quite drowning out the squawk and chatter of the seagulls. Elderly couples sat on benches to watch the world go by, self-consciously holding hands. Youths sauntered along their noses buried in their mobiles, oblivious to their surroundings. A small queue was waiting patiently at the parked ice cream van, as an old woman checked the menu board of pictures to decide which cornet she would have.

Further down the quay a woman standing in front of a blue painted wooden sentry box called in a loud voice extolling the attractions of a trip up the river. It was a litany she repeated almost without thought for most of the day and was spoken with little enthusiasm.

A few yards away Ben Trelask, or 'old Ben' as the locals called him, sat on his boat which was moored against the stone steps of the quay bobbing gently on the glittering water, and quietly smoked his pipe, content that the chalkboard advertising trips around the harbour and estuary mouth would bring in his punters without the need for all that shouting. With his worn old blue jumper and battered seaman's cap perched atop his still curly white hair, he looked every inch the competent boatman that he in fact was. His white beard was trimmed and neat after the attentions of his long-suffering wife the previous evening.

CHAPTER TWO

"I'm going to trim that," she had scolded him as he had sat in the kitchen drinking his tea, "you look like a bloody tramp." He grinned now at the memory. He had been doing this for many years, and although he would never be a rich man, his boat brought him in more than enough money during the summer for he and his wife to be able to survive fairly comfortably through the winter months when he added his 'odd jobs' money to the pot which also included their state pensions. He was in his mid-seventies now and although he had enjoyed better, more responsible jobs in earlier life, this would do now. He was far from thinking about retiring properly – what would he do all day? – but he was not averse to the thought of taking things a bit easier. He often quoted one of his favourite lines from 'Desiderata' the homily on life: 'Take kindly the counsel of the years, gratefully surrendering the things of youth'.

His pipe had ceased to draw so he tapped it against the wooden gunwale of his boat 'Esme' and emptied the spent tobacco over the side into the water. He had taken two groups of tourists for a chug around the estuary mouth so far today, and now for the moment was content to sit and enjoy a pipe. It must be nearly lunchtime and he was about to check the plastic sandwich box that Annie, his wife, had given him as he left the cottage earlier, when a shadow fell across him. Someone was standing on the quay directly above blocking out the sun.

"Mr Trelask?" It was not a local's voice; the accent was from somewhere up country.

Shielding his eyes from the sun with his free hand, Ben gazed up at a youngish man in jeans and a hoodie standing irresolutely above him, looking out of place amongst the tourists.

"Yep, that's me."

"My name's Dave. I think Helen Reade has mentioned me to you."

Ben looked the younger man slowly up and down, then laid his pipe down on the top of the waterproof which lay beside him.

"Yes, she did. You're her lodger, is that right?"

"Yes," said the figure above, offering nothing more.

"Well come on board," said Ben. "I'll get a crick in my neck looking up at you." The words were not spoken unkindly, merely a matter of fact.

Doing as he was told, Dave stepped aboard and at a gesture from Ben sat down on the other side of the boat, his back to the quay above him.

Ben looked him over once more and was not impressed. This chap looked positively shabby, there was an unkempt air about him. "Young Helen tells me you're looking for a job."

Dave nodded. "Yes." Again, he offered nothing else.

'Well,' thought Ben, 'He's no talker that's for sure.' "How long have you known Helen?"

"I don't really know her well at all," said Dave. "She was very kind to me a couple of weeks ago when I was looking and feeling like a drowned rat and gave me shelter for the

CHAPTER TWO

night at her place. The following day she offered me the use of her back bedroom until I'm on my feet, but I want to pay me way. I don't like accepting charity, especially not from someone as decent as her."

Ben nodded. This chap was not what he had expected, which was an up-country smart arse full of his own self-importance and overconfident of his appeal to women. The man opposite was self-effacing, shy almost. He'd seen better days, that was for sure, but he did not want to rely on someone else to solve his problems for him; Ben liked that in a person. Stand on your own feet was Ben's motto.

"So, you need a job?"

Dave nodded.

"Well, I don't know what young Helen told you, but I can't afford to pay you much, this boat doesn't earn big money."

For the first time the younger man gave the ghost of a smile. "Anything's better than the nothing I have now. The money I arrived with has almost gone, and well, I need to earn some."

"Do you know anything about boats?" queried Ben. He picked up his pipe and began stuffing tobacco into it as he spoke. "It's not as easy as it looks, you know, and I can't have the punters put in danger."

Dave glanced around at 'Esme'. She was an old clinker-built wooden boat about thirty feet long. A small half cabin at the front with a spoked wooden steering wheel and a throttle. Wooden slated seats lined the sides of the boat. She was probably licensed to carry no more than ten he guessed.

"I've sailed since I was in my teens, dinghies, that sort of thing, and in later life I've been on boats whenever I could. Couple of holidays afloat." He smiled at the memories and Ben found himself answering the smile. First impression was that he liked this chap. He always swore by first impressions did Ben.

Ben did not answer immediately, his attention taken by striking a match and lighting his pipe. He puffed until it was drawing well, then removed it from his mouth, emitting a cloud of smoke. "Well now," he said. "It just so happens that I was thinking maybe to take someone on for the season. General dogsbody, deckhand, that sort of thing. Maybe even take the old girl out on your own once I'm satisfied that you know what you're doing. I'm getting a bit long in the tooth for this caper, and the wife gives me hell about getting some help." He gave Dave a sharp glance. "You're not in any trouble, are you, with the police I mean?"

Dave shook his head. "No trouble, not like you mean, not with the police."

Ben's keen eyes missed nothing, and he could see the conflict raging within this man. "Why not go to the dole?"

Dave looked away down the estuary and shook his head again. "Can't," he said, "nor draw money from the cashpoint off my card. Too easily traced." He shook his head. "It's nothing illegal, believe me." He sighed and peered straight at the older man. "Look, I just don't want to be found at the moment, that's all. Need a bolt hole."

CHAPTER TWO

Ben glanced up at the quay and noticed there were two couples peering down at him who were obviously waiting for an invite to come aboard. This young man intrigued him, but he had work to attend to now and after all it was none of his business.

"OK," he said, making a decision. "Let's give you a week's trial. Be here tomorrow at nine sharp. I have a mackerel fishing trip. Got any waterproofs?" Seeing Dave shake his head he hurried on. "Never mind, I've got some spare you can use."

As Dave stood Ben looked up at him. "Final thing." His glance was stern now, and it crossed Dave's mind that this man would have been a handful in his prime. "I've only known young Helen for a couple of months, but she's one of the good people; you mess her about, and you'll answer to me, OK?"

Dave climbed on to the quay, leaving the way clear for the punters to get on board. "Clear." He smiled down at Ben. "And you're right, she's the kindest person I've ever met. No problems from me." He started to move away but remembered he had not fully introduced himself and turned back. "I'm Dave, by the way," he said, "Dave Mason." Without waiting for an answer, he strode away into the crowds.

Ben settled his customers in the seats he pointed out and climbed up on to the quay; he had noticed Annie arriving with his knapsack which he knew would contain a flask of soup. "Hiya Girl," he greeted his seventy-year-old wife in his usual way. "That's great, thanks."

Annie was wearing an old overcoat across her shoulders covering her jumper and gypsy skirt. She nodded after the retreating figure of Dave. "Who were that?"

"That's the stray that young Helen sent my way," he explained. "Seems a decent sort, I've agreed to give him a trial."

"Looks a bit scruffy," said Annie.

"Yeah," said Ben, checking his knapsack for what else it contained and noting with satisfaction there was a chocolate bar. "But he seems OK. There's a story there somewhere I'm thinking. Every year they turn up here running away from God knows what, thinking they'll find the answer." He turned to step down into the boat again. "Oh well, none of my business; see you later, girl."

Annie gazed at the retreating back of Dave, then gave a snort of disinterest, turned on her heel and walked away.

***

The old grandfather clock set against the wall of the tiny so-called museum ticked loudly as it had done for over one hundred years. Where it had come from no one could remember, despite Helen's enquiries. She had been instructed to wind it every three days when she took up this post and had done so assiduously. She liked the sound it made on the hour, the muted bonging from deep within its workings giving structure to her day.

CHAPTER TWO

The museum, if you could call it that, was in fact an old Methodist chapel that had not been used as a place of worship for seventy years and had been designated as the town museum a long time ago. Two uncarpeted wooden floors crammed with artefacts from the centuries, many of them with a maritime history, were all it constituted, but she had grown to love the place. Her office, if you could call the space at one end of the upper floor that, was hardly larger than a big cupboard. Just large enough for a desk, a swivel chair and an old, battered filing cabinet. Two green baize noticeboards were packed with her post-it notes, scraps of lined paper with her research, or postcards of some of the exhibits. After two months' work, she was beginning to make sense of the chaos she had inherited, but it was slow going.

Just at this moment, however, she was not doing anything at all. There were no visitors in this granite-built little chapel squatting as it was not far from the quay and between the town aquarium and a pub. The wooden floors ensured she could hear anyone anywhere in the building from where she was sitting at this moment, leaning back in her seat with her legs crossed on the desk. The black slacks that she wore were an acknowledgement that she was at work as was the dark blue blouse and matching cardigan.

Her youth demanded that she needed to add gravitas to her presence when she was required to speak to a member of the public.

She was staring out of the old arched window at the gathering dusk. It would soon be time to close for the night.

Her thoughts had been revolving around David for the last hour and she had barely noticed the passing of time. What was happening in her life? Her ordered if solitary existence had been turned upside down two weeks ago by him. Asking him to stay the following morning after his dramatic arrival had been the only decent thing to do, hadn't it? He had been clearly distressed, and she had a spare room doing nothing. She had uttered the invitation almost before she had decided what to say. He had looked so pathetic that morning, sitting there at her small kitchen table clasping his mug of coffee between both hands, as if he needed to draw some warmth from it. He had refused at first and was obviously embarrassed at the predicament he had placed her in, but she had assured him that she would like a bit of company, 'really', she had coaxed. 'Just until you sort yourself out.' So finally, he had gratefully accepted her offer. But she was finding she actually enjoyed his company. She liked sitting in the tiny lounge in the evening talking about many things, or nothing at all. He had an easy way with him and seemed to instinctively know if she wanted to be left with her thoughts. They would just sit in companionable silence staring at the flames from the little fire or listening to the radio. He had not made one lascivious remark, or one lewd suggestion in all this time. She was not an innocent and knew that such would not have been the case with most of the men she had known. In their own twisted little minds, they would have read far more into her invitation than was actually there and acted accordingly. But David had done no such thing. Not once. She found that she was liking

CHAPTER TWO

him more and more as the days went on and looked forward to going back to the cottage in the evening. Twice when she arrived home, she found he had cooked a meal for them both. Nothing fancy, just pleasant home cooked food, and he would do the washing up as well! Whomever he was married to had trained him well. 'No,' she corrected herself, 'that's no way to look at it, Helen, he's just a nice bloke.'

Her smile faded as she recalled once or twice glancing at him when he did not know she was looking and seeing the pain in his eyes as he stared at the flames. Seeing that he was far away in that other world that he had left behind and she could see his anguish, his torment.

What had he run from? She knew he had a wife and two children back home so why had he just turned up here? She had delicately broached the subject on two occasions, and he had deftly turned away her question with a self-deprecating laugh and told her he would tell her sometime, that it was nothing horrendous, but he did not want to talk about it at this moment.

The old clock broke her reverie as it bonged and clanked the hour. It was time to go. Quickly, she tidied her desk, walked downstairs to the main door and turning off the lights locked it behind her. It was still quite light as early summer evenings are, but the sky was already turning to purple and black at the edges and there was a hint of cold breeze in the air.

Donning her fleece and zipping it up, she noticed him sitting on the wall just across the cobbled road, watching her. His legs were dangling down and he was swinging them like a little boy. He raised his hand and grinned at her. "Hi," he called. He was wearing the old, faded jeans that he had purchased from the charity shop along with his ageing fleece.

"Hi, you," she said with a real thrill of pleasure that he was there. "How's this?"

"I got the job." He grinned. "Big thanks for sending me to that mate of yours, Old Ben. He's taken me on for a week's trial, so all being well I can get out of your hair soon."

Ridiculously she suddenly felt sad that he would be leaving. "Oh, there's no rush," she said, crossing over to him. "Why are you meeting me?"

"I thought I'd buy you a beer." He grinned up at her. "That's if you want to. By way of a thank you and a celebration."

She laughed infectiously and gave a slight bow. "Lead on, sir," she mimicked, "my time is yours." There was no awkwardness in their banter – after the last two weeks they were easy with each other.

He levered himself down off the wall and pointed to the little pub next door. "Is there OK? I don't know which are the good places and which are the bad in this town."

Spontaneously she slid her arm through his and walked alongside him as they made their way back across the road. "This one's fine," she laughed.

The dusk was falling fast now, and the call of the seagulls was muted as they found a roost for the night. The lights from the pub gave off a warm glow as they headed for it. She looked up and said something to him and they both laughed as they disappeared inside.

CHAPTER THREE

A week passed. May seeped into June and the spate of showery weather morphed into sunny days albeit with colder nights. The world carried on as usual, oblivious to the troubles of four little people. Politicians lied, babies were born, old people died, and the tides came in and went out twice a day as they always had. The young laughed at life and the old folk regretted decisions they had made when they themselves wereND gloriously young. Life continued.

***

Pam hated this bloody hoover, hated it with a vengeance. Her revered old vacuum had finally given up the struggle to stay alive a couple of months ago and David had come home with this damn thing. She always forgot what it was called but it was supposed to have a good name. She swore under her breath and rubbed the brush across the carpet with an anger that matched her mood. She was venting her frustration on the rug. The blaring radio was only just discernible above the vacuum's loud drone.

It was three weeks now that she had been alone, three weeks since that awful day when Dave disappeared. Still no word, not a bloody word. She rubbed harder still. Maggie had stayed for a week, which would have been the duration of her stay in Corfu but had then reluctantly had to leave to go back to her flat and return to work.

True, the 'dear old mate', as Pam always thought of her, telephoned most nights and popped in whenever she could, but it was not the same.

The kids had gradually gotten used to 'Dad' not being there or so it appeared on the surface, but they had been 'Grizzly' as her mom called it on several occasions recently and she knew the real reason why. She glanced down at her watch now and realised it was only an hour until she would have to fetch them from school.

"Oh, fucking hell," she said aloud and leaned down to turn the hoover off. It was a blessed relief as the noisy whine of it faded away and the radio invaded the airspace. Irritably she leaned over and turned that off also.

It was then that she heard the doorbell ringing loudly and by the length of time the button was depressed she guessed it had been ringing for some time. She had obviously not heard its insistent clamour above the din. She was not in the mood for visitors. "Oh, that's all I need," she groaned and looked down at herself dressed in her oldest scruffy jeans and a worn-out battered jumper. Her hair looked like a disturbed bird's nest, and she was barefooted; oh well, what did it matter?

CHAPTER THREE

Wrenching the front door open she found herself looking into the bland smiling face of Roger from David's office. Neat as ever in a well fitted suit and flowery tie. Behind him lurked an older man, small beady eyes glaring from a bland pale face topped by a shock of grey hair.

"Hello Pam." Roger smiled. "Hope it's not inconvenient. Can we come in?"

Pam shoved her hand through her hair and composed herself. She smiled uncertainly. "Yes, sorry, Roger, I was in the middle of something." She took a step backwards. "Come in."

Both men followed her into the lounge and at her gesture sat awkwardly on the edge of the sofa. They perched there like two uncertain pigeons, glancing around at the furnishings, and scattered toys.

"Excuse the mess," began Pam. "I wasn't expecting visitors."

"No problem." Roger nervously smiled. He had not been into this house before, despite knowing David for some years. He half turned his head towards his colleague. "Pam, this is Mr Willets, my manager."

Willets nodded down his nose. "Pleased to meet you, Mrs, erm, Mason." He did not seem pleased at all, in fact he seemed very uncomfortable. His black briefcase was across his knees as if he intended at some stage to open it.

Pam stared at them, waiting for them to speak. "Can I offer you a coffee or tea perhaps?" She did not really want the fag of making a drink, but social niceties demanded she ask.

"That's very kind, Pam..." began Roger but Willet's nasal voice cut across him.

"No, very kind, Mrs Mason, but we are in somewhat of a hurry."

"Oh. OK," said Pam and waited.

Willets opened his briefcase as if it contained jewellery and took out a sheet of typed paper.

"Now I understand from our personnel department, Mrs, erm, Mason that your husband David has been absent from work for three weeks now and we, that is the company, have received no valid reason or explanation for this. Is that correct?"

Pam looked out of the window and hesitated. "Well," she began.

Cutting across her again, Willets interrupted – it was obvious Willets was used to interrupting. "I also understand from Bennet here–" he nodded his head at Roger– "that it appears from the information you have supplied that your husband David has, how shall we put this delicately, done a bunk." His expression was blank, totally unaware of his lack of tact.

Pam looked at Roger and then shifted her glance to Willets. "It's true, Mr Willets, that at this moment I am not entirely sure of my husband's whereabouts. But I'm sure it's only a matter of time before…"

For a third time Willets crudely butted in: "He has not contacted you at all during the last three weeks?"

CHAPTER THREE

Pam felt herself flush with the first intimation of anger. "If you had let me finish, Mr Willets, I was about to say exactly that."

"Pam." Roger held his hand up in placation.

Willets appeared not to notice. "Dear me," he tutted. "Highly unsatisfactory, quite a problem."

"Quite," said Pam. "Myself and the kids all jump whenever the phone rings. They are upset of course."

"Oh yes I can imagine, and I'm not unsympathetic, Mrs Mason, but I was thinking more of our problem at the office." He peered at the typed sheet he held as if it would provide some clue to his errant employee's whereabouts.

Pam took a deep breath; 'who is this wanker?' she thought. To calm herself she stood and, crossing to the window, adjusted the curtain a little. Two old ladies from just up the road were walking past the front garden peering with interest at the 'bosses' barge' of a car that Roger and Willets had arrived in.

Turning, she looked at the pair squatting on her sofa. "A problem? I'm sorry, I don't follow?"

Willets replaced the paper back into his briefcase, "Your husband, Mrs Mason, holds a position of some responsibility within the company. Several of our younger members of staff rely on him to monitor their activities. This situation is extremely troublesome to us."

There was a brief silence as Pam digested this remark. Leaving aside his total lack of tact at the reality of her situation, his tone was cold, dismissive. "But surely, I mean," she began. "He's been passed over for promotion several times during the last three or four years. He can't be that important."

Willets looked up at her and gave a small condescending laugh. "Mrs Mason, it adds tremendous kudos to a company such as ours to employ a number of university graduates for fast tracking through the ranks. Once on our books it is beholden of us to offer certain incentives to ensure that they stay. We view them as future assets."

Now it was Pam's turn to interrupt, annoyance adding an edge to her voice "By incentives you mean promoting them above my husband who has been with you for fifteen years?"

Willets looked at Roger for back-up and back to Pam. "Be that as it may, we cannot have a pivotal member of staff disappearing on a whim, leaving younger employees unable to complete their duties. You must see it can…"

Again, Pam interrupted, real anger pumping into her voice. "Let me get this straight. These 'graduates'–" she held up both hands and waggled her fingers in the universal sign language for apostrophes– "these little darlings you are so anxious to employ, and have promoted ahead of my husband, cannot do their jobs unless he is there to wipe their arses for them?"

Roger stood up and once again held a placatory hand out. "Pam, please, this is not helping."

Pam ignored him, her eyes boring into Willets. "True or not true, Mr Willets?"

CHAPTER THREE

Willets stood up awkwardly. "I wouldn't put it quite that way," he blustered, clearly unused to having his authority questioned.

"I'll bet you wouldn't," blazed Pam, really angry now. "I'll just bet you wouldn't."

Roger took a step forward. "Pam, this is doing no good. I suggest we meet again in a few days."

Pam turned her taut angry face to him. "Shut up, Roger, just shut the fuck up."

Both men looked shocked at the language. Willets turned and made a move to the door. "I don't have time for this, Bennet. Mrs Mason, be so good as to tell your husband if he contacts you that he is in a great deal of trouble; I do not take disloyalty lightly."

Pam took a step forward, attempting with her anger to force them through the door. "What I will tell him, Willets, is to tell you to shove your job right up your skinny arse. Is that clear enough for you? Now I suggest you both leave my house and go and tell your overpaid little darlings to learn to do their jobs properly and not ride on the back of someone like my husband."

Willets was clearly dismayed at the way the conversation had deteriorated. "I'm not listening to language like that; I'm walking out now."

Pam screamed at them as they hurried into the hall and towards the front door. "I suggest you *run* out, you pompous prat."

As a last gesture Roger turned around on the front doorstep. "I'm sorry, Pam, really I am, if there's anything I can do…"

"Out," screamed Pam. And slammed the door in his face. Then turning, she stomped back into the lounge and sat down heavily into her chair. She giggled at the result of her anger, but the anger quickly turned to tears and she rubbed her eyes. "Oh David," she whispered as the tears fell onto her jumper. "Where the hell are you?"

***

Some hours later in a small waterside pub in the West Country, Helen stood at a crowded bar ordering two drinks. She had needed to shove her way to the mahogany counter through intransigent groups of large men who were loudly telling jokes, or swapping stories about their day, and were oblivious to a slim young woman trying to get served.

There were extra staff on tonight as not only was there a band playing later but a group of large racing yachts engaged in a round Britain race and each with a substantial number of tanned and beefy crew had stopped off in the estuary for the night. Pre-warned, the manager of the pub had seen the chance of a large payday and arranged accordingly. The harassed manager's wife had seen Helen's plight and decided to serve the only woman at her bar, crammed as she was between the big sailors. Heavily made up and sporting a flouncy blouse and leather skirt, she placed the drinks in

CHAPTER THREE

front of Helen. "There you go, Darlin" she said, "a pint of best and a gin and tonic. Is that all?"

Helen assured her that it was, paid her money over and turned to fight her way back to the table in the corner which was being saved by Dave.

Sitting comfortably in the small window seat, he watched her come towards him with pleasure. A small voice echoed in his brain: 'What the hell are you doing, Dave? This has got disaster written all over it.'

He turned his head to look out at the darkening water glinting with lights from the far shore, and from small boats which still scurried back and forth. Unbidden, the faces of his children appeared in the reflection in the mullioned glass and he almost groaned. They were better off without him. He knew that, had decided that after agonizing nights thinking of little else. Friends and family would rally around Pam and his kids, and things would get sorted out. Yes, that was it, that's what would happen. He nodded to his reflection. He was sure. Wasn't he?

During the last three weeks his relationship with the young woman who had rescued him probably from a police cell or a hostel for the down and out had deepened and become almost intimate. They were close friends now, they liked each other, confided in each other. Nothing physical, not yet anyway, she was just a good mate, and so what if she was a woman? He owed her a lot, and not just money for his bed and board. He had some money in his pocket now after his first week on the boat and could at least give her a contribution. He was annoyed that she had insisted on getting and paying for the drinks as soon as they entered the pub, but he knew the icy glare of an independent woman when she thought her equality was being questioned so he had quickly acquiesced.

Emerging from the crowd, she placed the drinks down on the small wooden table and slumped down beside him, grinning.

"What a scrum," she laughed. "Bunch of Hooray Henrys in on some yachts, sorry I was so long."

He grinned back at her and felt his maudlin mood disappear instantly. "No worries." He grinned back at her, lifting his beer.

"Cheers."

Laughing, they clinked glasses and drank.

Placing his beer back on the table he said, "Hooray Henrys – what sort of a phrase is that?"

She laughed out loud. "My dad used to say it, it means toffs, you know posh people."

She was wearing a dark green v-neck sweater and black jeans and he thought the top matched her eyes perfectly. His glance lingered longer than it should have on her face and her eyes widened a little as she noticed.

"So," she said breezily. "First week done. How do you find old Ben?"

"He's really great," answered Dave, taking another sip of beer. "Doesn't suffer fools gladly, mind – you must do what he tells you and quickly. Plus, I have the feeling he has been watching me, checking out my skills with the boat." Dave was also sure that Ben was in his own way looking out for Helen, his penetrative gaze Dave was sure, missed nothing and there had been several sharp questions regarding his background during this last week, but he kept this information to himself.

Helen smiled and nodded. "Yeah," she said, "he and Annie are good people. When I first arrived here, there were several things not working in the cottage, some lights, one of the cooker rings, that sort of thing. The town council who rent it to me as part of my contract were not much help but on my third day I ran into Annie in the local shop, and we got talking. Next thing you know they both appeared at my door, Annie with a hotpot for me to warm up, and Ben to fix everything that was wrong inside of two hours." She smiled at the memory. "We've all been good friends since."

Her face clouded. "They had a daughter about my age who died some years ago, don't know why, they are not very forthcoming on the subject, and I don't like to ask. Anyway, I think they have sort of adopted me." She chuckled and took another sip of her drink, leaning slightly against him. He enjoyed the familiarity of her contact and smiled.

"You look sad tonight, Dave." Her voice was low as she peered at him.

"Do I? Sorry." He gave a half smile intended to be reassuring – he did not want a 'deep' discussion this evening. "Never mind, I'm ok now." He wanted to change the subject and gazed around the pub. "Hey look, the band's about to start."

A couple of ageing men with beards and chunky jumpers had moved into the far corner behind two small mike stands and were tuning up a fiddle and a guitar. "Looks like folk music," said Dave, glad of the diversion. "I like folk music. Do you?"

Helen nodded, her voice low and husky. "Yep, as much as I like any other music." Her eyes were still on Dave's face, reluctant to let him avoid her question so adroitly. Every time she wanted to find out more about him, she had this problem. He was not unfriendly at all, just evasive. Again, she acknowledged that she liked this man, liked him a lot. But finding out anything of him was like doing three rounds with a candy floss – you could not land a punch. She knew he was married, had kids, whom he missed terribly, and for some reason had just upped and run away, but that was it. The sum total of her knowledge. She shrugged and for the moment gave up. With a small sigh of exasperation, she raised her glass to him. "Cheers."

He turned to look at her, his troubled eyes on hers and raised his own glass. "Here's to the lost." His voice was low. He sipped his drink.

Her eyes were serious now. "Here's to the lonely," she whispered.

Something was happening between them, and they both sensed it. The music began and they both tore their eyes from each other to watch the band. He lifted his drink once more. His free hand was resting on his leg, and spontaneously with the innocence and trust of a child, she

CHAPTER THREE

reached out and took it. Casually, without looking at her, he interlaced his fingers with hers. Neither said anything further for a long time.

They were content to sit in the crowded pub and listen to the music, holding hands as if it were the most natural thing in the world.

***

Ben made good money this week. The boat had earned its keep and more, so he allowed himself an extra tot of rum in his tea. He liked to drink it from the battered old enamel mug that Annie had repeatedly tried to throw out over the years but had always failed. He had rescued it from the bin on a number of occasions and even once found it nestling in the compost heap at the back of the small garden. He liked it, had used it for years and felt the tea tasted better from it. One should be comfortable with one's possessions, Ben thought. Wear the clothes you liked, use an ancient and trusted pair of shoes until they fell apart, smoke a pipe that was an old friend, no matter how battered it became. His philosophy was not based on miserliness, just on comfortable lessons learned from a lifetime of experience. In a world that was increasingly demanding and 'throw away', aged and trusted possessions gave one a sense of permanence.

Again, he looked down at the figures in the old children's notebook in which he had itemised the outgoings and incomings for 'Esme' during the last five years at least. There was no doubt that it had been a good week, especially when one considered that it was still quite early in the season.

He knew the reason of course. It was Dave. He had quickly realised during this last week that the young man knew boats and how to handle them efficiently and safely. More than that, he was personable and friendly with the punters. They liked him and responded to his chatter with appreciative smiles and even comments. 'Esme' had been a happy place this week and punters spoke to each other in cafés and pubs in the evening and he had found with some surprise that on three occasions this week there was a small queue of people waiting for him to start her up in the morning despite the loud rantings of Dora Penhaligan standing as usual in front of her sentry box just down the quay. He smiled at the thought as he remembered her increasingly shrill voice cajoling and even pleading with passers-by to enjoy a trip on her husband's boat the 'Sea Spray'.

He leaned back in the creaky wooden kitchen chair and slowly filled his pipe from his 'baccy' pouch. Annie bustled into the kitchen from the garden and smirked at his self-satisfied expression.

"Ah ha," she said, her voice taking on the timbre of a school mistress which in fact she had been at the local primary school until her retirement five years ago. "Feeling pleased with ourselves, are we?"

He grunted good naturedly and sucked on his pipe. "Aye," he said. "Best week in a long time."

CHAPTER THREE

Wiping her hands on a tea towel, she sat opposite him across the old wooden dining table that had seen better days. The kitchen half beamed and full of hanging copper kettles and a crowded Welsh dresser was the room they 'lived' in mostly. The front room being kept for best, and special occasions, which were an increasing rarity as they grew older.

If she looked hard, she fancied she could still see vestiges of the man he had been, the strong, honest, no-nonsense beefcake that she had married all those years ago. He was still the only man she had ever wanted, but age had done its work well and the picture was blurred around the edges, and wrinkles and laughter lines heavily creased the once handsome face that wore a permanent deep tan from a lifetime in the open air.

Grief after the death of their daughter Mo had left a lasting mark on him and there had been two years when she could not remember him even smiling, let alone laughing. But gradually they had both moved on from that hateful time and found a way of enduring life, and even functioning with some degree of normality. He was still the love of her life, and she cared deeply for him, so it was deeply gratifying to see him smiling in that self-satisfied way.

"Why is that, do you think?" she queried. "Is it the spell of good weather?"

He removed the pipe from his mouth. "Partly. But you know what, old girl? I think it's Dave. He makes a difference, people like him, and they come back for a second trip. They tip him, and I let him keep them even though he offered them to me. How's that for honesty?"

"It's working out then?" said Annie. It was rare for her to hear Ben praise anyone. One had to earn it, and most did not.

"Aye," he said again. "Yes, it is. You know, I only took him on for young Helen's sake, agreed to give him a go that is, but he'll be an asset to us, I'm sure of it."

"You like him, don't you?"

Ben nodded slowly as if the thought had only just occurred to him. "Yes, I do, he's a decent chap."

Annie nodded and smiled to herself. Ben mistrusted people as a matter of course, but once he liked you, he liked you for life, there was no middle ground.

"Found out anything more about him," she said and standing added, "want some more tea?"

He nodded. "Yes please." He sucked on his pipe some more. "No, I haven't, not really. You could hardly call him a chatterbox. There's something there, something gnawing at him, but he never speaks of it, and I'm not going to ask. If he wants to tell me he will."

She held the kettle under the tap and considered this remark. It was so typical of her husband not to pry. He considered people's business their own and would never ask what he called 'private' questions.

But she was inquisitive herself about this newcomer into their lives, especially as it now appeared he would be a permanent fixture for the summer at least. She made a mental note to ask young Helen what she knew the next

CHAPTER THREE

time she saw her. A thought occurred to her.

"So," she said as she put the kettle on the hob of the range that spread along one wall of the old kitchen. "Does this mean you will be able to have the odd day off so we can have a day trip out or just go shopping together?"

Ben gave a start as if he had received a mild electric shock. "Well, let's see how things go," he said, rather too hurriedly. "It's early days yet after all."

Annie chuckled and shook her head ruefully. He was so easy to read. You could almost hear his thoughts 'shopping? shopping?'.

"Young Helen likes him," she offered as she leaned against the range. "She doesn't say so, but I can tell. There's a light that comes into her eyes when he is mentioned."

Ben muttered something to himself.

"What?" she said. "Speak up, you old bugger."

Ben removed the pipe from his mouth. "I said he'd better not mess her about, she's a good lass."

Annie busied herself taking a cup down from the dresser, giving herself time to consider before she answered. "Yes," she said finally. "She is. I like her a lot, and so do you." She hesitated not quite sure whether to continue but decided to. "She's a lot like our Mo, don't you think?"

Ben turned around to look up at her. "Yes," he said contemplatively. "Of course I do. But I don't think of her as a replacement, don't you go thinking that for a minute."

Annie reached out and laid a hand on his shoulder. "No," she soothed, a slow sad smile raising the corners of her mouth. "Of course, I don't think that, but she's a decent kid nonetheless, and if she likes him, I trust her judgement."

Ben leaned back again in his chair and replaced the pipe in his mouth. "Well we don't have a choice, do we," he said, peering through his pipe smoke into the future.

***

It was approaching closing time when they finally left the pub. The two-man band had been very good, and a crowd of happy slightly tipsy customers dribbled out on to the quay that was now lit by the multi coloured lights strung between the waterside lamp posts. At the rear of the last group to exit came Dave and Helen, laughing at some comment that had been made. There was a gentle hubbub of voices all along the quayside. People strolling in the evening air, youths standing in groups quietly talking into the inevitable mobile phones. A middle-aged couple sat unselfconsciously eating chips from paper wrapping, watching the last of the small boats as they busily found their moorings for the night, small green and red navigation lights flickering out on the dark water.

As full darkness descended it had turned chilly, and Helen found that her jumper was nowhere near adequate against the breeze. She shivered involuntarily and without conscious thought Dave wrapped his arm around her shoulders. She loved the feeling of warmth and affection that came with that gesture and curled her own arm around his

CHAPTER THREE

waist. Together they strolled slowly along the quay towards her cottage. Neither wanted to ruin the moment with a banal comment, so they just walked slowly and smiled to themselves as their thoughts went ahead of them.

They passed the small quayside restaurant that served its customers outside in the summer. The forecourt was crowded, people sat on small wooden chairs that surrounded red and white gingham tableclothed tables, loaded it seemed with steaming plates of food and bottles of wine. The hum of good-humoured conversation and laughter was backed by muted samba music from inside. The air was tainted with the delicious smell of cooked fish, garlic, and heady wine.

Helen and Dave hardly noticed, he was very aware of the perfume she was wearing, and she for her part was glowing with the avalanche of feeling that personal contact with another human being whom she liked very much was bringing. Both suspected what would happen when they reached the cottage, and both had decided just to go with it. The night had been lovely, and it did not have to finish yet, did it? Time would tell. For the moment the reserve of the careworn, guilt-ridden Dave had been overridden by four pints of Best and some great music. The cautious and responsible young woman with him was just 'going with the flow' as her friends used to encourage her to do back when the world was young. The gods would decide what would happen.

CHAPTER FOUR

The little boy leaned out over the gunwale of the boat staring transfixed at the myriad tiny rainbows that danced in the white water thrown up by the bow of Esme as she ploughed through the sparkling sunlit sea. His mother anxiously grabbed hold of the back of his jumper. "Be careful, Georgie," she said. "Not too far or you'll fall in."

The little boy turned his pink-cheeked, excited face to her and chirped, "But, Mom, you can see rainbows in the water, wow it's great."

His mom, infected with the glee of her six-year-old, laughed spontaneously. "I know but be careful."

She turned to look apologetically at Dave who was grinning at them from the wheel of the boat. "Sorry," she called.

Interrupted from his commentary to the passengers about things of interest to look at, Dave nodded indulgently. "It's OK, I know what kids are like, but you'll need to pull him in shortly. I'm about to turn back into the estuary to go

CHAPTER FOUR

back up to the town and coming across the wind the water will chop up a bit."

She nodded and hauled her protesting son back onto the bench seat running along the length of the boat. "Come on now, Georgie, sit by me. The man says it's going to get a bit rough now."

The boy looked up at Dave with a vaguely accusing stare. Grinning, Dave leaned down and handed him a toffee that he had taken from his pocket "There you go, young man." He laughed. "That's for being a good boy."

The boy smiled politely and, taking the sweet, quickly unwrapped it and with a deft movement of long practice popped it into his mouth, the rainbows on the water forgotten. His mother smiled up at Dave and mouthed a thank-you.

Dave turned his attention to his position on the water and noted his sighting points on the shore which gave him his 'heads up' to turn the boat and head back up to the town quay. Here where the river met the sea the water was always a little choppy with short steep waves and you had to be careful to keep the boat steady. The steep hills either side of the estuary glowed bright green in the morning sun. Sheep dotted the fields that were interspersed with stands of dark trees, beech and oak, occasionally larch. Here at the headland where the land disappeared into the sea it reared up to show bare rock, lapped at the base by a froth of white as small blue-green wavelets broke inoffensively against it. On the left-hand side, the ruins of one of Henry the eighth's small forts built to dissuade the French from venturing into England's anchorages stuck up from a stand of trees like a rotting tooth. Above it all the sky was a clear sheet of azure blue with just the odd strand of wispy cirrus cloud high up. It was one of those mornings when everything seems to glow.

People not used to a boat's motion quickly become alarmed when they start to rock and roll even gently. The two old ladies who were 'regular' passengers laughed and whooped with delight as they imagined they were living dangerously. They had been sharing a packet of humbugs and both hurriedly popped another one into their over lipsticked mouths to offset any feelings of seasickness, congratulating themselves for being seasoned sea-goers. Dave as usual had provided some sort of commentary during the short trip; these old ladies knew his patter off by heart but still they politely peered at him with feigned interest.

The boat was quite full this morning, eight passengers, plus Dave, and a last-minute surprise guest Helen. Being a Wednesday, it was her day off and she had walked Dave down to the boat with no real plan other than a breath of fresh air, and perhaps to do a little shopping for a few items. They had chatted desultorily of many things as they walked, but she realised that he was still somewhere else, distracted by their earlier conversation and she had asked old Ben who was down at the quay prepping the boat if it was OK to accompany Dave on the 'trip' this morning.

CHAPTER FOUR

Ben had given her that condescending indulgent look that he always wore when he spoke to her. "Of course you can, girl, the fresh air will do you good. No need for waterproofs this morning; it's going to be a fine day." He placed the inevitable old pipe back into his mouth and returned to fiddling with a piece of rope. Suddenly he remembered something. "David, when you come back in later, take her out to one of the buoys in the middle of the channel and tie her on for an hour. In fact, you and young Helen can have your lunch out there."

Helen laughed out loud and patted Ben's shoulder. "What a great idea, I won't be long," and saying no more she scuttled off down the quay to buy sandwiches and juice. Both men watched her go, her light summer dress billowing around her legs.

"She seems on good form this morning." Ben grinned. "You're doing her good, young Dave. I've never known her so happy."

Dave nodded smiling, his eyes still appreciatively following her. "Yes." He grinned. "She has this way of lifting your spirits." Then he remembered what he wanted to ask.

"So why do I need to take Esme out into the estuary?"

"There's a marine inspector doing the rounds today, checking everyone's paperwork, insurance, state of the passenger carrying boats, all that sort of nonsense. Now there's nothing wrong with the old girl and all my paperwork is in order, but I still don't want some officious town council lacky poking his nose around my boat, so just for an hour when he is around, keep her out there." He pointed out into the glittering water.

Dave remembered this conversation now as he skilfully steered Esme between a flock of moored boats bobbing on the water, towards the stairway set into the grey stoned wall. He scanned the busy quayside for any sign of the 'inspector' but could see nothing out of the ordinary. Tourists ambled up and down or stood eating ice cream, watching his approach. Boats seemed to fascinate people on holiday, and they liked nothing better than to watch local working craft bustling back and forth earning a living.

He gave the boat's throttle a practised burst of reverse and Esme slowed, stopped and gently kissed the stone steps where she rocked gently on the placid water. Dave expertly tied her to the iron ring set into the wall and stepped ashore to help the passengers over the side. Helen heard the chink of small coins as they all without exception tipped him and thanked him for the trip. The middle-aged married couple, the old man with a bird spotting book and binoculars, the usual mix. "Very nice, young man," said one of the old ladies as she clung to his arm. Casually she put two ten pence pieces into his hand. "Edna and I will be back tomorrow; you mark my words."

Dave grinned at her. "You'll be very welcome, my love."

Helen watching him felt the usual wave of affection for this man sweep over her and make her smile with joy. Everybody liked him, and she liked him more than any of them. She found solace with him, yes that was it, solace. He was her answer to the ills of the world, her way of coping

CHAPTER FOUR

with life. He was her friend, her confidant, and now her lover. She coloured slightly as she reflected on this – she was still not too old to blush. He looked totally different now with his lengthening ash blond hair fluttering in the small breeze, his tan, and his ready smile. His faded jeans, patched by her, his old hoody sporting the motif 'Sailors do it with a boom', completed the picture of a local enjoying life. So different from the pale, haggard, careworn chap in his crumpled work suit that she had met on this very quay only a few weeks ago.

But then she remembered that things were not always so perfect. Her smile faded as she recalled their conversation of earlier this morning as they lay folded into each other in bed. It was that conversation that was the reason for her presence on the boat this morning.

She could not remember how they had begun a conversation about taking kids to school. Maybe it was the laughter of the children on the quay below their open window waiting as they did every morning winter or summer for the little ferry to take them over the water to school. Dave smiled and nodded at the window as they listened. "I used to take my kids to school whenever I could, usually two or three days a week," he mused. "If the timings were right, and mostly they were, I could do it and still arrive at the office on time. I loved it, walking from the car to their classrooms amongst the crowds of moms, dads and grandparents all doing the same thing. Children laughing and talking all carrying backpacks almost as big as they were. My kids one on either side of me, each holding my hand. The chatter of their voices as they told me something terribly important about their day, or just chimed at each other. That feeling of their warm hands in mine is something I shall never forget." He raised himself slightly and looked out at the water.

She forced herself to remain silent, willing him to continue – he was finally talking about them. "Although they would always have had breakfast before we left the house, their schoolmates queued every morning outside the school canteen for two pieces of toast in a napkin."

He mused: "It was a service the school offered for just a few pence so of course my kids would insist that we had to queue as well, and they would chatter and laugh with their friends as we did so." He peered into the distance, not really seeing anything. "It was…magical."

He turned his head so that she could not see his face but before he did so she had seen the emotion playing there. "Loved it," he said, again his voice so low he might almost have spoken to himself.

They were lying together in the big bed; he was propped up against the old wooden headboard. Both were naked and she was wedged comfortably against his chest. It was Wednesday morning, so she did not have to be up for work, and he did not have a 'trip' to take out until ten o'clock.

The sash window which was right next to the bed looked out right across the estuary. Through it they could see the usual hustle and bustle of early morning as boats of

CHAPTER FOUR

all kinds scurried back and forth across the choppy water. It was going to be a lovely day, the sun was already carrying with it some warmth, but neither of them felt inclined to move, so snug was it lying entangled together beneath the huge duvet.

He sighed and leaned down to kiss the top of her head. He could smell her hair and breathed it in deeply. Knowing what he was doing she chuckled contentedly and stretched her arm further across his bare chest.

They had been sleeping together for two weeks now since returning from that lovely night at the pub when, whilst watching the local folk group, things had been said and emotions had surfaced and been given their head. Their relationship had deepened, and loneliness and longing had developed into a deep affection and trust which might, someday soon, develop into love.

But there was always the underlying tension within him, the angst that was ever present marring his enjoyment and contentment. He never said as much, but she could sense it whenever they were together like this. They had woken early and made long, uncomplicated love and were now lying in the afterglow idly talking about everything and nothing. Sensing an opportunity, she had asked about his children and for once he had opened up a little. It was rare for him to mention the life he had left behind at all.

He made no secret of it, did not seek to deceive her, just did not talk about it, so with tentative guile she had gently probed and questioned.

He sighed again. "I wonder what they think of Dad now?" he continued harshly. "No doubt Pam's mom has told them I am every bastard under the sun". He lifted his free arm and idly stroked her hair. "And you know what? She's probably right."

Helen lifted her head to stare into his troubled eyes. "No, she's not. Don't beat yourself up like that. You're a decent man and whatever it was that made you do what you did–" here she stopped and chose her words carefully– "I'm sure you did for the best of reasons." There was a silence. He did not answer but stared out of the window again. "I know you will tell me about it when you feel it's right," she continued. Still, he said nothing, and she realised that for the moment that was the end of this conversation.

'Oh well, no sense making a drama of it,' she thought. 'Let's not start the day with negativity.' With a convulsive leap she threw the duvet aside and stood up. "I'll put the coffee on, you'd better think about moving too, you don't want Ben after you for being late." She leaned forward and affectionately tousled his hair.

He smiled up at her, as with a flash of pale buttocks, she primly disappeared through the bedroom door, and he heard the clump of her feet descending the narrow steep stairs to the kitchen.

***

CHAPTER FOUR

It was quite breezy when you got out into the park. Pam hadn't realised until she had gotten out of the car. True, the sun was out, and after all it was late June, but she should have put a coat on and not just her jumper and jeans. She released Jenny the golden retriever from the back of the car and carefully checked that there were no other dogs around before unclipping her lead. With a grateful glance up at Pam and a little yip of excitement, the old dog bounded off a few yards to explore.

There was the pap of a car horn and she turned to see Maggie had entered the little parking area and was climbing out of her red sports car with difficulty. Maggie was sporting a designer Spanish-style short jacket and tight white jeans which looked to be on the verge of splitting.

"Bloody hell, Pammie," she laughed. "I really should get rid of this thing. I can hardly get out of it now without an effort." She laughed at herself and strolled over to her old friend. "And let me tell you," she continued, "wearing a skirt in this cowing thing is a complete no-go, not unless you want everyone and his uncle to see your knickers as you get in or out of it."

The two women grinned at each other and enjoyed a quick hug.

Maggie had telephoned a little earlier to ask if Pam fancied meeting for a coffee or something. "I've wagged the day off," she said simply.

"I've got to take Jenny for a walk shortly," said Pam. "Mom's got the kids this morning, taking them to soft-play and giving them lunch, so I'm a free agent. Want to come?

And we can grab a coffee afterwards."

Maggie was no great lover of the 'outdoors' as she called it, but agreed anyway.

Arm in arm they strolled across the sun-kissed grass as the dog careered back and forwards between the flower beds, called to by Pam now and again when she strayed too far.

Maggie put a hand to her tousled hair. "You haven't got an aspirin with you, have you, Pammie? I've got a terrible headache."

Pam laughed. "You mean a hangover? When are you ever going to learn, Mags? Honestly." She rummaged in her pockets for show, but she knew she had nothing of the sort on her person. "What was it this time"?

Maggie chuckled with embarrassment "Some of the guys and gals at the office were popping for a quick one at the new wine bar on the high street when we finished work. 'Genoa' I think it's called. I thought I'd just go for half an hour. Well, you know me."

Pam laughed out loud. "Oh yes, I know you. What time did you get home?"

Maggie ruefully smiled at her oldest friend. "About eleven I think." Then feeling she should say more she added, "Well I was enjoying myself, wasn't I?"

They were passing close beside two large oak trees and the breeze was strong enough to cause a loud rustle of leaves and a moan among the branches. Simultaneously they both looked up and walked on a little faster, eager to be out from under.

CHAPTER FOUR

"So!" said Maggie. "I haven't spoken to you for three days – any news?" She kept to herself the almost certainty that there wouldn't be.

"Nah," said Pam, "nothing. I've had a letter from the bank telling me our joint account is overdrawn, well over the overdraft limit. Great. I went in and spoke to some kid who said he was in charge and was about as responsive and understanding as a robot."

Maggie snorted. "Oh I know the type, let me guess, immaculate suit, immaculate hair, and no understanding of real people's lives whatsoever?" She halted to check an obscenity. "Wankers!" she settled on and said it to no one in particular.

"He said I and my husband were in what they call 'Persistent debt' whatever the hell that is. I said I bloody well knew that and had he ever been married and had kids?" Stopping abruptly, she turned and called to Jenny who was almost out of sight and waited until the dog began running back towards them. "Wrong thing to say really. It's no good getting angry with these little kids, they have no idea what life is about, all they care about is the printouts from their laptops."

"Hmm." Maggie decided to be non-committal. "So how did it finish?"

"I told him the situation I was in, and that as soon as I could rectify the situation I would. They like gobbledegook speak like that 'rectify the situation'. What a prat." She withdrew her arm from Maggie's and pulled the hair away from her eyes. "Anyway, for the moment they seem to have accepted that. We'll see."

She bent down and picked up a stick which she expertly threw for Jenny who gave another yip of excitement and chased after it.

"That's not the worst of it though."

Maggie sensed there was a lot more and just waited.

"I've had a letter from the Mortgage company saying we are six months in arrears and what are we going to do about it."

"Bloody hell, Pammie!" Maggie was shocked. "No bloody wonder you are down. What the hell?"

They had reached a battered park bench, and both sat down heavily as if they had walked many miles. Maggie withdrew a packet of cigarettes from her small jacket pocket and lit one, then feeling a gesture was required offered the packet to Pam, who hesitated before surprisingly accepting one. "What the hell, I need it," she said.

They sat companionably smoking for some time, each lost in their own thoughts. Finally, Maggie said, "So what happened then?"

Recalled from her own musings Pam said, "Who, the mortgage company? I was totally honest with them and gave them a brief rundown of what had happened." She took a deep drag of her cigarette and exhaled a great cloud of smoke. "Actually they were quite good about the whole thing. Told me they would give me two months to sort something out before they had to take things further."

Maggie snorted. "Big of them."

CHAPTER FOUR

Pam had no answer. "Yeah," she said finally. "Yeah."

"Come on, Pammie," cried Maggie, jumping up. "This is depressing. Let's take this bloody dog back and dump her at your place then you and I are going for a drink. A proper drink. I'm buying."

Despite herself Pam stood up and hugged her friend. "Oh Mags," she laughed, "I do love you."

Twenty minutes later they were in the 'new' trendy wine bar which had been visited by Maggie the previous evening. Almost every surface was mirrored, and black leather and shiny chrome bar tables and stools reflected the trendy lighting. Muted jazz piano music was playing to the dozen or so drinkers who perched like so many sparrows on the high stools, feet balanced on the foot-bars. There were large black and white photographs of a picturesque Italian town on the walls and Pam assumed them to be of Genoa.

True to her word Maggie had ordered a bottle of ice chilled white wine and they sat sipping their drinks, dividing their time between talking of mundane things or gazing around at the surroundings.

"How are you sleeping?" queried Maggie, finally feeling the need to return to the problems that were troubling her friend.

Placing her wine glass down on the chrome tabletop, Pam gave a small snort. "Don't laugh, but I line the pillows up down the side of me as if it's someone there."

She looked across to see if this was going to draw a derogatory remark, but Maggie just stared back. "Sometimes when I wake up, just for a moment, I think he is there. That it's David lying there and not just two old pillows. Stupid really."

Maggie reached over and touched her oldest friend's hand. "Oh Pammie, what are we going to do with you?"

Pam gave a small, embarrassed laugh. "Yeah I know, ridiculous, isn't it?"

Seeming to decide how she was going to say something, Maggie said, "You probably don't realise this, but I've really envied you all of these years, you know?"

"Who, me?" said Pam incredulously. "Why?"

"You've got it all or had it all. Everything I've ever wanted. Married to a great bloke, children. A home, family around you." She faltered under Pam's gaze. "Everything," she said.

They both turned around as a minor altercation flared in the corner. Two youths who were not really the clientele this establishment wanted were trying to brow beat the barman in liveried shirt and waistcoat to put the TV on for the sport; he was having none of it and eventually they banged out of the door, sulking.

"I've had my chances to get married as you well know," continued Maggie, reluctant to let the conversation lapse. "But somehow there was always one more interesting bloke, one more promotion to push for, one more party to go to, and then suddenly you're over forty and offers don't seem to come around much anymore."

This was all said in such a rush that Pam realised her old friend had spoken these words to herself on many

CHAPTER FOUR

occasions. One made decisions in life, sometimes they were right, and sometimes they were wrong. But none of us were free of regret.

Attempting to lighten the mood a little she said, "And of course you're as old as Methuselah now, you old crone, and on the scrapheap forever." She paused to sip her drink. "I thought I was the one with problems here." In fairness she could not blame her friend too much, wine loosened tongues and the truth was spoken, secrets unfurled.

"To some of my work colleagues I am as old as Methuselah, Pammie," said Maggie, "and if I've learnt anything it's that I am getting older now and I don't know anything, haven't learnt anything."

This was becoming maudlin and exactly what Pam did not need. "Come on, Mags," she soothed, "don't be daft."

"Daft is it," replied Maggie. "I overheard some of the young girls in the office the other day talking about the old dragon. I didn't realise until sometime later they were talking about me. *ME!* The playgirl of the western world." She sighed hugely and taking a large swig of her wine reached out and poured more from the bottle into her glass. "I could have broken down and cried right there in the office, nearly did, what a prat." She took another sip. "So yes, Pammy, I've envied you with your settled life, successful marriage, kids."

Pam interrupted, her voice derisive: "Oh yes. Bills, arguments, nappies, bills, cooking, cleaning, more bills, husbands' moods, nappies, yet more bills, debts."

Maggie looked directly across the table at her. "Companionship, someone to share your troubles with, warmth, laughter?"

Pam took a sip of her own drink to allow herself time to think. "You know, Mags," she said eventually, it's funny, but you never notice those things, until they're not there. Oh God, Mags!" Her control was almost torn apart.

Maggie noticed the depth of her despair then and felt guilty about this turn of conversation. "He'll turn up, Pammie," she soothed. "You mark my words, like some bad penny, you'll see."

"If I want him to."

"Do you?"

Pam rubbed her eyes. "Oh I don't know, Mags. Do you know if he walked through that door now, I'm not sure if I would run to him and throw my arms around him or beat the shit out of him, the unfeeling wanker."

Maggie gave a little smile. "I guess you'd just have to follow your feelings."

"In what way?"

"Well, I meant it as a calming joke, but the truth is if that happens just do what *you* want to do. Not what you think I would do, or what your mother wants you to do, but what *you* want to do. Let's order another bottle," she said and without waiting for an answer she raised her hand until the barman noticed, then called for another bottle of the same.

"It gets complicated, Mags," said Pam peering at her reflection in the table as if the answer was down there

CHAPTER FOUR

somewhere. "When you get married suddenly it's not the same. Somehow, it's not just the two of you anymore. Your families, they put pressure on you, force you to consider their feelings and what they expect of you, so you modify your behaviour a little and when kids come along then Jesus the shit really hits the fan."

She stopped as the barman brought over the second bottle and Maggie paid with her credit card. When he had gone, Pam continued as if he had not interrupted, her words flowing quickly now that the floodgates were open.

"And somehow in all that fuss you lose each other a bit. You're still together but in another way, not your own. And as I've said, money, or the lack of it, leans on you, grinds you down, and suddenly you notice you've lost each other a bit more."

She stopped as if she was breathless and topped up her glass. "Do you understand what I am saying?"

Maggie for the first time fully understood the feelings churning around in her friend's head. "Yes, I think so," she said, feeling that her response was totally inadequate. "Look," she said. "Let's lift the mood and have another drink, eh?"

Pam sat up straight, pushed back her shoulders and smiled. "Yep," she grinned. "The hell with it all."

Maggie leaned over and clinked her raised glass against Pam's. "The hell with it all."

***

Helen could not remember feeling so happy and carefree in years. Happy was perhaps to pedestrian a word for the bubbling joy she felt each morning when she awoke. She was not alone; someone was next to her in those first few moments when she opened her eyes.

Someone was warm lying next to her, someone she cared increasingly for with each passing day. She could not help but smile most of the time although she realised this must make her appear addled if she was walking down the street. But she could not help it, laughter was always just below the surface and occasionally bubbled out of her like champagne.

It was down to Dave, she knew that. She had spoken to herself sternly the other day, telling herself to 'grow up' and 'get a grip'. This could yet all go wrong, that she knew, but for the moment let it run, just live in the moment. At Dave's prompting recently she had called up a copy of 'Desiderata' and read the whole thing, wondering at its centuries-old wisdom. The last paragraph was what had moved her most: *'With all its shams drudgery and broken dreams it is still a beautiful world'*.

To add to her pleasure her dad had telephoned her yesterday to ask how she was. Her mom was being obdurate and as she predicted, and it had become a 'thing' between them, each one waiting stubbornly for the other to ring. So as usual her dear old dad had stepped in and played the diplomat. Dad, her lovely dad, with his calm wisdom, his patience, and his awful jokes. She knew that every daughter probably felt

CHAPTER FOUR

like this about their dads. For the first years of your life, you put them on a pedestal but as you grow older you realise and accept that he was just a man, doing his best, trying not to appear too foolish in front of his children. Whenever she thought about him, she smiled, and that was a testament of his influence and importance in her life, and the effect he had on her.

She was pleasantly sleepy lying here on the warm floorboards of 'Esme' as the little boat bobbed gently on the sun kissed water, tied to a mooring buoy in mid estuary. Dave was a little distance away tinkering with the engine that was beneath a wooden cowling in between the bench seats which ran down either side of the length of the craft.

Sensing her eyes on him, he looked up at her and smiled, his teeth white against his tan. "I thought you'd nodded off." He grinned. "That's the problem with drinking a glass of wine in the middle of the day. I was just taking a quick moment to check the oil level on the old girl, won't be a minute." He wiped his hands on an old rag and began to replace the cowling.

Helen felt so relaxed and replete she could not even be bothered to reply but just grinned back, stretching out her legs in the sunshine. She'd allowed her summer dress to ride up her thighs deliberately by accident and felt a thrill of pleasure as she saw he could not stop his eyes from staring.

Moving over to her, he sat down next to her, leaning his back against the wooden transom at the back of the boat. She leaned her head down to rest on his shoulder. "This is heavenly," she breathed. He nodded his head and murmured agreement. Raising his head, he looked over the gunwale and noticed that a trawler was crawling past and knew the wake would rock them in a moment. He loved the motion of the boat, any boat, loved the way the movement stayed with you even when you had been back ashore for some hours. It was so peaceful here, away from prying eyes, away from the troubles of the world.

"We'll have to move soon, you know," he said regretfully, "I have another trip in about half an hour. Are you coming or going back to the cottage?"

Reluctantly she levered herself upright and looked around her at the busy water and the quays in the distance. "I'll leave you to it this afternoon, my lover," she said, smiling at how accurate the old West Country phrase was at this moment. "I've got things to do. I'll see you back home later." Home! Was that how she saw it now, home? It was tiny, and a little untidy, and she knew that at some stage she would have to leave it, but for the moment that's exactly what it was: home.

He looked at her and stroked his hand down her cheek. "OK," he said and sighed. "I was just thinking when I was checking the oil, wouldn't it be fantastic if we could live like this for ever."

It was as if a small cloud had moved across the sun, a shadow of doubt flitted across Helen's face. "Can't we?" she said, her voice so low he almost did not hear.

CHAPTER FIVE

"Righto, ladies and gents, could we have all the bride and groom's immediate families please? That's moms and dads, brothers and sisters, uncles and aunts, old Uncle Tom Cobley and all!!!"

There was a chorus of good-natured laughter as around fifteen people all nervously self-conscious in their best suits or diaphanous wedding outfits and big hats shuffled into place in front of the camera tripod.

Everyone except the newly married couple themselves were being extremely polite as positions based on order of precedence were decided and shuffled into. Two little page boys looking extremely uncomfortable in their neatly pressed white shirts, red shorts and red dickie bows were hustled to the front where they stood frozen into immobility by embarrassment. Maggie, resplendent in her lilac silk 'maid of honour' concoction stooped and straightened Pam's voluminous white skirts before taking her place next to her. The other two bridesmaids Sharon and Celia, two more of Pam's old school friends, their lilac outfits not quite so glamorous as Maggie's, were standing the other side of Dave, giggling self-consciously as they held the front of their skirts off the ground in movements designed not only to avoid marks on their dresses but also to show off their strappy white high heeled footwear.

Above them all from within the warm, one thousand-year-old stone of the church steeple came the ancient sound of church bells as they began to ring in honour of the vows that had just been taken.

"That's it, folks!" called the cameraman, resplendent himself in a dark three-piece suit and sporting a red flower in the buttonhole. "And hold it there, big smile everyone." There was a pregnant pause as everyone awaited the click of the lens. "That includes you, the groom," called the cameraman, his eye glued to his eyepiece. "Smile, young man." There was a smattering of laughter and someone from the watching crowd of friends gathered behind the cameraman called, "Come on, Dave mate, it's not that bad, is it."

Dave smiling broadly held up his hand to apologize. "Sorry!" he called, cursing himself for frowning at such a time. In truth he had been worrying that everything at the reception would go without a hitch.

He so wanted it to be a special never-to-be-forgotten day for Pam.

"Right, here we go again," called the cameraman. There was a machine gun staccato of clicks as half a dozen photographs were snapped in quick succession. "Thanks,

CHAPTER FIVE

everyone, that's a wrap. See you at the reception," he called. "Try not to spill anything down yourselves as I will be taking more shots later."

The assembled group all laughed and there was a smattering of applause. Pam turned and looked up into the face of the man she loved. He looked down at her and winked. Neither moved, engrossed as they were in the moment. Confetti drifted on the breeze between them.

'I do love him,' she thought, 'I really do.' She was thinking back to a conversation with her old mate Maggie two nights ago when they had gone out for a pre 'hen night' drink, just the two of them as old mates do. She was becoming ever more nervous as the big day arrived, and was starting to fret a little – had she made the right decision?

"Don't be daft, Pammie," Maggie had said. "It's just pre-marriage nerves, you know it is. You love him, don't you?"

Pam hesitated. "Mags, I'm not sure. I like him, like him a whole lot, but love? I'm not sure. Am I doing the right thing? Or am I marrying him because it's what's expected, or because Mom and dad want me to. They've liked him from the moment I first brought him home. But they are not marrying him, are they?"

"Well," said Maggie, "They are in a way, you know. He's becoming part of your family, as you are becoming part of his. That's what they say, isn't it? Marriage is not just about you two. Families marry each other, sad but true. That's the way it is."

Pam nodded, unsure of her own thoughts. "Maybe," she said.

"And anyway," continued Maggie breezily, "if in six months' time you discover you really don't love him, well 'fuck him off'."

They both laughed at this outrageous statement and Pam's doubts were dispelled for the moment. She raised her champagne flute. "Absolutely, Mags," she said. "Simple really." Again, they both laughed and clinked their glasses.

Now, standing in front of the cameraman, oblivious to anything else but each other, uncaring of the crowd of relatives and family who began making their way to cars and the reception, she chided herself for those negative thoughts. Yes, she most definitely loved him, and they would have a great life together. He was a nice man, not bad looking and above all, he was kind, that was important. He was her Dave. They would be fine. What on earth was she thinking of the other night?

He laughed at her face lost in thought as it was. "Hey, wife of mine," he chuckled, "are you hungry?"

She leaned into him and laughed. "Yep," she said, "ravenous, let's go, hubby." She hugged his arm and felt a small thrill as it rubbed her bosom.

He did not move but looking down at her his face suddenly became serious, the smile disappearing. The tapestry of blue sky and scudding white clouds behind his head seemed to be moving in a strange way. His eyes took on a malevolent glitter. "In fifteen years' time I'm going to

CHAPTER FIVE

bugger off and leave you all alone with our kids. Won't that be fun." He laughed a harsh mocking laugh.

It was then that Pam awoke and gave a little mew of anguish. She opened her eyes. It was morning, she could see her bedroom clearly in the pearly grey morning light that filtered through the thin, drawn bedroom curtains, and she realised with a rush of relief that she had been dreaming. She was perspiring and felt clammy, her nightdress was clinging to her body, and for some reason she could not move her legs. 'What a bloody awful dream,' she thought. Some of those pictures from her wedding had lain unremembered in the darker recesses of her mind for years. The people's faces, some of them dead for years now, their clothes, everything. Not only how people looked but how it felt that day, it had all been so vivid. She struggled to sit up, fighting with the damp sheet, and felt calmer once she managed it, more in control. She took a long shuddering breath and stretched her bare arms up towards the ceiling, hearing her joints crack. She would have a quick shower. Yes, that's what she needed, then a strong coffee. 'Come on, Pam,' she said to herself, 'get a grip, girl.' She saw that Jenny had padded silently into her room in the night and taken up residence on the bottom of her bed. That was why she had not been able to move her legs – the dog had been lying across them.

The snoozing hound was lying on her back with all four legs in the air, long pink tongue lolling from the corner of her mouth. It forced a smile from Pam and the anxiety dissipated completely.

"What's the matter, girl," she said affectionately to the recumbent form, "are you missing him too?" Rolling on to her side the retriever looked at her with brown baleful eyes. "I know," soothed Pam, "we all do."

She glanced at the clock on her bedside table and could not believe her eyes, the luminous hands said it was seven o'clock, and it was a school morning. Quite clearly from the silence shrouding the house the kids were not awake.

"Oh, bloody hell! she said aloud and raised her voice to shout. "Kids, it's seven o'clock. Get up now or you'll be late for school."

Still grumbling to herself she leapt from the bed and headed for the loo. It would be a few sleep-befuddled minutes yet before she realised it was July and the kids' school had closed for the holidays.

***

How long had it been since they had done this? mused Annie. She and Ben, sitting with some old friends in a pub at lunchtime, just having a drink and chewing the fat. It must be years. Idly she tried to calculate but gave up, it was too much like hard work. With real pleasure she glanced around this small table. The six of them were grouped together in the dark corner of the homely if a little scruffy half-beamed lounge of the local pub. This place was not really frequented by the tourists, as it was a little way from the water. She remembered nights in this place going back

CHAPTER FIVE

fifty years or more, and in that time, nothing appeared to have changed. The old decorative patterned glass lamps still hung from the ceiling beams; horse brasses still littered the walls interspersed with old, framed sepia photographs of locals long gone to their graves. The dingy windows were too small to let in much light, so the small wall mounted lamps their tasselled shades scorched by years of hot light bulbs needed to be lit all day, which added to the cosiness.

The room was still reverberating from the recent entertainment. A group of old locals were sitting in the opposite corner, singing songs as they had probably done for forty years or more. No one minded, it added hugely to the atmosphere and was all done with great good humour. Some of the songs were old sea shanties, and some were old melodies from way back in the fifties and sixties. Occasionally one of the group sang a 'new' song from only twenty or thirty years ago. For Annie the highlight had been the last number they sang which signalled the end of the impromptu concert before the singers settled down to talk about football. The obvious leader had stood up from his stool and started the falsetto wah wah of the intro to be joined in perfect harmony as if they had rehearsed it by the rest, all singing the old Beach Boys feelgood song 'Don't worry baby', which set the whole room laughing and clapping joyfully. The place was still reverberating or so it seemed with the song.

The two couples sitting with Ben and Annie were their oldest and dearest friends. Saul and his wife Clara, and Finlay and his wife Molly. They had all gone to the same school when they were tackers, all shared their youth and early adulthood with each other, and now as they were all well into old age, they felt comfortable with each other like putting on an old cardigan. 'All passion spent' as someone had once said. They had all experienced pain and heartache in their lives and through it all had learned to rely on each other and trust each other implicitly. That's what real friendship meant, wasn't it? To have seen everything that life throws at us and still be all together. Annie nodded to herself imperceptibly as she thought about this. Some people she knew seemed to sail contentedly through life with everything working out as they wished. 'The rest of us just have to make the best of what comes along,' she mused. The homespun wisdom of this statement gave her comfort. She allowed herself a slow smile. Thank God for David. His handling of old Esme and the confidence Ben now had in him allowed time for lunchtimes such as this. It was long overdue. She glanced at Ben; his face animated as it had not been for a long time as he related some tale to the amusement of everyone. 'He looks ten years younger,' she thought. 'Some of the strain has gone from that dear old face, the lines around his eyes look at this moment like laughter lines and not stress marks. Bless, David, long may he be here. I wish it could be forever.'

Feeling her glance, Ben turned to look at her, fearing she would criticise the story he was telling, but to his relief she only smiled and nodded encouragement at him to continue. Losing their daughter Maureen ten years ago had hit him

CHAPTER FIVE

terribly hard and there had been times when she thought he would never get over it, never be her Ben again. But like human beings do, he had staggered on through life and found a way of handling it. She had learned that grief is a journey, that everyone has to take during their lifetime. People die and indeed everyone does in the end, so grief is inevitable. He felt guilty somehow, she knew that. As if a dad could stop disease. He had cried in anguish once when Mo was dying aged only thirty-five, that he was her dad and *should* be able to sort it for her. But of course, he couldn't, he was just a man, it wasn't up to him who lived and who died. She had soothed him with this fact, but it had only enraged him further. For a while he had cursed God and refused to go to church – not that they went much anyway, just high days and holidays – but the anger in him needed someone to focus on, someone to blame and he chose God. Now years later he was, at least on the surface, reconciled to what had happened and took some comfort in the fact that he would one day meet his beloved daughter again, or so he had told himself.

'What morbid thoughts for a nice day with friends in the pub,' she chided herself and with an effort forced a smile onto her lightly powdered face. There was a spontaneous burst of laughter from everyone as Ben finished his story. Having no idea what he had been saying, she joined in with the laughter anyway and took a long sip from her half a pint of lager.

"Where's the old boat today, Ben?" queried Saul, a giant of a man with a shock of iron-grey hair topping a broad red face. His chunky grey fisherman's jumper sporting two or three holes.

"Mackerel fishing trip," answered Ben. "Out past the point over near the cardinal buoy. There should be some fish there to keep the punters happy."

"That David seems a decent chap for an up-country bloke," chimed Clara, her eyes looking huge behind the powerful National Health spectacles that she now wore. "I had a quick chat with him the other day on the quay and I liked him."

Ben nodded sagely. "Yes. Decent he is, and good with the boat. He and young Helen seem very happy."

"Anything in that?" Finlay joined in, his completely bald head glinting in the low lamp light. "I was passing their cottage the other day as they came out. They walked off arm in arm, laughing like children at something, some joke or other. They didn't even see me."

"We don't know," interrupted Annie a little sharply. "We don't ask. But you're right, Fin, they seem on the face of it to be very happy. Her face lights up when he's around. It's nice to see."

They all nodded.

"Anyway," announced Ben, anxious to move the subject away from the girl he now almost considered a surrogate daughter and her chosen beau. "Is it your round, Saul?" He knew it was. "Only, I can see you." He held up his empty

CHAPTER FIVE

pewter pint mug that had a glass bottom and peered through it at his old friend.

Everyone laughed.

"OK, OK," said Saul ruefully. "I'm going. Same again, everyone?"

They all nodded and smiled. He levered himself up off his stool and lumbered off to the bar.

Annie leaned closer to Ben. "We must do this more often," she said, "I haven't seen you laugh like this in a long time."

He chuckled good naturedly. "Get away with you, girl. You'll turn me into a toper." He chucked her under the chin as he had used to do when they were still wonderfully young but did not know it.

She smiled broadly and patted his leg. "Shall we have some crisps?" she asked artfully.

At that very moment the two people they had spoken about, and who were now an important part of their lives, were engaged in very different tasks. David was handing out cold bottles of beer that he had removed from the cold box aboard Esme to his punters. The four fishermen, all clad in waterproofs despite the sunshine, were very jovial as they were reeling in wriggling silver mackerel almost as quickly as they could lower their hooks into the water. They gave a small cheer as the beers were handed out and Dave smiled broadly. Happy fishing guys usually meant a nice tip. He glanced up and took a visual bearing on the huge yellow and black cardinal buoy a quarter of a mile to his west, and back towards the mouth of the estuary with its red and white safe water buoy half a mile to the east. Yes, he was still in position. Another half an hour and he would tell the guys that it was time to call it a day and head back in with a very happy boat indeed.

Helen at that moment was in the bathroom at the cottage, excited beyond words, a broad grin insuppressibly on her face. She had just discovered something incredible.

***

Pam still wasn't sure about this, why had she let them talk her into it? The holdup stockings that she had never worn in her life and the somewhat skimpy dress that Maggie had loaned her combined to make her feel a little like a skinned rabbit. To go out of the front door wearing this outfit would need all her courage and a large portion of 'I don't give a shit'.

Maggie had turned up yesterday evening with her work mate Laura in tow. Pam had only met Laura, a brassy blonde divorcee, on a couple of occasions and was not very impressed. Maggie's work mate had been to the house once before when they were all three going for a drink and she seemed to use a lot of eyes whenever Dave came into the room. Last night all three women had sat in the lounge drinking wine – was it two or three bottles? Pam wasn't sure, and somehow, the other two had convinced her that she needed a night out. One Thursday in every month the local nightclub hosted an over

CHAPTER FIVE

30s night, or as it was disparagingly known 'Grab a granny night'. The music was 80s and 90s and there was absolutely guaranteed to be no Rap, garage or grunge. "Come on," Laura had urged, "it'll be fun."

Pam sensed some earlier collusion but ignored it. Their intentions were good.

Finally, after a long and persuasive discussion, she had relented and agreed to go.

"Pammie, I'll bring you round some stockings and a nice dress, I know you and nothing you have in your wardrobe will be suitable, trust me."

Now twenty-four hours later standing in front of the full-length bedroom mirror, critically assessing the mid-thigh length strappy black sequined number that Maggie had foisted on her, Pam was not so sure this was a good idea. She almost decided to march downstairs to the lounge where they were waiting and announce that she had changed her mind. But no, that would not be fair, they were all dressed up and ready. Maggie had bought the tickets, and the taxi was ordered. "What the hell, let's do it," she said aloud at her reflection. The kids had gone to Grannie's for the night. Thank God her mom was not baby-sitting here, she would be generous with her disapproving looks.

An hour later, with two large Negronis inside her, she was feeling a lot better and decided that maybe this wasn't such a bad idea after all. The music was much louder than she ever remembered it being when she was a club goer, but one got used to it. The repetitive throbbing disco beat of the bass, which seemed to be the same whichever song was playing, had almost become unnoticeable so relentless was it, and if you leaned slightly forward towards whomever was speaking to you and utilised a bit of lip reading, you could almost have a conversation.

The lighting was poor, and she was appalled to notice that the ultraviolet rendered your underwear almost completely visible as if your dress was see-through. Oh well, everyone was in the same boat, and no one seemed to mind. So far, she had not glimpsed anyone obviously 'on the pull'. In fact, everyone seemed quite nice and just intent on having a good time.

The three women had danced a little and laughed a little, chatted amongst themselves and even sung the odd song together. 'Yes,' Pam decided, she was feeling much better. This was quite nice.

A middle aged 'hen' party was in, and although raucous were harmless. 'Probably somebody's second time around,' mused Pam.

The bride was self-consciously wearing a flimsy white wedding veil which clashed horribly with her yellow trouser suit and high heels. Some wag had pinned a note to the back of her jacket with a drawing of a male phallus on it and the legend 'I like it up the arse'. The bride-to-be, blissfully unaware, danced and swayed in the middle of the laughing group.

Donna Summer was singing loudly about 'Nappy Love', wasn't that what they had always used to call it? Pam was

CHAPTER FIVE

smiling broadly as she recalled this, and Maggie arriving back from the bar with two glasses of wine was gratified to see her old friend looking happy. This had been a good idea.

"Laura's gone off for a dance with some bloke she knows who was at the bar," she mouthed, handing the glass over to Pam who nodded her understanding.

"Does she know about Dave?" shouted Pam, peering through the gloom to check that Maggie had heard.

"I think she's guessed." Maggie's face was altering from red, to blue to green and back to red as the coloured lights flashed incessantly. "All I've said is that you are on your own. She's probably worked it out, but would never say anything."

Pam nodded; she did not want to keep shouting. The wine was ice cold and slid down her throat too easily. She peered around her again at the dance floor which was packed with gyrating couples, all laughing it seemed. The actual dance floor she noticed kept changing colour in time to the beat.

Turning back, she saw with a start that Maggie was talking with two men who had sidled up to her. It was obvious from the way they were all comfortable that she knew them. They each had suit jackets on and open necked expensive shirts. In the dim multi-coloured light one of them seemed to have amazingly white teeth.

Seeing Pam looking at them, the taller of the two held out his hand and shouted, "Hi I'm Phil, I'm an old friend of Maggie's. This is my mate Chris." His grin was friendly and infectious. She took his hand and briefly shook it, repeating the process with his mate. He said something else to her, but she could not hear and politely shook her head, pointing to her ears. Maggie handed her glass to her and sidled off for a dance with Chris.

Phil tried to say something once more, but meeting with the same response nodded and gently taking her elbow led her a few yards to an alcove where there was a small round table with a seat circling it. It had just been vacated by three youngish women all busy peering into their mobile phones. How had he spotted it in this semi-darkness? She had no idea but realised that he was obviously a regular and knew all these little nooks. They both sat down, and Pam suddenly felt ludicrously self-conscious. She was alone with a man, a complete stranger, in a nightclub.

He noticed her discomfort and leaned across the table towards her. "Maggie and Chris have gone for a dance. They'll be back in a bit. You're stuck with me I'm afraid." Again, he grinned and again it was infectious; she returned it.

'What was his name again?' Oh, Christ, she could not remember. 'Phil, yes that was it, Phil.' She took another sip of her drink. She was not used at all to talking with strange men in a nightclub. It had been years since she had even been somewhere like this. He was speaking again, and she quickly leaned forward to listen.

"Maggie tells me you're her oldest and best friend."

She nodded. "Yep, we've known each other a long, long time."

CHAPTER FIVE

He laughed loudly. "Well, not too long I hope, you don't look like a pensioner."

She smiled ruefully. "Well no, I suppose you're right. But it seems like a long time. We were at school together."

The stilted conversation of two people just passing the time carried on for some minutes. She could not find anything off-putting or obnoxious about him; in fact, he was quite good looking in a craggy middle-aged sort of way. The fact was she was just not comfortable doing this and it showed.

"Look," he said finally, "I'm not on the pull or anything. I wouldn't insult you by trying any teenage antics. I'm just here for a few beers with a mate, and he fancied a dance when we ran into Maggie." He peered at her to see if she had heard. "OK?" he said.

She looked at him and nodded, smiling. "OK."

After that she relaxed a little and found that she was enjoying his company. Someone who knew nothing about her, or her situation.

Someone who did not know her husband or her kids. Someone who just wanted to talk to her, Pam Mason. Suddenly she found that she was telling him everything. Why she could never imagine. About her husband who had left her, that he was 'God knew where', about her problems, everything.

The music was a little lower now as the evening was moving on and they could converse more easily. Maggie and Chris had returned briefly, red-faced and perspiring, to check on them. Laura had disappeared completely, and Pam guessed she would not be back.

"We're gonna have one more dance, then I'll be back, Pammie," Maggie announced as she and Chris weaved away through the throng.

Phil was finishing his drink. "Look, I've got to go soon, I've got an early start in the morning. A meeting up north, sorry." He lifted the small bottle of beer he was drinking from, obviously, to finish it.

Pam gave a small laugh. "That's OK, nice to have met you." She was rummaging in her small handbag for her wallet. She must get Maggie a drink when she returned, she was not going to let her friend buy all the drinks tonight. She placed her wallet on the table and opened it to check her notes. A photo of Dave was under a clear piece of plastic embedded in the leather.

Idly Phil watched her and then spotting something he jerked forward to get a better look. "Hey wait a minute," he exclaimed. "That's Dave."

Pam gazed back at him, stunned. "David, yes. That's David, my husband."

"You're not telling me it's Dave who's run off and left you, surely? Dave is your husband?"

"Yes," she said, vaguely hostile. "Yes, he is. Do you know him?"

He chuckled loudly. "I should do, love; he works for me."

She was frozen into immobility and realised that she was staring open mouthed, foolishly. "What do you mean?

CHAPTER FIVE

That's not true. David works in the centre of town for an insurance company; you must be mistaken."

Noticing that this pleasant woman was becoming agitated, Phil leaned back a little and smiled reassuringly. "Well, I don't know what he does for a full-time job, but he has worked part-time for me for over a year. Two nights a week and Sunday mornings." Seeing her confusion, he added by way of explanation, "I own a betting shop in the high street. Dave cleans for me."

She could not have been more shocked if he had told her that she had won Miss World. "But," she stuttered. "But Sunday mornings he always takes our dog for a good walk. Some nights in the week too."

Phil nodded. "Yep. Jenny the retriever. Lovely old dog, all the staff love her and give her treats whilst Dave's working. He's a really nice guy. I wondered why he had disappeared. I had no address or anything, just paid him out of petty cash which he always said suited him." He shook his head. "Well well, this is a surprise."

Maggie and Chris arrived at the table and Phil immediately stood up, allowing Maggie to take his seat. Seeing the look on Pam's face, Maggie said, "What's up? Pammie, what's the matter?" She glared around at Phil. "You haven't tried anything, have you, Phil?"

Phil held his hands up in a placating gesture. "Hey whoa. No way, Maggie. Pam will tell you. She's just had a bit of a shock. Look, sorry, all, but I've got to go." He smiled at everyone, wishing them goodnight, not wanting to become involved in some sort of trauma and moved away through the crowd followed by the still gently sweating Chris who looked back and waved.

Pam was obviously not ready to speak, so Maggie stood up again. "I'll get us another drink. Never mind a wine, you look like you need something stronger, Pammie. When I get back you can tell me what's wrong." She elbowed her way towards the bar.

Pam had hardly heard a word that anyone had said for the last few minutes. Dimly she was aware that the men had gone, and just caught Maggie's words about getting another drink.

Jimmy Somerville was singing in his high falsetto about 'Not leaving him this way', but Pam barely noticed. She was peering at the plastic covered photograph trying to absorb what Phil had just told her.

She couldn't take it in.

"Oh God, Dave," she whispered. "Why didn't you tell me, you bloody fool?" Tears oozed from her eyes and rolled slowly down her cheeks onto the table.

CHAPTER SIX

He must do some exercise, he decided, do something to get fitter, he was puffing like a grampus. What a bloody silly saying that was, what the hell was a grampus? It was the heat, that's what it was, it was too damn warm for this caper, either that or he was too old. Was a man too old for anything at forty-two? 'Of course not, don't be a prat.' He grinned through his distress and felt the sweat running down his spine.

Dave stopped climbing this steep grass-covered hill and stood up straight, re-settling the heavy knapsack across his shoulders. The straps had dug into his flesh through the flimsy tee-shirt he was wearing; it was that bloody wine Helen had insisted on putting in there at the last minute. The sandwiches, the strawberries, and the plastic plates and cups weighed virtually nothing. Bloody wine.

July was proving to be a lovely month, and although it was nearing its end the balmy sun-kissed days continued. Day after day of cloudless blue sky, hot sultry sunshine, and very little breeze. The beaches in the area were packed from early in the day until the sun went down in the west with spectacular sunsets. The ice cream vendors and pubs were all enjoying a bumper season, and they needed to after the last few years. August then September would be here all too quickly and the suntanned hordes would return home to their jobs and their real lives.

Turning, Dave glanced back to Helen who was climbing the hill a little way behind him and seemed to be strolling easily. She was wearing a pink gingham sundress and very little else by the look of it. Strappy leather sandals, and a pair of dark sunglasses. Mind you, she was carrying the blanket that would double as their picnic tablecloth, he thought. It was clutched easily across one of her bare arms. The bright sunlight seemed to bounce off her and make her even more radiant. Seeing him looking back at her, she waved and grinned with a flash of white teeth against her tan.

Behind them the view was panoramic. It was yet another brilliant day, and the aquamarine sea that surrounded the headland on three sides glittered and lazed in the heat. The coastline disappeared into the southwest with a series of headlands and bays that gradually vanished into the blue haze. They were climbing the hills behind the little town.

On the other side of the estuary, he could see the usual white froth where the sea met the land, but today it looked benevolent, little waves rolling gently in as if a breeze was moving under a tablecloth. Further out towards the horizon where the sea was a darker blue, he could see the odd looming silhouette of a big ship moving away down the

CHAPTER SIX

English Channel towards the Atlantic.

The steep meadow they were climbing was alive with colour. The luscious green grass and fern were almost knee high in places and speckled with summer flowers. Pinks and mauve coneflowers jostled for position with poppies, daisies, and columbine. Helen had told him what their names were of course. What he knew about plants you could write on the back of a postage stamp.

She drew up beside him, and despite her obvious fitness he could see that she was breathing quite heavily herself. "What's the matter, love?" she laughed. "Run out of puff?"

He returned her grin. "No," he lied. "Just stopped to look at the view and wait for you."

She reached out and touched his cheek with a cool hand. "Liar," she chuckled. "Anyway, we're almost there, just a few more yards and there's an old dry-stone wall to lean against and we can look at the view then." She moved her sunglasses up onto the top of her head and it seemed to him that even her eyes were smiling. The freckles across her nose seemed more pronounced today and in his biased opinion made her even prettier.

They had climbed steadily since leaving the little town via a succession of steep stone stairways which gave way to a narrow dirt track between foliage tangled hedges and then once through a five-barred gate onto the meadows. Clear of the obstruction of the jumble of buildings, every step seemed to enhance the view as they moved upwards. The rag tag of tiled roofs was far below them now, and although they could still see the usual bustle on the estuary as boats of all kinds busily moved back and forth, there was no sound up here save the singing of birds and the occasional seagull's plaintive cry. The locals said that a seagull's cry was the souls of drowned sailors calling out for release. He thrust this uncomfortable thought aside. The day was too idyllic for such morbid fancies. He breathed in the scented air until his chest could expand no more.

"Right," he said, "let's get there. I'm starving."

Ten minutes later they were comfortably settled, leaning against the warmth of the old drystone wall, a plastic cup of coffee each in their hands. Dave had forgotten that in addition to the wine Helen had also slipped the flask into the bag to add to his load. But he didn't mind. Why was it that drinking coffee from an old plastic cup when you were out in the sunshine was so enjoyable?

He stretched out his legs, bare to the sunshine because of the shorts he was wearing, and felt the rays warm his flesh. Helen, slouching beside him, had pulled her dress up to allow the sun to reach the full extent of her legs and further deepen her tan. Seated next to them on the checked blanket were the ham and cheese sandwiches that she had made, and a packet of small sausage rolls. These, together with a couple of apples and the small punnet of strawberries, made an ideal picnic in this heat. The wine was still in the bag, which was shoved behind Dave, in a futile attempt to keep it cool.

Helen had planned this outing for over a week and wanted everything to be perfect. The location, the weather,

CHAPTER SIX

the food, everything. She gave a slow little smile and relished the secret she held. Hers alone for just a few more minutes.

A bee appeared from nowhere and buzzed around them briefly, the sound adding to the somnolent atmosphere, until it decided there was nothing here of interest, glided over the wall and was gone.

They ate slowly, savouring the impromptu meal, chatting desultorily, easy in each other's company. The wine was opened and poured into more paper cups. This almost finished Dave off who was now more relaxed and content than he remembered being in a very long time.

Helen glanced affectionately at him. He was leaning back comfortably, arms folded, eyes shut, an old baseball cap that he had bought from a market stall last week tipped over his eyes to keep out the glare and decided that this was the time. He was barely awake, his eyelids heavy. Again, she enjoyed a little secret smile, the corners of her mouth lifting slightly, leaving dimples in her cheeks. She was so thrilled she could hardly speak.

She turned and lay on her back, her head in his lap, uncaring of the tangle of her rucked-up dress. What did it matter? There was no one about, no one at all to invade their perfect little world.

"Hmmm," she crooned, "what a lovely day."

Dave murmured an assent.

"It's picture-book. The town below us, the sea, the blue sky," she continued. "Don't you think?"

Again, he murmured "Hmm".

"Pig!" She chuckled. "You're not listening, are you? You're almost asleep."

He grinned and nodded. "I am listening, I've heard every word," he soothed "and," he hurried on anxious to placate, "you look absolutely beautiful today."

She feigned annoyance. "How can you tell, your eyes are closed."

"It's a gift I have."

"Well, sit up, my gifted friend, we need to finish the sandwiches before the flies get them and I need to speak to you."

"Let them have the food, I'm full." He was very reluctant to move at all; this was perfect.

Down in the town the church clock chimed the hour and began chiming off twelve.

"Listen," said Helen, her voice low. "There's something lovely about church bells, isn't there? I've always liked them. Just … lovely."

He lifted the hat from his head and glanced down at her with a smile. "It's no good, you're not going to let me doze, are you?" He chuckled. "Is that your word for today 'Lovely'? That's about five times you've said it this morning."

She lifted her head up from his lap and leaning on her elbow gazed at him. "It's how I feel today. Lovely. Say it, go on, roll it off your tongue lov-e-ly. Everything's lov-e-ly."

He reached out and tousled her hair. "You're mad," he said softly. "But lov-e-ly."

CHAPTER SIX

She grinned. "Yeah that's it, lov-e-ly. Here, have some more wine."

He held out his paper cup and she poured a little more of the now only slightly chilled rosé into it.

"I've got something to tell you." She smiled broadly as she moved to sit next to him, leaning into him. The excitement bubbled within her.

He turned to look into her eyes, which were very green today and flecked with strands of hazel, and for the first time realised something important was about to happen. "Oh, yes?" he said almost but not quite dreading what she was about to say. "And what is that? Is it lov-e-ly?"

Her smile disappeared as she had a sudden and unexpected thought that he might not be thrilled as she. Taking a deep breath, she said softly, her eyes never leaving his face, "I'm pregnant".

There was a silence. She could see the play of emotions flit across his face. Pleasure, doubt, dread, fear, and back to pleasure. "I'm sorry, love," she hurried on. "Perhaps we should have been a bit more careful, but I never thought, you know, never dreamed, well that's it." She leaned away from him a little, still scrutinizing his face intently. Eager for his approval, eager for him to say something, anything.

It was a complete shock to him, had taken his breath away. It was the very last thing he had expected her to say. 'Oh my god,' he thought and remembered just in time not to let such a thought show in his face. This changed everything, didn't it?

"Well, that's brilliant," he said lamely, and realising she was now close to tears he reached out and pulled her towards him. "Really, I'm pleased honestly, it's just a bit of a shock, I mean I'm an old man?"

"Old man!" She laughed now. "You're forty-two. You're right: let's order the bath chair now, and the ear trumpet. Would you like a foot stool?"

He nuzzled the top of her head, smelling the warm earthiness of her hair. "Bitch." He smiled. "I just wasn't expecting it, that's all. Give me a few minutes to get used to the idea."

They sat quietly for a while, neither wishing to destroy this moment. He felt her body tremble as she suppressed a laugh and realised, she was finding his shock and dismay funny.

"Are you having a good time?" he said ruefully; his voice was more like his old self now, light and carefree.

"I always have fun with you, Dave." She turned her face up to him and kissed him. "I love you, Dave."

He chuckled. "I know."

"You pig," she chided, punching him lightly in the ribs. "You're supposed to say it back."

"That I know also." He smiled. "I love you too," he said, his eyes suddenly serious. "Really I do."

She sat forward quickly, clasping her hands around her knees. She was keen to continue the conversation without it lapsing into a petting session. "I've been thinking about names," she said. "How about Lucinda?"

CHAPTER SIX

'My god,' he thought, she's already talking about names. "Names?" he said lamely. "How long have you known about this, young lady?"

"Oh, about a week," she said primly. "I wanted to choose the perfect moment to tell you. This was it."

He nodded, chuckling. "You are a conniving cow." He laughed. "So that's why you were at such pains to arrange all of this, I wondered what the sudden desire to go for a picnic was." He lifted his cup. "Any more of that wine left? I think I need a drink."

Gleefully she poured the last of it into his cup. 'It's done,' she thought. 'It's done, and he loves it, I can relax.' She had been both dreading and looking forward to this for many days now. Who knew how a man would react when told such news, especially when he had a wife and children somewhere else. For her it was one of the greatest moments of her life, but would it be for him?

He was squinting off into the distance, sipping his wine, a quizzical look on his face as if he could not quite believe what he had heard.

She took a sip of her own wine. "So what do you think?" she said. "About Lucinda I mean."

"Bit odd for a boy, don't you think?"

"Don't be an idiot," she snorted good naturedly, but in truth she had never considered it might be a boy. In her mind's eye for the last week, she had been planning little girl outfits, all ribbons, lace, and pastel colours. But he was right of course, it might be a boy.

"No chance," she said. "It's going to be a girl, a daughter, I'm sure of it."

He chuckled. "I see. Well, it's a bit story bookish, isn't it?"

"Exactly, like a lovely story."

"There you go again, lov-e-ly."

"Pig," she chortled again unimaginatively.

There was a silence. The bee had returned and buzzed amiably around them to see if there was anything new to interest it. Both were staring at the sea, but neither was seeing anything. One was too full of joy; the other was almost happy but also apprehensive.

Dave reached out and picked a blade of grass which he inserted into his mouth like a cigarette. There was something he had to say, and he felt guilty because it might mar her obvious pleasure.

"It's not all lov-e-ly though, is it?" He dared not look at her.

Her face suddenly became serious, her green eyes troubled. "Not today, Dave, eh?" she murmured. "Let's leave it for today. I know there's things to discuss, but just for today sitting on this hillside, together in the sunshine, let's have one beautiful day to remember."

He turned to look at her. "What do you mean remember?"

Helen sighed. "I mean who knows how this is going to end? Do you think I'm a fool? Do you think I don't see the pain in your eyes. Do you think I can't feel the tension in your body when you hold me in bed in the night? When I know you're pretending to be asleep but you're really lying awake thinking about them, worrying about them, wondering how they are."

"Helen I…"

She cut him off. "Wait, stop." She leaned over and placed her hands either side of his face. "I love you, Dave, and I know you love me, but that's not always enough, is it?"

He looked at her, at the concern on her face. 'God, she's so pretty,' he thought, 'what the hell have I done to this girl?'

"Hey where did this come from?" He breathed.

"No! I said leave it for today." Her voice was almost inaudible, but her face was so close to his they were almost kissing. "It's such a gorgeous day, and we're enjoying ourselves. We'll face what's to come when it comes." She kissed him; her lips were cool, and he was engulfed in the aroma of the delicate perfume that she always wore. "So, let's savour the rest of this day, OK? It's just for you and me today, the sunshine, this hill, the sea, the whole world out there. For this moment it's ours, and no one else's. The memory of this moment will last us into heaven. Something for me to remember when I'm old."

It seemed to him the most perfect thing to say, and he could only nod lest he betray his feelings with a quavering voice.

He watched mutely as she knelt to repack the backpack, wondering how on earth he had become involved with this beautiful young woman. She was so strong willed, so independent, so unlike the young woman at work that he was used to. The girls in his office were vacuous by comparison, interested only in make-up or clothes or who they were going out with. Some of the books that Helen owned which lay scattered around the cottage made his head whirl with their incomprehensible subjects. How could someone so pretty and vivacious be so clever and interesting? Only two nights ago he had enjoyed a long lecture about why modern humans had survived whilst Neanderthals didn't. She had convinced him of her theory, not that it took much persuasion due to his complete lack of knowledge on the subject. She had been a member of many academic groups covering a variety of subjects, until that idiot she married had been unfaithful to her within six months of their marriage and turned her into the introverted, semi reclusive, lonely woman that he had met that day on the quay. It had been a delight to see the ebullient, interesting and playful woman in front of him re-appear over the last months.

He smiled now as he remembered the earnest intensity of her diatribes. The last lecture was made even more piquant as she was squatting in front of the slow burning lounge fire clad only in her underwear at the time.

The conjured picture aroused certain feelings and he had to catch hold of himself. 'Enough of that, mate, time to move.' He scrambled to his feet and continued their conversation as if there had been no pause.

"Yes," he said, leaning down to pick up the pack and hand her the blanket. "Yeah, you're right. Let's work off this bloody wine with a stiff walk over the cliffs. What do you think?"

CHAPTER SIX

She laughed and stood up quickly, the sombre intense mood instantly dispelled. He could clearly see the outline of her body through the thin stuff of her dress. "Yeah, good idea," she laughed, and kicked him gently. "Come on then, old man. Think you can make it?"

"Ow," he laughed, "that hurt."

***

Petey was asleep now. His regular breathing deep and untroubled. Pam looking down at him, smiled and gently smoothed his tousled hair. Very gently so as not to wake him, she moved the curls away from his sticky forehead. The Calamine lotion made him look like a ghost child, and he had quite enjoyed the theatricality of it.

She leaned back against the headboard of his tiny bed and sighed with relief. Thank God for that. He should stay asleep now until the morning. The dose of Calpol she had just made him swallow should ensure that. She looked across the bedroom to the other tiny bed and noted with satisfaction that little Darcy slumbered on oblivious. She was going back to her nan's today and was excited about it.

Both children had contracted Chicken Pox within a few days of each other and although it was a mild enough attack, and every child contracted it at some stage, it still brought with it sleepless nights as slightly feverish and uncomfortable children, especially when they were only six and eight, found it difficult to drop off.

More distressingly, for two nights running the sensitive little boy, now lying with his head on his mom's lap, had cried out for his daddy.

She shifted her position as she tried to re-arrange her nightdress that had rucked up underneath her.

She knew that a fever, however slight – and with chicken pox it was only slight – still brought dreams and a troubled mind. He was a tough little lad, her son. He had never once wept because one of the rocks and foundations of his young life had suddenly disappeared; not once had he asked where Daddy was. Perhaps he had left that to his 'big' sister who constantly demanded information as to what was going on. No matter how old these two lived to be, and that as ever was in the hands of the gods, she would always be his big sister.

Pam knew that her own mother had been disparaging in her remarks about her errant son-in-law, and she had eventually had to have a stern word that it was not at all acceptable to lay her anger about Dave onto his children. They had enough to deal with without 'Nanny' bad mouthing their dad.

She knew that for some weeks before the school broke up Darcy had fielded classmates' gossip about her daddy running off, but when she asked Pam about this had just been told to ignore them, and they would get tired of mentioning it. "Daddy will be back before we know it. OK." The little girl had nodded uncertainly. "OK," she had said and gone upstairs to tidy her dolls and teddy bears.

CHAPTER SIX

She noticed that the children were 'clingier' these days, both with her, and each other. There were only rarely the shouting matches between them that had been a daily occurrence since they were old enough to play with each other. They were quieter certainly, and one day last week investigating a worrying silence from their room, Pam had found them poring over an old photograph album that contained several pictures of Dave.

She glanced over at the plastic owl clock on the wall. Two large yellow plastic hands moved around a dial whilst the eyes above moved from side to side as it ticked. It showed it was 5.30. Well, she had enjoyed a few hours' sleep before Petey's distressed calling had brought her into the kid's room half an hour ago. Should she get up and make a coffee?

She guessed that she would not fall asleep again now, and even if she did, chances were that she would miss the alarm call, be late jumping out of bed, and her office supervisor would want to know why she was not 'on-line' at 9.00 AM sharp. "Oh, bloody hell," she muttered under her breath.

Gently moving the sleeping Petey's head from her lap onto his pillow, she shuffled sideways off the mattress and stood up. What day was it? Thursday, yes that's right it's Thursday. That meant it was Darcy's Brownies night this evening, and her gran was taking her swimming too, so before she made that coffee, she'd better get her kit and towel ready and put them in her backpack.

She tiptoed as silently as she could down the stairs, wondering where the hell her slippers were. There was a full-length mirror in the hallway just inside the front door and she caught a glimpse of herself as she passed and chuckled out aloud at herself. A middle-aged woman albeit still not bad looking in a crumpled up old blue nightie with her shoulder length tawny hair all awry and sticking up. "What did you come as?" She grinned. "Arrived on a motor bike, have you? God what a sight."

Ten minutes later, with a glorious steaming cup of strong coffee clutched in her hands and one of Dave's anoraks over her shoulders, she squatted down in the lounge and turned on the TV. It was the endless round of news and weather followed by news and weather, and then more news and weather. 'Was it on a loop or did these immaculately dressed young men and women actually sit there and read the autocue over and over, time after time? What a bloody silly way to earn a living if they did.'

An over jolly young woman appeared standing in front of a large map of the UK and grinning like an idiot advised that a large storm was coming in from the Atlantic and would bring heavy rain and strong winds across the country for the next two days. It had already hit parts of the southwest and was moving steadily northward. Pam did not take much notice, being more diverted by the fact that this woman in a pink smock affair was quite heavily pregnant. It looked as though she was about to give birth at any time. How many of these weather girls had appeared recently looking huge in some maternity construction? She had lost count. What did these women do when they were

CHAPTER SIX

not broadcasting – shag all day?

It was beginning to get light outside and she decided to get dressed and put a load of washing into the machine. It was new and quiet so it would not wake the kids.

She remembered that once she had readied Darcy for the day and handed her over to her mom who was calling for her, there was something she wanted to do today, something important. A call to make which might add to the picture she was building up about a possible reason for Dave to do what he did.

It was important.

***

When Annie came down the stairs into the kitchen, Ben was already up and dressed and about to go out, even though it was only 7.30. He was finishing the last dregs of coffee from his enamel mug and was gazing out of the small half-paned kitchen window at the day. The hollyhocks that grew against the outside walls were bent over at an impossible angle and but for the trellis to which they were attached would have long since broken in the strong wind. They were tapping the window glass as if they wanted to come in. Up high, streams of flimsy white cirrus clouds were moving across the blue of the sky very quickly, heralding as usual a change in the weather.

"How's this?" she asked. "I didn't think you had much to do today."

He grinned at her, and she was reminded how he used to look when he was young and in his prime. Despite being well into his seventies now, he still had that wonderful boyish smile and that twinkle in his eyes. His hair although snow white now was still thick and wavy. She knew that many men would give their eye teeth to have kept such a head of hair in old age.

"You mean you hoped I didn't have much to do today. I refuse to wander around another bloody supermarket with you, girl." His laugh was infectious, and she returned it.

"I like going around supermarkets with you. I've not had much chance to do that living here, and going with you gives the added bonus that I don't have to carry anything." She did not have to add that the nearest supermarket was twenty miles away, so it was indeed a luxury for her to be offered so much variety for something as simple as groceries.

"Well, be that as it may, I have things to do this morning." He was shrugging on an old thick check lumberjack style shirt over his T shirt, and she knew over it all would go his battered old seaman's denim smock. "Bad weather coming in I'm thinking, the boat will probably be redundant for two days at least from tonight so I'm off round to the boatyard. I'll be asking Ron the mechanic there to have a look at that drive shaft for me. It'll be the ideal time. I need to have a word with David about taking her around with me, I've been meaning to introduce him to Ron anyway."

"Oh!" Annie was filling the old copper kettle, but her head came up with interest. "Why is that?"

CHAPTER SIX

"Well, he needs to meet young David anyway, as it will probably be him that takes her to him in the future." His tone was casual, but Annie sensed that he was hedging a little.

She peered across at her husband with interest. He was making a business of checking his pockets and obviously did not want to look at her.

"Are you thinking of making this a more permanent arrangement then? Is he staying, do you know?"

"I don't know and that's the truth of it. There's still something bugging the bloke, something on his mind and I can't get to the bottom of it."

"Is that why you insisted young Helen was offered the curator job full time because you knew he would stay with her?" Ben was a town council member and had lobbied assiduously for Helen to be offered a permanent post at the museum.

He grinned sheepishly. "Damn, girl, you've seen right through me, my lover." His face became serious again. "But I mean what I say, there's something wrong there and I need to know what it is."

"Don't be so nosey. If he wants to tell you, he will. He only works for you, you're not his father, you old bugger."

Ben chuckled despite himself. "Yep, you're right I know, but I like him, and he's made a big difference to us, girl. Not only to the money in our pockets but to the time we can spend together, and that's no mistake. Truth be told, I was thinking to ask if he wanted to come in with me, maybe as a partner, junior partner of course, but, well there it is."

ONE DAY I'LL FLY AWAY

This was a long speech for Ben, and Annie nodded indulgently, smiling gently. "And of course, the fact that he makes Helen happy has got nothing to do with it." She lit the gas under the kettle and sat down at the table.

Ben nodded. "Perhaps," he conceded. "They're two nice people, and we all need nice young people in our lives as we get older. They remind us of how we were." He chuckled. "Blimey, I'll be writing songs next."

Again, she was surprised at his frankness. She loved it; she was married to a nice man, she knew that, but he was not always open about what he was feeling, not always able to put into words his thoughts. He tramped up the narrow stairs in search of his wallet, and this gave her time to consider what he had said. The strengthening breeze rattled the back door – they must get that old latch fixed before winter set in this year.

"Well, you do what you want, it's your business and your boat," she said as he re-entered the kitchen.

"Ours. Our business and our boat."

She nodded and looked him squarely in the eyes. "You have my blessing, Benjamin." The kettle began to sing, its whistle shrill, and insistent. "You do what you think is best. If it means they both stay around here, I'm all for it."

He gave a low laugh and reaching out mussed the top of her head. "Thanks, girl." He headed for the back door.

"Oy! I've just brushed that, you old coot," the rueful good-natured shouting followed him out into the blustery day.

CHAPTER SIX

***

"Good morning, Willis, Harvey & Stein, how may I help?"

The receptionist at the other end of the telephone line tried her best to sound genuine but when you have repeated this phrase fifteen times already this morning and it was barely ten o'clock, it was difficult.

"Good morning," said Pam. "Mr Bennet in claims please."

"Putting you through."

Pam was perched on one of the battered stools in the kitchen, her coffee before her on what she and David laughingly called the breakfast bar. It was the ironing board that for many days each week was permanently erected and leaning against the worktop by the window. As she waited, she took a long sip and tried to rehearse the question she must ask.

There was a loud click and Roger's voice: "Bennet".

"Hi Roger, it's me, Pam."

"Oh, hi Pam, this is unexpected. How are you? Any news from old Dave yet?"

His voice, she thought, sounded guarded.

"I'm fine, well almost fine, and no, nothing yet."

"Oh dear." Roger's voice was lowered; she knew he was in the general office and obviously didn't want anyone else to hear. "Listen, Pam, I'm really glad you've rung, I wanted to apologise for the old man's behaviour that day."

"What?" said Pam and then realised what he was referring to. "Oh forget it, Roger, I have. It's not important. Look…"

"I was highly embarrassed."

"No need, I'm a big girl now and can look after myself. Anyway, what I wanted to ask was…"

"Anything. You know that."

Pam took a deep breath. A rebuke for his repeated interruptions was stifled before she spoke – it was not his fault, any of this.

"OK. Look, I wanted to ask you…"

"You must be worried stiff."

"Will you listen!" Pam's voice was raised. She relented almost immediately. "Sorry, Roger, but there's something I need to know."

"OK." Roger sounded contrite. "Fire away."

"That last day, the last day Dave was there, did anything happen?"

"About what? Sorry, I don't understand."

"I don't know, an argument? A reprimand? Was he upset about something? Anything?"

Helpfully, Roger was thinking, you had to give him that, Pam thought, he was trying.

"Erm, let me see. Well, there was a collection for old Foster in accounts who was retiring after thirty years. Jesus, can you imagine thirty years at the same place? Bloody hell." He laughed at his own worldliness.

"And?"

"What? Oh well as usual Dave couldn't afford to put much in. We all chucked in a fiver, but I think by counting his small change he managed a couple of quid, and he did

CHAPTER SIX

take some ribbing about that." There was a pause; he was thinking again.

Pam tapped her finger on the ironing board unwilling to interrupt him.

"Oh, hang on," continued Roger. "He did overreact a little a bit later, but we all put it down to a follow-on from the holiday thing, you know."

"No, I don't know. What holiday thing?"

"Well, me and some of the guys had popped down the pub for a swift half lunchtime and as usual Dave said he didn't have time."

"Could not afford it, you mean."

"Well, yes, I suppose so, but it's always been a mystery to us what he does with his money. I mean, come on, it's only a quick lunchtime drink."

With an effort Pam held her temper. "And?" she snapped.

"Well, we had been talking about our holidays and carried it on when we got back."

"Oh God."

Roger hurried on, oblivious now to Pam's tone. "I'm taking my lot to Florida again. Lovely place. Ever been?"

"No."

"You should. You'd love it. Anyway, Adrian from finance is taking his family to St Lucia, and Mick who works with us is off to Sicily. Now there's a place I'd like to go. Maybe next year."

"And Dave said..." Pam could now suspect what was coming.

139

"Said he had booked up to take you all for a week in a caravan to Cumbria." Roger burst out laughing. "He took some severe ribbing I can tell you. I mean, *Cumbria in a caravan, come on.*"

He waited for a comment but was met with only silence, so he cleared his throat to hide his uneasiness. "Pam, are you still there?"

"Yes, I'm still here. Go on."

"Well, that's it really, it carried on a bit into the university thing, but it was nothing, Dave took it all in good part."

"University thing?"

Roger did not like the menacing tone in Pam's voice but had said it now, so he decided to carry on. "Adrian's eldest son is about to go to Uni, Cardiff I think, and we all got talking about how much it costs. I said, and I only meant it as a joke, Pam, really. I said to Dave that never mind, his kids would be invaluable serving my kids fries and a burger whenever they were home from Uni for the holidays." He guffawed at his own mirth. "But again, he appeared to take it in good part, although come to think of it he was very tetchy for the rest of the day. But hang on!" he said suddenly remembering something. "Hadn't you and he had some sort of a row the night before? Something about money again he said, if I remember right."

Pam's voice was flat, emotionless as she thought about that night. "We'd had an argument about something and nothing, I don't even remember what now, but we ended up shouting as usual. I told him he was useless to me and

CHAPTER SIX

a hopeless father who could not support his family. Oh Christ." She almost sobbed but stopped herself in time.

Roger's voice was lower again now; he could sense her distress. "Don't get your knickers in a twist over it, Pam. He's a tough cookie, our Dave, he can take it."

"Can he?"

"Yeah. I'm sure of it. Look, great to hear from you but I've got to go now." He was suddenly all haste and efficiency – obviously someone senior had walked into the office.

"Yep, me too," hurried Pam. "Bye Roger." He had started to say something else as Pam cut him off.

She looked sightlessly out of the window and noticed that the sky had started to cloud over as the predicted storm front was moving slowly up the country.

"Oh, bloody hell, Dave," she breathed. "I'm sorry. I didn't mean it, you daft bugger."

CHAPTER SEVEN

The islands of Great Britain jut out into the vastness of the Atlantic Ocean just off the coast of mainland Europe. They are prone to changeable weather patterns because of this exposed position and because they are surrounded by the sea.

Much of the UK's weather originates far out in this vast expanse of ocean when a depression forms as cold air moving away from the poles collides with warm air moving away from the tropics. The warm air sucking vapour from the sea rises and the cold air descends beneath it, at which time the whole thing begins to spin. These depressions make their way north-eastward across the Atlantic in a series of whirling cloud and rain masses known affectionately by many as 'The Pearl necklace'. The results can either be heavy rain, or high wind, or in some cases both, which then becomes an Atlantic storm. The seas around the UK are not warm enough for a hurricane to form but nevertheless storms of some ferocity occasionally lash the southwest of England, and when these coincide with a high tide called a

CHAPTER SEVEN

'spring' tide – although it has nothing to do with the season – flooding can occur and regularly some loss of life.

It was one such storm that now began to move ponderously across southwest England in late August.

Tourists who yesterday had been strolling casually along the estuary quayside in t-shirts and shorts were now huddled in cafes and bars, their waterproofs dripping puddles onto the floor, and the windows steaming up in consequence. If they ordered one more cup of lukewarm coffee from the harassed waitress who was not used to the café being so crowded this early in the day, they could stay another half an hour, couldn't they? Campers had battened down as best they could their canvas homes and retired to their cars, or a hurriedly booked B&B for the duration. The local beaches, recently crowded and noisy places echoing to the sound of children's laughter, and music and smelling of sun block, were now deserted and wind-blown. Sand lifted by the high winds swirled and swooped across the empty expanse, pattering with increasing force against the closed and shuttered beach huts, and ice cream advertising hoardings. Seaweed lifted from the rock pools by insistent gusts conglomerated in smelly piles against sea walls and benches, sheltering amongst its olive-green and yellow sticky fronds the occasional small crab who had been picked up with it.

The small decorative trees along the waterfront, planted there to give patches of shade in a hot day, were now bent over like so many old people at a bus stop before the howling wind. The rows of suspended coloured lights which were draped from one wrought iron lamppost to the next now danced and swirled wildly.

Annie, peering out of her cottage window down to the town quayside, had not seen the water in the estuary this high for years. The windblown and swirling waters were just inches from the top of the stonework and small waves were regularly washing on to the roadway running in rivulets to lap against the far kerb. The small boats that were moored just off the quay were high in the water and level with the roadway, bobbing and twisting furiously like horses trying to escape from a rope held by their groom. One or two small clinker-built rowing boats had actually escaped from their lines and were now nestled against benches, having been washed across the road. They rocked gently against the faded and chipped wooden seats with the benign and smug attitude of sailors who have escaped from an angry sea.

Craning her head to look down the estuary towards the open sea, Annie could discern no difference between the slate grey water and the lowering pewter sky above it, and could only tell where one finished and the other began by the line of white spray as the turbulent waves at the river mouth churned and frothed against the incoming tide, throwing huge amounts of water high into the swirling air.

'Thank God they took Esme around to Ron's boatyard late last night,' she thought. It had been blustery and raining even then, but she realised now the wisdom of such a move and once again acknowledged the lifetime of common sense where the sea was concerned gained by Ben. 'Clever old

CHAPTER SEVEN

bugger,' she murmured. Half an hour ago she had seen the lifeboat, stationed as it was about half a mile up the estuary, power down towards the sea, white bow waves arcing high into the air on either side of its prow as it battered its way through the resisting waters. The bright orange of its superstructure standing out starkly against the greyness all around it. 'Someone was in trouble out there,' she thought, 'probably a yachtsman who had taken no notice of the 'imminent gales' warning broadcast by the BBC.' She let the small curtain fall and turned away from the window. 'Some of these people never learn,' she muttered, 'bloody fools.' She filled the kettle and put it on the stove. A cup of tea was called for.

Helen had arrived at the museum expecting a quiet day but had been rudely surprised as a procession of waterproof-clad soaking and dripping parents with sulking children in tow trooped in through the doors the moment she opened them. They slouched around both floors, peering with scant interest at the maritime exhibits, but glad to be in out of the rain, and intent on 'doing' something. The pools of water gathering on the bare floorboards as rain sluiced from their waterproofs were growing larger by the minute and although she resented having to make the effort, Helen realised she would have to ferret out a mop and bucket soon. If nothing else it was a 'Health and Safety' issue, and although she hated with a vengeance that phrase, she acknowledged that there was an element of truth this time. The last thing she needed was to be comforting a distraught pensioner lying prostrate on the soaking floor as she hurriedly summoned an ambulance. Inwardly she groaned: it was going to be a long day. She had been sick this morning, as she had for the last few days, and was beginning to realise that perhaps pregnancy was not the mystical happy and fulfilling time that she had envisaged.

***

At that very moment Dave and Ben were crouched in the small half cabin at the front of Esme, which gave them some protection from the incessant rain and wind. They had brought the boat around into the creek where Ron's boatyard was last evening and now thanked God that they had. She was moored against one of the small floating pontoons awaiting to be called forward to the ramp, and with a foresight born of many years, Ben had tied her up last night head to wind so that they could sit in relative comfort as the little boat bobbed and strained against her mooring ropes.

Ben had brought a large flask of tea in a backpack and as he poured a generous steaming measure into each man's plastic beaker, he fished from somewhere in his voluminous fisherman's smock a small hip flask of beaten metal and deposited a large measure of rum into the piping hot swirling brown liquid.

They had walked the half mile from his cottage earlier on and arrived buffeted and soaked but pleased that the

CHAPTER SEVEN

forward planning had thus far paid off. The narrow lane that led from the town across the small, wooded hill to the creek and the boatyard had been littered with fallen branches and flotsam, the air filled with the ominous creaking of trees which bowed before the howling wind.

On their arrival, Ron had told Ben he would be about half an hour and would call them when they should manoeuvre Esme onto the strops to be lifted out of the water. Glancing towards the boat shed now, Dave could see that it would be a few minutes yet. The large wooden slatted shed, pink faded paint flaking in several areas, looked dilapidated in this weather – the rain almost obscuring the large black lettering along the frontage advertising 'RON TEAGUE. Marine Engineer. Boat Maintenance & Chandlery since 1892'. Fronting the shed was a crude quay and the concrete ramp into the water astride which crouched like a giant spider the lifting crane, its webbing strops hanging loose and swaying in the wind awaiting Esme. Around the shed a detritus of old partially dismantled boats, and pieces of old machinery, jostled for position amongst newer white plastic yachts chocked up on wooden stilts. Ron was in deep conversation with two younger boat owners, their expensive yachting waterproofs in luminous greens and yellows in sharp contrast to the oil and paint stained overall and shabby flat cap worn by the huge figure of Ron, all crewcut and tattoos. He was a perfect fit for his yard and gave off an aura of calm efficiency and competence. He was wagging his head morosely and you could make a guess that he was informing the pair in front of him that whatever they wanted done to their craft would have to wait until next Thursday. Dave grinned; it was the litany of workmen in demand since time immemorial: "Oh not today, guys, sorry, not a chance".

Still grinning, Dave turned his head to find Ben crouched on the opposite side of the cuddy regarding him intently. "Have a sip of your tea," said Ben. "It'll do you good."

Obeying, Dave took a swig of the hot liquid and felt his eyes water immediately with both the scalding heat and the large alcoholic content of the evil brew.

"Bloody hell, Ben," he managed before he had a fit of coughing. "What the hell are you trying to do to me?"

Usually, Ben would have laughed, but strangely he did not. Not today. He had planned this meeting for two days and rehearsed what he wanted to say. It was not the time for jollity. This was serious. There was a silence as he gathered his thoughts. The rain pattered against the cabin like shrapnel and just down the creek in the estuary proper the wind boomed hugely.

"Son, we need to have a chat," he began, then seeing Dave's look of consternation he held up a hand. "Nothing to worry about, no great dramatics, but I have a plan which I've discussed with Annie, which involves you if you're interested, but before we come to that I need to find out a bit more about you than I know now." He broke off to take a swig from his own mug. "Which isn't much." He softened his words with a smile: "Is it?"

CHAPTER SEVEN

Dave looked at this man whom he'd come to like and admire greatly, and to whom he already owed much. He nodded slightly, frowning. He had half expected this conversation for some time, but that did not make it any less daunting. If he could sidestep it, he would, but knew that he must not, not anymore.

"No," he finally spoke. "No, it isn't." He took another smaller sip from his tea as he composed his thoughts. "You've been very good to me, Ben, you and Annie both, and I suppose I do owe you some explanation. I'm sorry."

"No need to be sorry, son. I gave you a chance on the boat mainly because young Helen asked me to, but you haven't let me down at all. In fact, the business side of Esme is doing better than ever, and it's mostly down to your hard work. I thank you for it, Annie thanks you for it for different reasons. But moving forward…" Here he peered intently at the younger man. "And let's hope we *can* move forward; we need to know who you are and what you are. Does that make sense?"

Dave nodded again. "Yes," he said.

"You're a nice enough chap," continued Ben, "that much is obvious, and young Helen thinks the world of you, that too is obvious." He looked down at his sea boots and then back up at Dave. "But there's a darkness in you, something is wrong, and I can't put my finger on it." He half smiled. "Don't get me wrong, I'm not criticising, God knows I hate a gabby bloke, but gabby you most certainly are not, and Annie likes you, that goes a long way with me, she is never wrong about someone." He took a sip of his tea. "So that's it. I, that is Annie and I, have a bit of a plan, but before we go there, I need to know a bit more about you, son. OK?"

Dave nodded back, thought for a moment and then took a deep breath. So, it was here, the conversation he had been dreading. These next few minutes would probably see the end of his budding friendship with this man, probably seen him thrown off this boat and told never to show his face again. But he had put it off for long enough, there was nothing for it now.

"OK, Ben here we go. I'm just going to tell you the worst, and please let me finish before you speak. You won't be impressed, I know that for nothing, and let me emphasize that everything I am now going to tell you Helen has known right from the get-go. I've never for one minute kept anything from her, OK?"

Ben nodded imperceptibly. "Righto," he murmured.

Dave looked up and down the creek, seeking inspiration, but finding none just launched in a rush into it, his words falling over each other as he spoke. He told Ben that he was married with two children up country. That his wife was a good woman who as far as he knew had never let him down. He told him that he had a job in an office, that his kids, a son, six, and a daughter, eight, were the love of his life, and that he missed both them and his wife every day. But he could never ever go back.

Ben's face remained impassive throughout this telling, but inside his mind was in some turmoil. 'What the hell?'

CHAPTER SEVEN

he thought. This was the last thing he had expected to hear.

He was about to speak when Dave held up his own hand to still his words. "Let me finish, Ben, please." It was as if he could not stop, now he had started, all the angst and anguish spilling out as if he was throwing up. He was emptying his mind, telling it all before he could stop.

"Then two years ago it all started to go wrong." Somehow, he stopped the flow of words and took a sip of tea as he composed himself again. "Pam, that's my wife, Pam had a miscarriage. She'd gotten pregnant because we weren't careful; at first, we were horrified, but we had both come around to quite liking the idea of another child. Five of us instead of four." He gave a half smile at the memory, but it quickly disappeared. "Anyway, she lost it, and we were devastated. Couldn't get it out of our minds, you know? So, I took her away for a four-day break abroad. Left the kids with her mom. We couldn't afford it, I knew that our finances were always stretched to the limit, but what the hell, neither of us was thinking straight. So off we went. It did no good, of course, we both came back still miserable, but tired and broke now as well."

A heavy gust made Esme lurch and both men looked up from their mugs in surprise, but it swept on past, and the boat settled back down to its bobbing again.

"Anyway, things got worse ever after that. I got behind with the mortgage, couldn't pay bills properly, went to a finance company and got ripped off with paying massive interest payments. You've heard the stories, must have. It happens. But no matter what I did I couldn't sort it. I twisted,

I turned, I ducked and dived, I got a second job, but nothing helped. The kids still went without new clothes, we all went without holidays, we survived on a diet of crap." His voice was rising as he became more agitated. "And just recently I began to see grey appearing in Pam's hair. Grey hairs in her mid-forties! And me? I could do nothing about it. Not a damn thing. I had tried everything."

His hands were shaking a little with emotion now, and he lifted his mug to take another swig. "We had started arguing a lot as well, about silly inconsequential things, unimportant things, things that didn't matter. Arguing all the time, in front of the kids who would start crying." His face had darkened with the memories. "I would stay away for hours rather than go home, rather than see their faces looking accusingly at me, telling me to stop shouting, Daddy." He pinched the top of his nose in an effort to stop tears – that would be the ultimate show of weakness in front of this kindly old man.

He took another deep breath and sipped his tea until the spasm of emotion passed. Ben realised the emotion at play and just let him sit.

"So! Then I began to think, well Pam's a good-looking woman. If I wasn't around, she'd find herself another bloke, a decent bloke who could give her the life she and the kids deserve, you know." He rubbed his freehand across his eyes. "So, one day I got up, made her a cup of tea, checked the kids were still asleep, backed the car off the drive, and instead of driving to work drove down here. You know I wasn't

CHAPTER SEVEN

even sure, thinking back, where I was going, or what I was thinking, if I was thinking at all, I just drove just away."

He placed his now empty mug gently onto the deck between his feet and looking up, stared straight at Ben. "So that's it, mate, that's the whole story. If you want me to get off the boat and walk away right now, I'll understand. I'm not sure what my reasons were, suddenly it all got too much, not a break-down, just an overload, a fuse blew." Again, he rubbed his eyes. "No. That's a load of crap, I was a coward, a failure, I just ran."

He could not look at Ben, could not look at anything, he just sat staring at nothing, feeling vaguely cleansed, empty. There it was told, that was it. Whatever happened now was out of his control.

Ben finished his mug too and placed it on the wooden bench seat next to him. He had been shocked at what he had heard; it was not what he had expected at all. "A sad tale, son," he said, "though I think you're being a bit hard on yourself."

He wanted to say something more but did not want to appear to be in agreement with this troubled young man opposite. Who knew how anyone would react in a similar situation? He hoped he himself might have done things differently, have faced up to his problems better, but who knew?

The human mind was a strange thing. He remembered that it was only Annie who had stopped him going off the rails completely when Mo had died. But for her he might have done anything, done terrible damage to anyone, or to himself. He knew what it was to temporarily lose your wits, your reason.

"Look," he said finally. "We'll move Esme over to the ramp as soon as Ron calls, and then you and I will walk back and have a beer at the pub. I was going to propose something to you, but I'm not sure this is the time, now, and I'm not sure it would work anyway."

Dave looked up at him and nodded, a half smile belying the bleak look in his eyes. "OK."

"But," Ben said, "just before we finish here, you know you're going to have to go back sooner or later, don't you, son?"

"Yes." It was the first time Dave had said it out aloud. "But we'll talk about it some more over a pint."

There was a shout almost drowned by the wind. Ron was waving at them. It was time for Esme to be moved over to the crane.

As they both stood up, Ben said, "Fire up the engine, son, I'll get the lines."

Dave said, "Ben, there's something else."

"What?" said Ben, climbing over the gunwale on to the pontoon and leaning backwards to rub his aching spine.

"Helen's pregnant."

"Oh Christ, son."

CHAPTER EIGHT

One-minute little Damien was there and the next he was not. His young mom Karen couldn't believe what she had just seen. Paul, her husband, had just come back from taking their other son Tyler for a pee in the public toilet and was kneeling to fasten up the little boy's waterproof. "There you go, little soldier," he was saying. "Is that better now?"

There was a shrill cry and both parents looked aghast as their younger boy, the little four-year-old, was physically picked up off the quay and thrown into the swirling muddy grey waters by a huge gust of wind. It occurred to both parents now that it was too late, that perhaps in this weather, they would have been better off staying inside the B&B instead of bringing their two young children for a walk along the front, certainly not so near the edge of the quay. True, there were many other people around intent on not letting the weather ruin their holiday, but perhaps not with children so young.

Paul stood and rushed to the water's edge, a cry of panic and anguish howling from him. He was dreadfully aware even in those few seconds that he should have learned to swim at some stage in his twenty-six years, should have taken his father's advice. His little son was already twenty yards out and being swept downstream by the outgoing tide. The turbulent water whipped as it was by the wind and the rain looked like the inside of a washing machine. The little boy hampered by his wellingtons and his voluminous red waterproof was just managing to keep his head out of the water as he doggy paddled furiously, wailing in fear for help.

Non swimmer or not, Paul did what any father would do and started to kick off his own boots. He was going in. Going into the water with no thought of how he would get to his son, or how he would get back to the quay, he just had to get out there. Karen was wailing and shrieking, gazing at her disappearing young son, her reason gone.

As Paul struggled with his second boot, a figure in an old and faded anorak ran past him and without hesitation dived hugely into the raging water. The speed of his run taking him yards out into the turmoil. A head surfaced between the short steep waves and turned back and forth seeking the whereabouts of the child.

Karen, and two or three others who were already at the water's edge were pointing and shouting, telling him the boy was 'over there', and to 'be quick'.

Dave had not consciously thought about what he was doing. He and Ben, having seen Esme lifted from the water and swung onto the quay dripping water hugely as she hung on the crane strops, had been walking slowly back

CHAPTER EIGHT

to the town, and the pub. Their conversation was deep and intense, so much so that it was not until the child cried in panic that they had raised their heads and seen the danger.

His old wellingtons kicked off in an instant, Dave ran as fast as he could and did not stop or pause at all when he reached the edge of the quay, but just launched himself off it, his speed taking him far out. Surfacing, he could not believe the cold, it took his breath away, and he had a moment of panic as he realised, he might not be able to breathe or swim out here. His instinctive gesture when a child's life was in danger might end badly for both of them.

His anorak was flooding, and he tore it off, feeling much more in control as the drag of it left him. His stockinged feet, unencumbered by boots, were kicking hugely, allowing him to make some headway in the churning waters. Where was the boy? Treading water, he looked back at the quay now some thirty yards away and could see a small crowd now gesticulating and calling madly. They were pointing to his left, downstream. He caught a glimpse of Ben talking urgently on a mobile phone.

He struck out to his left overarm, the power of the current carrying him forward swiftly. How he was going to swim back against it to get to land he had no idea. Just get to the boy, that was his only thought. The cold was numbing, the rain and spray stinging his eyes. The short choppy waters seemed intent on hampering him as much as they could. Keep it calm, he was telling himself, panic is your enemy, just find the boy.

Suddenly there he was, a dark-haired little head only feet from him. He kicked forward and grabbed a handful of sodden hair. The little boy was almost unconscious, his small strength long since dissipated. He was just fighting to stay afloat.

"OK, little man," said Dave as calmly as he could. "It's OK now. I've got you."

Panicked and terror-stricken eyes turned to him, and a scream of fear came from the little mouth. Dave raised his voice. "It's OK. We'll get you back to your mom, OK?"

If he understood at all, the child gave no hint but just continued to scream. Trying doggedly to remember his life saving classes whilst still at school, Dave turned the child around to face away from him and slid an arm under the boy's chin. The lad struggled feebly but all of his small child's strength had gone, and he could not break Dave's grip.

Feeling his own strength failing, Dave began the long pull back to what he hoped was the shore. The current was so strong, the wind was not helping, blowing spindrift into his face. Small sharp choppy waves kept washing over his head making it difficult to take a breath. With his free hand he wiped his eyes as he trod water. 'Where the hell was the quayside?' He was being carried past a small, moored boat but as he emerged from its shadow, he glimpsed the bank.

"DAVE!" Ben's voice, very loud, was shouting from somewhere over there; instinctively he began kicking towards it. "DAVE, HERE!" Again Ben's huge voice, guiding, encouraging. 'Keep swimming,' he told himself.

CHAPTER EIGHT

'Come on, Davey boy, kick out now, keep swimming.' He was so tired now. Exhaustion and the insidious beginnings of hypothermia were making him feel drowsy. The child had stopped struggling and was passive in his arms. 'Hope to god he's OK,' he thought. He had not had a young child so close to him since he left home all those weeks ago, and it had resurrected feelings that he had kept hammered down deep inside.

"DAVE, HERE!" Once again Ben's voice but sounding much closer now. He stopped and raised his head. The quay was only thirty feet away and topped by quite a crowd. He had been swept at least one hundred yards downstream, followed by the shuffling crowd moving along the bank keeping pace, and Ben was standing on a set of stone steps set into the wall. He was gesticulating and pointing at the steps, urging Dave to come there. Dave was almost spent now and knew he could not go much further. His lungs were bursting and there was a strange fluttering darkness, his grip on the youngster maintained by willpower alone. He could feel his own little daughter's arms around his neck as he bent down to kiss her goodnight as he did every evening when she was freshly washed with hair neatly combed and smelling of talcum.

'Night night, poppet,' he would always say, 'sleep well.' She always curled her little chubby hands behind his neck and whispered, 'I love you, Daddy'. He would always smile and reply: 'Love you too, little maid. Now go to sleep'. He almost cried out now in his near collapse so vivid was the memory.

He was fading fast, the child small as it was a dead weight. Then suddenly with a splash there were two other men in the water taking the lad from him, and Ben up to his waist on the lowest step grabbing the scruff of his sodden jumper "Come on now, son, we've got you. Well done, that's it, you made it."

People all around him, helping him up the steps, pounding his back, shouts of 'well done' and 'hero'. He felt faint and reaching the top of the steps had to sit on the nearest bench, whilst someone draped a blanket around his shoulders. He was shivering hugely, couldn't stop it. A coughing fit swept over him, and he threw up a load of estuary water, which made him feel a little better.

Suddenly a young woman was hugging him, crying and laughing at the same time – it was the boy's mother. "Thank you, oh thank you." She kept repeating it as if she could not stop. Dave just smiled and nodded. He lacked the strength to do anything else.

Someone thrust a plastic cup of coffee from the nearby café into his trembling hand and told him to 'get that down you'. He did as he was told, it was scalding hot, but he did not care; his shivering became less. He felt almost human again. A youngish man appeared and knelt in front of him. He was terribly grave, and shock was forcing his eyes very wide indeed. "You've saved my son's life," he said. "If there's anything, anything I can ever do for you, just ask". He leaned forward and hugged Dave, who again just nodded and gave a slow smile.

CHAPTER EIGHT

"The boy's OK?" he croaked; his mouth tasted of the salty sea.

"He's had a terrible scare and he's swallowed a lot of water, but he'll be fine," nodded the man. "We'll take him to the nearest A & E right now just to be sure, but he'll be fine thanks to you. I'm a doctor."

Dave did not really know what to say, but just stared into his coffee. "Only what anyone would have done," he managed.

"There's nothing as precious as a child is there?" It was a loaded statement but only he knew it. He was very tired now and tears welled in his eyes as the enormity of what had just happened began to overwhelm him and fear and exhaustion were coming through as tears. A strong arm encircled his shoulders and Ben's deep strong voice said, "Come on then, son, let's get you back to the cottage. A good fire and a lot more tea with a good shot of brandy in it is what you need."

Dave felt himself almost lifted off the bench and with a lot of help from Ben on one side and another man on the other, he began to make his way on wobbly legs down the quay.

He was only half conscious and concentrating just to put one foot in front of the other, so he failed to notice standing in the crowd that was quite large now, a brassy, blonde-haired woman leaning on the arm of a much younger man with whom she had come to the coast for a dirty weekend, peering intently at him.

***

Helen's mobile rang as she was explaining to an old couple the intricacies of the decoration and its production process of the iron age bowl in the glass cabinet in front of them. They were nodding politely even though her technical explanation had gone a little over their heads. 'What a pleasant and knowledgeable young woman,' the wife was thinking, 'so rare to find such manners in one so young these days.'

The jarring tinny tones of Laura Marling erupted from Helen's slacks pocket. "Excuse me," she apologized, "I have to take this." Turning, she walked slowly away, holding the phone up to her ear.

"What!" they heard her say, clearly shocked. "Is he OK? Thank God for that. I'm coming straight over."

Turning, Helen raised her voice to address the dozen or so people that were meandering around the exhibits on this floor.

"I'm so sorry, everyone, but due to an emergency I'm going to have to close the museum for a short while. I do apologise."

There were a few groans but in the main the browsers were a relaxed, amiable bunch and, accepting her news with resignation, shuffled towards the exit. Helen took the stairs to the upper level two at a time and shouted out the same message with similar results. Soon the museum was empty and ensuring that all the lights were turned off – they had

CHAPTER EIGHT

been on despite being the middle of the day because of the darkness of the storm clouds – she was able to lock the big double doors and donning her waterproof hare off to Ben and Annie's cottage.

Annie had been quietly preparing vegetables for a hot pot this evening when Ben phoned her to tell her what had happened and to ask her to sort out a clean and dry set of his old clothes for David.

She was glad of the interruption, it sounded as if young David was going to be fine, and now she had something to do. As she had stood at the sink, she had been morosely peering through the rain-lashed window in front of her at the lowering clouds lumbering across the sky. She was a bit down today. For some reason memories of dear Mo kept springing unbidden into her mind. She couldn't stop them. It was on such a day as this that their daughter, after a long and brave fight against a remorseless enemy that gave her no quarter, and no mercy, had left them. They knew she was going, had been advised by the doctor and the nurse that this was probably the day. She and Ben had sat either side of her hospital bed, holding her hands and trying with the force of their will to keep her here. But they knew it was hopeless. She was unconscious now and seemed to struggle for every breath. No one was saying anything, what was there to say? They had sat and listened to the heavy rain outside patter and thrash at the windows.

Slowly they watched her drift away like an outgoing tide disappearing off a beach as night falls and the sinking sun flares in the west. Raising her head for the umpteenth time, Annie had peered at her daughter's worn and thin face and realised she had gone.

"Mo," she had said softly. No answer. "Mo." Again, nothing. Those lovely China blue eyes so full of love and laughter would never open again.

Ben, on the other side of the bed, raised his head and looked at his beloved daughter's face. He sighed hugely and raising her hand kissed it. "I think she's gone, girl" was all he could manage. He turned away and looked out of the window.

With an effort Annie pulled herself back into the present. No sense brooding on all that now, bloody weather. She shook herself, dispelling the ghosts; she had things to do. Ben had asked for a set of dry clothes and a hot drink. Lots to attend to. She took off her apron, threw it onto the kitchen table and ran up the stairs.

When Helen arrived at the cottage Dave was sitting comfortably in front of the blazing fire in the small lounge. His feet in an outsize pair of fisherman's grey woollen socks, perched on a small stool in front of him. He looked like a small boy who has stolen his dad's clothes – despite his age Ben was still considerably stockier. Huge chunky faded blue jumper and outsized combat trousers completed his ensemble. He was grinning sheepishly and hugging a steaming mug of cocoa between his hands.

He was feeling almost human again now and was secretly enjoying the attentions of Annie who fussed around

CHAPTER EIGHT

him like a mother hen. He nodded to Helen as she came in and could not repress a chuckle.

"Before you ask, I'm fine," he said. "Lot of fuss about nothing."

Helen walked over to him and hugged him to her. "You bloody fool, love," she said. "You could have been killed."

"Nah," chuckled Dave. "No chance."

"There was every chance, son," interrupted Ben who was perched on the arm of the small settee opposite. "It was a brave thing to do and no mistake."

Dave shrugged self-consciously. "Well I had no choice, couldn't let the kid drown, could I?" His face looked very gaunt and drained in the firelight.

Helen squatted down next to his chair and laid a proprietary hand on his leg. "What happened, Ben?" she enquired.

Annie bustled in from the kitchen with a cup of tea for her which she took gratefully. "Thanks, Annie, you're an angel." She sipped appreciatively.

Ben told her the whole story quickly and without embellishment. Dave thought it sounded far more dramatic than it in fact had been and said so.

"Bloody hell, love," breathed Helen when Ben had finished. "I can't believe it. How did the little boy get to be in the water anyway?"

Dave opened his mouth but got no further as Ben butted in and explained in greater detail, finishing with: "It could have ended badly, young lady, but thanks to your man here it didn't. Thank the Lord".

Annie looked at her husband sharply – it was the first time he had mentioned God since Mo.

"Amen to that," echoed Helen. She suddenly burst out laughing, both with relief and humour. "I've just remembered I've closed the bloody museum. Just told everybody to leave, hustled them out and locked the doors. What was I thinking?"

Ben chuckled. "I think in this instance we can forgive you."

Annie had moved back into the kitchen to fetch herself a cup of tea and now returning sat down next to Ben. "Did you two get chance to have a chat?" she asked artfully, looking up at Ben.

Helen peered enquiringly at these two elderly people she loved dearly. "A chat?" she queried. "What about?"

Ben was dismissive and it was obvious to Annie that he did not wish to talk about it at this moment. "Yes and no, girl, yes and no, but it'll do for another day now. OK?"

Annie acknowledged with the familiarity born of long years together that was almost telepathy that Ben did not wish to discuss things at this time. They would talk later when they were alone.

She nodded slowly and took a drink of her tea.

Helen looked from Ben to Annie, and then to Dave. All three seemed reluctant to take this conversation further and she was sensitive and astute enough to realise she could get all she wanted to know later from Dave, so she let it go.

CHAPTER EIGHT

Ben sighed and realised that he could not avoid telling his wife of the ruin of all their plans. He must tell her what he had learned from Dave. Must tell her that there was very little chance, if any at all, that this young couple who they had taken to their hearts would settle down in this little town. He knew how much it would wound his wife who had a surrogate daughter now to replace at least a little dear Mo. His own plans and dreams were lying in a ruin, but he knew Annie would take it much harder. He was not looking forward to that conversation at all.

Talk continued in a desultory manner as Dave slowly regained his colour and the warmth of the fire and two cups of hot cocoa and a brandy laced mug of tea began to make him feel more human. Ben now knew the truth of his predicament, and so later would Annie. He had not been immediately shown the door by this old man he liked and admired, and hopefully Annie would be counselled by her husband. He needed to make some decisions. Big decisions, and quickly before he hurt Helen much more than he needed or intended to. She had sat down on the floor between his legs now and was chatting quietly to Annie; her head was resting on his knee. Idly Dave was running his fingers through her hair. It was all so natural, he thought, so easy, but he knew now as his mind was beginning to function properly for the first time in many weeks, that it could not last.

From the chair opposite Ben was gazing at them both with something like benevolence but also something else, a sadness. He liked these two a great deal and had the nagging feeling that time was running out for them. Yes, that's what it was, Dave decided as he peered back, the old man looked sad as if he knew what was coming and did not like it.

Grabbing hold of the young lad in the river had sent a shock of realisation flooding through his body like electricity. It was the first time he had touched or even been close to a child since he arrived here and it had brought home a tidal wave of emotion and awakening pain, the realisation of what he had done. The enormity of his betrayal of Pam and his children. God knew what had been happening to them whilst he lived the dream down here in the southwest. What on earth had he been thinking? What must his kids think? He could imagine what Pam would have to say to him when they met again, as they must. He was aware for the first time in months that in his distressed state his mind had shied away from any thought of the consequences of his actions. Not considered at all what he would have to face sooner or later. He had kept thoughts of his old life locked away deep down inside his inner self. Had not, dared not, let them out. Until now. The feel of a young life in his arms had awakened his dormant parental feelings. That huge well of emotion that anyone with children knows only too well.

That source of boundless joy, comfort and optimism that unconditional love brings had been absent from his being for too long now, and suddenly it was back. Back with vengeance. What had he done? What on earth had he done?

"Are you alright, David? You look tired and troubled."

CHAPTER EIGHT

The question from a concerned looking Annie penetrated his thoughts and brought him back to the present. With an effort he managed to smile.

"Yep, thanks, Annie, I'm fine. Just a bit spent is all."

Standing, Annie smoothed down her apron. "Right, one more cup of tea to keep out the chills." Her tone was matter of fact, but it fooled no one to the fact that she was seeking to hide her concern with a mundanity.

"I don't think..." began Dave but he was halted as Helen raised her head and turning to look at him, smiled that lovely twinkling smile that he adored so much. The dimples on her cheeks making her look years younger than she was.

"Just one more, love, I think you need it." She squeezed his knee to emphasise her words, peering into his eyes, pleading for him to agree, and he realised the need to stop was hers, and suddenly with a jolt of awareness and pain it dawned on him that she knew what he was thinking. Knew that this could not last, knew that he was only here for a short while. That he was not hers.

Dumbly, he nodded, not trusting his voice to say more than "OK".

Later that evening Ben and Annie were sitting comfortably in their armchairs placed as they had been for years on either side of the fireplace, the small flames licking the few lumps of coal giving off a pleasant, homely glow. Mozart's 'Concerto for flute and harp' was playing low on the stereo unit in the corner. It was one of Annie's favourites and she always played it when she was troubled. The swell and dip of the music soothed her anxiety. She was knitting automatically, her fingers almost unbidden going through the motions. She knew that her Ben was putting off the moment when he must tell her of his conversation with young David and that did not augur well for what he would say. Ben looking at her from his chair idly reloading his pipe, gave a sigh knowing that he was about to shatter her hopes and plans about the future. Sensing his look, she gazed back at him and stopped knitting.

"Did your mange to speak to David?" she said. "Before all this happened, I mean?"

He nodded. "I did."

There was a pause; he did not know how to continue.

"Well?" said Annie impatiently. "Did he like the idea. What did he say?"

Outside the storm was abating now, all its fury spent, but it was still blustery, and the wind still gusted strongly enough to rattle the doors and windows of the old cottage. Rain still pattered against the window.

"It's a non-starter, girl. I'm sorry."

Annie was nonplussed, even though it was what she had expected from the moment he had prevaricated earlier. "But why?"

Taking a deep breath, Ben told her. Told her that Dave was married with a wife and children up country, that eventually, probably soon now, he would have to go back, that Helen knew all about it, had known from the beginning, and accepted it. He told her that their plans for

CHAPTER EIGHT

the two young people in their lives to settle down here and eventually inherit the business were for nothing. He told her that the ideas for her and Ben to have some sort of idyllic retirement, instead of having to scrimp and save and devote every hour of the day to just surviving, was a pipe dream.

When he had finished, Annie was sitting weeping quietly. The knitting lying in her lap forgotten. Bitter tears of self-pity running unchecked down her old cheeks onto her lap. They would get by, she knew that. They always had. But for a brief moment the possibility of a different sort of life had opened up for her. A life where the man she loved had opportunity and leisure in his day to spend time with her, to go and browse around shops with her, to go drinking with old friends, to laugh, and love. To be like it was all those years ago. A lifetime ago. Now suddenly all her plans were in ruins, and a chasm of emptiness was yawning before her.

"But I don't understand," she cried. "What was he thinking?"

"I don't believe he was thinking at all, girl," said Ben gazing into the flames. "I'm no psychiatrist but I think the boy had a sort of mental breakdown. I don't think he planned any of it. What he ran from I only know bits he told me this morning. Who knows what goes on in people's minds? I lost my head for a while after Mo, didn't I, who knows what any of us will do?"

Annie thought of Helen gazing lovingly at David, of the light in her eyes when she was with him, of the same light in his eyes. Of the life they could all have had together, and she shook her head. Reaching up a hand, she wiped her eyes fiercely, willing the tears to stop, but they would not.

"You know when we're young we think by the time we get old we'll know all the answers, have everything straight in our heads. But we don't, do we?" She peered through wet lashes at Ben. "I'm an old lady now, and I don't understand anything anymore. Nothing at all." She plonked down her knitting on the floor beside her chair. "What I always hate in this life is the casual twists of fate that consign all our plans, all our striving, all our efforts, to nothingness." She produced a handkerchief from somewhere and furiously rubbed her eyes.

Standing, Ben moved towards the sideboard where he poured them both a large tot of rum. Handing hers to her, he rested his hand briefly on her shoulder before sitting down heavily in his chair again.

"Take a sip of that, girl," he said. "There's more."

Obeying, Annie sipped and felt the comforting warmth of the dark liquid snake down through her body. She felt a little better.

"More?" she said.

With an effort Ben raised his eyes to hers. "Young Helen's pregnant."

***

Two hundred yards away in her tiny little kitchen, the young woman being discussed by Ben and Annie sat at the small kitchen table sipping a cup of cocoa. Upstairs Dave

CHAPTER EIGHT

was soundly asleep, snoring gently. The events of the day, combined with the brandy Annie had forced on him and the large scotch she herself had insisted he down when they arrived back at the cottage, had finally caught up with him and she knew he would not wake until the morning.

It was fully dark outside now and the last vestiges of the storm were blowing themselves out in spent frustration. From the lounge came the choral sounds of a William Byrd Mass for four voices. It was one of her favourites and she needed the mesmeric cadences to calm her spirit and help her to think. She was going over the events of the day. A day that could have seen the end of everything. All that had developed during the last weeks and months could have finished in an instant, in an instinctive act of kindness and care by the slumbering man upstairs. How could he have been so reckless, she thought, when he knew how much she loved and depended on him, when he knew there was a child on the way? In a moment of madness, he had risked it all for a child he did not know. She took an angry sip of the steaming hot drink and felt the hot liquid calm her spirit. Of course, he had done that. Of course. It was what any decent ordinary man would have done, wasn't it?

Both Ben and Dave himself had been casually dismissive of the danger and risks involved, but she was not an idiot, she was aware that it could all have ended very differently. They had arrived home to find a down at heel reporter lurking around outside their front door, eager for details, names, anything to flesh out his story for the local county newspaper. She had curtly dismissed his enquiries, pleading exhaustion, and one look at Dave's haggard exhausted face had convinced the reporter that she was right, and he had faded away into the twilight gloom.

It had not occurred to Helen until just a few minutes ago that Dave's name would probably be plastered all over the local news for anyone to see. She could not stop that process but feared its repercussions.

As she sat, she was twisting over in her hands a small figurine of a fairy with tiny wings that she had found only this morning in the suit jacket that she had first seen him wearing down on the quay the day he arrived all those weeks ago. He had slung it casually on to the wardrobe floor in their bedroom when he moved into the cottage officially and it had not been touched since that day until this morning when tidying the room before she left for work, she had noticed it and picking it up to put on a hanger had detected a small bulge in one pocket.

It was his daughter's obviously, could not be anything else, but it had brought home to her with a jolt that his previous life was very real, and still out there somewhere. It wasn't just a hazy recollection of his past anymore. She was tired, she knew that, worn out with the stress of the day and the fear of what might have happened. Her mother had always said to her in times like these to 'get a good night's sleep, it will all look better in the morning'. Involuntarily she smiled at the recollection. She must ring her mom; they had not spoken in some weeks. She had not, dared not, tell

CHAPTER EIGHT

her about her pregnancy. She had only briefly mentioned her 'new' boyfriend Dave to her parents, and they had seemed mildly pleased that she was making a life for herself, albeit a long way from home. That she was carrying a married man's child was something she had not had the courage yet to disclose and she could imagine their reaction.

She returned her gaze to the little plastic fairy. "What's your name, sweetheart?" she whispered. "Do you miss the little girl who owns you?" Suddenly it was all too much and with an overwhelming feeling of sadness and impending doom, she gave a muffled sob, watching the big tears roll down her cheek and on to the yellow Formica top of the table. What on earth were they going to do? What did the future hold? For her, for Dave, for Annie, for Ben? It was too heavy to think about tonight and she stood irritably rubbing her eyes and placed the figurine on the windowsill. Tomorrow, they would talk about it and sort it all out tomorrow. Yes, that was it.

Having made this decision, she felt a little better, and moved into the lounge to turn off the stereo. Rain still pattered idly against the window and peering briefly out she acknowledged that out there in the dark the world continued to turn and would bring with it what it would. That's what everyone in the world must face, that in reality we have no control whatsoever over events and our lives, she thought. Oh well it would all look better in the morning. For now, she would climb the stairs, get into bed and cuddle up to Dave, feeling his warmth and comfort, and hope that sleep came quickly.

CHAPTER NINE

These places always smelt so nice and homely, didn't they. It was probably a cynical ploy by the marketing team behind this multinational, but it worked. The somnolent murmur of people's voices overlaid by the hiss and burble of the coffee machines. The occasional whoosh of steam as milk for another steaming cup was frothed; it was somehow comforting. The well-known branded coffee shop was barely half full as it was only late morning on a Wednesday. The subdued lighting reflected benignly off the mirrored ceiling support stanchions and the glistening polished metal of the giant coffee processors. The pastries and soft drinks illuminated in the spotlit counter display cabinets seemed to glow and beckon you on to buy them. The mock marble tabletops were all immaculately clean, each sporting a folded stand-up cardboard menu itemizing the large number of different coffees which one might enjoy here.

Outside in the street, shoppers rushed by, intent on the things they must do today, anxious and careworn, and always on a schedule. But inside, this side of the tinted

CHAPTER NINE

glass windows, all was quiet and calm. An oasis of refuge. A fleeting memory browsed through Pam's mind as she sat quietly staring. It was always an observation of David's that the people passing by each one of them, fat or thin, bent over or standing straight, reminded him of the ministry of silly walks sketch trapped in a Bruegel painting. 'Daft bugger' she would always retort when he said it.

Pam's large latte was beginning to lose its initial warmth and she toyed with the idea of going up to the counter for a replacement, but wanted to keep her small table for two by the window, so she decided to wait until Mags arrived, whenever that may be. She glanced down at her wristwatch. To be fair, Mags was only fifteen minutes late and that was nothing. She knew from long experience her friend's timekeeping was of the 'time will stretch' type. If you added them up over the last thirty years how many hours had she sat or stood somewhere waiting for her friend to finally make an appearance, breathless and full of apologies and a lengthy explanation? It had been the same when they were at school. Saturday mornings were sacrosanct and inviolate. Meet in town under the big clock at 9.30, go to the coffee bar and plan their day. Shopping, or rather window shopping and browsing, dreaming of the future when they would have money. Then maybe time spent in the local music store listening to samples in one of the booths. Did people still do that? It would be downloads now, surely. Come to that, were there CDs anymore? Download seemed to be the accepted way to listen to music these days, but it just wasn't the same.

Who knew. She smiled at the memory of music booths and once more glanced at her watch.

It was early September now so the kids were back in school for a large part of the day, which meant that with a little planning she could be available to 'catch a quick coffee' as Mags said. This time the summons from her old friend had seemed to be more important than usual, some undercurrent of urgency and excitement in her voice had piqued Pam's interest, so she had agreed to come even though her time on the phone these days, trying to boost her telesales figures and its vital commission payment was important.

Never had she felt so impoverished in her life. Dave had been gone almost four months and things were becoming critical. The bank was running out of patience, and the mortgage company were now issuing written threats with consequences laid out clinically in hard, dispassionate, plain script. She had a meeting with the local Citizens Advice Bureau tomorrow and hoped that they would be able to suggest a course of action that might make it possible for her and the kids to stay where they were, but she was not sure.

She thrust such thoughts irritably aside and drained the last dregs of her coffee. Well, she would give her old friend another ten minutes and then the hell with her. How rude to invite someone out for coffee and then be so late. Typical Mags. She well remembered an incident when they were in their late teens and had tickets for a teen disco at a local town hall. Mags had been almost a full hour late and they had almost but not quite fallen out over it. Pam had been

CHAPTER NINE

monosyllabic for some time after her apologetic friend had bustled up to her full of explanation. What made it more galling was that a little later, gentle, but cunning questioning had elicited the fact that even as Pam had arrived at the meeting place and taken up her position in a chilly spot in front of the local 'Boots' store, her friend was only just leaving the warm lounge where she had been sitting with her parents and was making her way upstairs to get ready.

Pam shook her head ruefully at the memory. Oh well it was a long time ago now. No sense in getting worked up over it. Where the hell was she? Outside the day was bright and still quite warm but the sun had that watery autumnal glare to it, not the full brilliance of a mid-summer day. Passers-by were not in warm clothing by any means, but there was a distinct lack of tee shirts and shorts, rather many men now sported thin jumpers and some women had decided on short leather jackets or pastel-coloured hoodies. Before long it would be October and then the cold would really start to bite, the days would get much shorter and they would be off again into another long dreary winter. Would she have anywhere to live by then? Would she have heard from Dave? Who knew. 'Put those thoughts aside, Pam,' she thought. Time enough for worrying and fretting when she was alone in bed at night and the demons came. How long had it been since she had enjoyed a good night's sleep? She couldn't remember. Her mom had been brilliant both in helping with the kids and, God bless her, with turning up on several occasions with two or three supermarket bags full of food. She had batted Pam's profusive thanks aside with a brief 'oh don't be daft, Pam, what else are mothers for? Do you think I am going to let my babies go hungry?'.

The glass door squeaked open and looking up she saw a dishevelled Mags almost fall through it. Her usual immaculate appearance for once marred by a short pink coat that was unusually hanging wide open, not primly buttoned up. The short navy-blue wrap-around skirt beneath it had somehow opened allowing the other coffee drinkers a glimpse of tan lacy stocking tops. Maggie breathlessly scanned the tables and spying Pam pirouetted her way across to her, dumping her voluminous brown leather handbag on the table.

"Sorry, Pammy, so sorry. Just as I was leaving, I had to take a call from an irate client and just could not get rid of him. I've run all the way here on these heels for Christ's sake, and almost thought you'd gone."

Despite her annoyance, Pam had to chuckle, it was so Mags, this stumbling through life hoping everyone would tolerate and even love her for her lack of order and planning.

"It's OK, Mags. You can make up for it by getting me another coffee."

"Done," said Mags. "But I can make up for it in a much better way than that." She gave her old friend a strange look. "Back in a mo." And she disappeared up to the counter.

There it was again, that oblique remark that promised something out of the ordinary. Pam was intrigued despite herself. 'Don't get excited,' she told herself. 'It's probably nothing more than some new bloke that she's met.'

CHAPTER NINE

Returning with a mug in each hand, Maggie placed the coffees on the table and plonked herself down opposite Pam. Casually she shrugged her coat off and draped it across the back of her chair. Her snow-white blouse did nothing to conceal the pink bra underneath, which clearly was a hit with two or three of the old men in the place as frank stares drew an angry glare back from Maggie.

"Let's have a slurp of this first, Pammy," she mouthed and proceeded to empty half of her cappuccino before replacing the huge cup onto its saucer. "Oh, that's better. I've been gasping for this for the last two hours. Really busy morning, you know how it is."

"I was busy myself, Mags," said Pam a little tersely, but smiling despite her mild irritation. "What's so important?"

Maggie took a deep breath and dramatically looked her old friend straight in the eye. "I *think* I know where Dave is."

The blood drained from Pam's face, and she felt herself stiffen with shock. "You what?" was all she could manage. "What?"

Maggie was a little taken aback by the look on Pam's face but continued. "I had a call from Laura last night. She's got a new bloke as you know, even younger than usual. This one's doing quite well, he's lasted three weeks so far, which for Laura is a long time."

"Mags!" Pam's voice was strained, anxious.

"Sorry, where was I? Anyway, she's just come back from a dirty weekend down near the coast somewhere. Not the greatest timing considering the weather over the weekend, which was much worse I understand down there near the sea. Knowing Laura, I don't suppose they went out much anyway." She laughed easily but seeing that Pam was not amused hurried on.

"Anyway, Pammy, she said that she could not be one hundred percent certain at first. Seemed she watched as Dave rescued a kid from drowning."

"What?" breathed Pam. "How on earth?"

Maggie held up her hand to stop Pam and continued, anxious now to reveal all. "But she spoke to a couple of old locals down there afterwards and she was right." Maggie leaned back triumphantly on her chair. "It was him alright, they knew him well."

She leaned on her elbows and took another sip of coffee. "I checked the local papers from down there online this morning. I've brought my tablet with me and have something to show you." She reached down into her bag which was on the floor at her feet and with a flourish produced a small pink laptop. Opening it, she expertly tapped the keys quickly cruising the internet until she found what she was looking for and twirled the machine around so that Pam could read what she had discovered.

Western Gazette. Dateline Sept 10th.

A Young boy was saved from almost certain drowning yesterday by the timely intervention of a temporary resident in our south Cornish estuary town.

CHAPTER NINE

Six-year-old Damien Mathews on holiday with his parents Paul Mathews a doctor from Reading and his wife Karen, was hurled into the flooded and stormy estuary waters by a strong and exceptionally powerful gust of wind, and but for the selfless actions of David Mason would have perished. Without thought for his own safety Mason dived into the turbulent waters and after a lengthy struggle with the elements managed to bring the youngster to shore.

The boy's father told this reporter that "But for Mr Mason's heroic act my son would have drowned. I cannot thank him enough. I and my wife will always be in his debt".

After a check-up at the local hospital Damien Mathews was discharged and allowed to go back to his lodgings with his family.

Mr Mason was not available for comment, but a local resident, Mr Finlay Pencarrow, said: "Dave's a very private person who has only been with us a short time, but he is already a popular figure amongst the locals and tourists alike. This action is typical of him."

Pam read the article through again, and then once more. Maggie, showing surprising tact, did not interrupt at all, allowing her friend to assimilate this cataclysmic news.

Finally, Pam leaned back in her chair and looked across at Maggie. "Bloody hell!" was all she could manage.

She lifted her cup and took a long slow sip; she needed time to think. "When was this?" she queried at length, even though she could see the dateline perfectly well.

"A few days ago, Pammy." Maggie grinned even though she realised it might not be appropriate. "Old Mags has gone and solved the mystery for you, my old mate."

"Did Laura–" Pam could not move her mouth properly, she had never until now understood the phrase 'tongue tied'. "Did Laura speak to him at all? Did he see her?" A thousand questions jostled for prominence.

"No," said Maggie serious once again. "I told you she was not entirely sure it was him, and apparently, he needed some reviving after the rescue and was surrounded by well-wishers. As soon as he could stand, he was hustled away by a crowd of locals."

Maggie hesitated briefly, unsure of how to continue. She glanced out of the window, seeking inspiration, but finding none decided to just get it over with. She knew she must now really upset her oldest and dearest friend.

"There's more, Pammy," she murmured, ludicrously keeping her voice low as if anyone else in the coffee bar would be at all interested. "He's living with someone." She nodded conspiratorially across the table. "You know. Living with someone."

"Living with someone?" Pam was confused, stunned. "What do you mean?" was all she could manage.

Maggie took a deep breath and said it in a rush: "He's living with a young woman, Pam. A real looker, according

CHAPTER NINE

to Laura. She asked around, you know how she is. He's been with her all along apparently. Since the day he left you."

It was too much to take in. Pam just stared; her coffee forgotten. She needed a drink, needed a good belt of something stronger than coffee, but there was nothing. She suddenly felt cold and hugged her coat tightly around herself. It was the shock, of course, she knew that, but that was all that registered for the present. Normal thoughts would resume shortly but not yet, not at this moment, all she could manage was to sit and stare.

"David?" she muttered. "I mean David. It doesn't make sense."

Maggie leaned across and rested her hand on Pam's arm. "You OK, Pammy?"

Pam could not answer, could not formulate one single response. She peered out of the window at the day that had suddenly changed forever; the world had been knocked off its axis.

"Fucking hell," she managed again, speaking almost to herself. "Bloody fucking hell."

***

Annie thought that this had been a great success so far. The evening was warm for mid-September and the campfire that Ben, Dave, and the others had built would keep out the chills as the temperature dropped. It had been her idea, of course. She had thought about it, and planned it, and badgered everyone who was here to come, had refused to take no for an answer. With uncharacteristic obstinacy and persistence, she had made it happen.

Having finally come to terms with the way things were and what would now inevitably happen with the ultimate catastrophic effects on hers and Ben's plans for their old age, she had decided that they must somehow mark David's time in their community, not just let him slip away one morning unnoticed, furtive, feeling guilty like a whipped dog. No, that was not going to happen.

She had camouflaged the event and its true meaning by telling everyone that it was a gathering not only to celebrate David's incredible act of bravery, but also to draw a line under the summer and look forward to the autumn and winter as people had done for millennia. Way back to the times of the hunter gatherer tribes of the early neolithic era people had thought it pertinent to note the change of the seasons and give thanks to the gods for their bounty and beneficence, and to celebrate the fact that they were all still alive and walking the earth. She smiled to herself, a slow secretive smile as she acknowledged that some of Helen's gentle, casual, and regular lectures on early prehistory had been retained in her old brain. Well, it just proved the maxim that you were never too old to learn.

Surrounding her on this shingly beach were most of the people she loved. Old friends, new friends. Helen who had almost filled the void left by Mo, almost but not quite, and Dave of course who had altered everything in such a

CHAPTER NINE

short time. A troubled stranger had crept into the town one morning and altered the dynamic of their somnolent existence forever.

It was twilight and whilst above them the sky was dark and pocked with the first hint of stars, out on the horizon where the sea met the sky it was still quite light with a luminous rose-tinted glow. Anyone between Annie and the sea appeared only as silhouettes. It made for a comforting scene. Just off to her right, the large fire built of driftwood by the men crackled and blazed contentedly and the warm glow from it coloured the figures seated around it, soothing their ageing faces like those in the paintings by Rembrandt or Caravaggio that she had seen in books.

There were about twenty people in all, men and women that she had known and loved for years, some that she had grown up with, gone to school with, and the occasional person not so well known to her who had been invited by others. The night was full of the sound of good-natured talk and laughter. Wine and beer had been brought in profusion and the men were roasting potatoes and sausages in the flames, as they had done when they were teenagers on just such nights as this. Someone had brought a small portable CD player and the relaxing gentle rhythms of a Miles Davis album provided a soothing background to the gentle chatter.

Only she and Ben knew the real reason for this gathering. The predicament that Helen and Dave faced was their business and theirs alone. Even they, the real players in this drama, had not realised or faced yet what the future held. But Annie knew. She had seen much more of life and its casual cruelty and disregard for people's feelings than had the two younger people. She could see Dave now standing down near the shore with a can in his hand listening with interest to some amusing story told by big Saul.

The sea after the recent storms was quiet and benevolent tonight. Small wavelets whispered and chuckled onto the beach leaving a frothy line like white lace when they slid backwards into the water. It was all so lovely, so peaceful. This was what life was really about, these little moments, these pictures frozen in time that remain with us for all of our lives. Quiet little fragments of happiness amidst the chaos, the heartache and the tumult.

Annie's thoughts were rudely interrupted as Helen, dressed tonight in jeans and a lacy white sleeveless top that seemed to glow in the twilight, suddenly appeared and slumped down beside her.

"Thanks for organizing this, Annie, it's wonderful."

Annie raised her glass of wine in salute. "You're welcome. Although it's not just for you, I thought after the last few days we all needed something to smile about."

Helen wrapped her arm around the old lady's cardigan clad shoulders and hugged her. "Well whatever the reason, thank you."

Annie nodded towards the silhouetted David down near the shoreline. "How's David? Fully recovered from his heroics?"

CHAPTER NINE

Helen nodded. "Yeah, he's fine. He was very tired the following day and the day after that, and I'm so grateful to Ben for giving him a couple of days off."

Annie chuckled. "The old boy was a bit worried about him, I don't mind telling you. Of course, he was there so he saw what might have happened. It could all have gone very wrong indeed. Thank the Lord it had a happy ending."

Helen raised her own can of cider. "Amen to that."

They watched as Dave and big Saul turned and trudged back to the fire still deep in conversation. Dave noticed them watching and raised his drink in greeting. He found a place in the circle around the fire and lowered himself to the shingle a little stiffly. His legs still aching from his recent exertions.

"He's come a long way since he arrived," mused Annie. "I hardly recognize him from that haggard, drained, pale-faced figure I was first introduced to all those weeks ago, and that's down to you, my girl."

Helen smiled softly as she watched David. "Hmm. Well, I think it's all of us, and this place of course, and Esme, and the sea. I get the impression he was living the wrong life, like a square peg in a round hole if that's not too simple an explanation."

Annie turned to look at the lovely young woman beside her. "And you look different, too, if you don't mind me saying so my lover. You used to look like a lost soul, wandering around the town aimlessly. Seeming to be in a world of your own most of the time. We had no choice, Ben and I, but to take you under our wing. Ben used to worry about you a lot. But not now. He looks at you and he's like a proud father who sees his daughter blossoming and making a decent life for herself. He feels gratified somehow." She chuckled deprecatingly. "Listen to me? Gratified indeed. Where did I get a word like that from?"

They both laughed companionably. Easy in each other's company.

Someone had told a funny story to the crowd around the fire and there was a sudden burst of laughter and outraged female shrieks as the punchline came. It was almost fully dark now and the warming glow of the fire reflected from the surrounding tanned, careworn faces, caressing the laughter lines, easing the strain of hard lives written in every wrinkle and crease.

Annie became suddenly serious. "Has he thought about what he is going to do, Helen? You know, about his other family?"

The pleasure drained from Helen's face, and she peered down at her drinks can as if an answer were in there.

She had almost forgotten that Dave's history and predicament were not a secret known only to herself anymore. "Not that he's told me. Oh, I know that it's on his mind. I see him go off into a trance sometimes, see the light go out of his eyes as he wrestles with some demon riding him. I don't like to intrude, don't want to push him about it. Don't want him to feel he's being forced to make a decision, until he's ready to. I think saving that little boy, holding the youngster close to him, brought memories flooding back to

CHAPTER NINE

overwhelm him." Her voice had become very wobbly, and a tear rolled slowly down her cheek, glinting in the firelight.

"I don't want him to go, Annie. Don't know what on earth I'll do without him. I've only known him for a few months, but he's the love of my life whatever that means. I never understood that phrase before. Love at first sight, and all those silly lines, I thought they were just for song writers, but they're not, are they?" A small sob escaped unbidden, like a cat running out of a front door. She sighed hugely. "But deep inside me I know that he has to go. He must. A wife and two kids? He has no choice, does he? I just don't think he has acknowledged it to himself yet. I think he shies away from the idea. Can't face it. If ever I've seen a man torn in two, I'm seeing it now."

She leaned back on her elbows so that Annie hid her from the fire, her face would not now be lit by the flames a few yards away. Her belly underneath the white top was distended a little already. Not much. Anyone not knowing the situation would just think she had put on a little weight. It was hardly noticeable yet, but it would be in a few weeks. It reminded Annie that she would have to deal with that situation as well.

She raised her hand and stroked Helen's hair. She almost felt like crying herself. She had no answers for this troubled young woman, no homegrown philosophy to offer the surrogate daughter she had adopted, and she felt helpless, impotent, unable to provide a solution. She was older, wiser some would say, but she felt useless, in some way failing this vulnerable young woman.

"One thing I'm grateful for just at this moment, Annie," continued Helen as if she were talking to herself, "I don't think that he has realised the inevitable. It hasn't occurred to him yet. I don't think he understands that he has no choice at all in the matter, no control, he *must* go back, he just doesn't know it yet. He's a good man, and even if he was returning to a horrible life, which I know he's not, he would still have to go. When he faces it, he'll feel it's his duty, because that's what a good man would do." She reached down and grabbed a handful of shingle, and allowed it to fall through her fingers like sand through an egg timer. "But he hasn't fully realised all of this yet, and I know I'm being selfish but I'm saying nothing to influence him, not a word."

She lay further back resting her head on the shingle and laid her bare arm across her eyes. Another small sob was choked back, she sounded like a wounded little girl railing at the uncaring world. Annie once more stroked her hair, wishing she could solve the young woman's troubles, but knew she couldn't, and it made her feel desperately sad. Feeling suddenly that she was being watched, she glanced up quickly and caught sight of Dave sitting the other side of the fire, a look of anguish and concern on his face as he watched Helen.

With a grief almost too sore for tears, Annie thought. "He *does* know."

***

CHAPTER NINE

He loved waiting outside the school gates for his kids. One minute all was peace and silence except for the gossiping housewives who, enjoying the company of their friends in an otherwise boring day, stood in clumps on the pavement, and the next minute it was utter chaos with screaming, laughing children freshly released for the day, darting everywhere like chickens after thrown millet.

He spotted his own kids hand in hand, much to little Petey's disgust. He was trying to pull away from the firm grip of his elder sister Darcy who was playing mother and holding on to him for grim death. Both were dragging their over-large backpacks along the floor behind them. The teacher on gate duty always insisted on having the collecting grown-up pointed out to her by the children and only let them go through the gate when she had received an answering wave. He grinned his thanks to her and knelt to hug them both as they ran to him. They were breathless and full of the day's news.

The red gingham school dress that Darcy wore was crumpled and had a grass stain down the front, and Pete's red school polo-shirt sporting the school badge on its left breast was covered in some sort of juice.

Dave laughed out loud at the pleasure on their faces. Their daddy had collected them, they always loved that.

The memory was so real, so poignant that even here sitting before a campfire in the dark on a shingle beach, Dave gave an unconscious mew of distress. The pictures disappeared and he realised the flames he was staring into had conjured up the past.

"You OK, son?"

He had not heard Ben come up and sit down next to him. The old man was slumped cross legged on the shingle, holding his hands out to the flames for warmth.

Dave shook himself. "Yeah, I'm fine. Someone just walked over my grave is all."

Ben nodded unconvinced but decided to accept this. "Hmm I know that feeling well enough. These old bones are beginning to remind me I'm not a young man anymore."

"Rubbish," chided Dave. "You're one of the fittest elderly men I've ever known."

Ben snorted. "And getting more elderly every day." He reached over for Dave's can. "Any cider left in that? Do you mind?" Without waiting for an answer he lifted the can and took a deep swig. "That's better." Casually as one would to someone whom you have known all your life, he passed the can back. "Cheers."

Dave nodded into the shadows towards Annie and Helen deep in conversation huddled together for warmth. "What are those two hatching, do you think?"

Ben followed his gaze and chuckled. "Putting the world to rights, I suppose." He would have said more but at that moment Saul's younger brother Ezra, sitting on the other side of the fire, fished out his old squeezebox from somewhere and to a chorus of cheers or groans started to play an old folk tune.

CHAPTER NINE

For a while everyone sat silently revelling in the haunting sounds, notes and lilting melodies from another century, a gentler century. The music was strangely soporific, and Dave felt his mood lightening a little. With a flourish the music came to an end and to scattered applause Ezra explained he needed to find another drink. Dave suddenly remembered something he needed to ask.

"Ben," he said. "The other day during the storm when we were sitting on Esme waiting for the boatyard to call her in, I had the feeling you were on the verge of asking me something. Telling me something certainly. What was it?"

Taken momentarily off-guard, Ben was silent, considering his answer before he spoke. "It was nothing, son," he finally settled on. "It doesn't matter now. Best forgotten." Nothing in his voice betrayed the dismay and sadness that the end of all his plans for the future had brought. They all involved this young man beside him whose continued presence here in this place was now in severe doubt. It was far better to leave it all unsaid.

Dave peered at his friend in the gloom and perceived something of the emotion behind this bald statement but decided not to pursue it.

"OK," he said. "No worries."

The women were coming over to them now and the men both made room. Annie slumped down between Ben and David, and Helen sat on Dave's lap facing the fire and leaned her back into him. It did not occur to Dave that Helen had deliberately sat like this so that he could not see her face. She shivered a little and held her hands out to the fire.

"It's getting chilly," she said.

Ben took off his fleece and draped it around her shoulders. "There you go, young lady. Don't get cold now. You should have brought a jumper with you; the temperature really drops once the sun goes down, you know that."

It was a gentle reprimand, the sort a father gives to his daughter and Dave grinned in the darkness as he noticed that Helen did not reply but sheepishly nodded, severely embarrassed. He felt so comfortable with these people. He could not believe that just over four months ago he did not know of their existence. Helen, especially Helen, and Annie, and Ben and Big Saul, and his wife Clara, and his brother Ezra, and Finn and Molly, and a dozen or so others who were all now sprawled comfortably around this blazing fire, talking in amiable and desultory fashion, with the sound of the gently breaking waves providing a backdrop to it all. Leaning his head back he looked up at the stars above him. They seemed very bright tonight and myriad.

The galaxies and planets, the black holes, and suns all wheeling above him following their pre-ordained tracks across the sky, uncaring and impervious to the troubles of a few little people on this tiny blue planet at the edge of everything. It made one feel both insignificant but also an integral part of something. Were their lives pre-ordained? Was everything as the Muslims believed 'written'? The Anglo-Saxons, Helen had told him, had called it Weart, fate,

CHAPTER NINE

the way things turn out. It was a mystery. All he knew was that tonight at this moment he felt at peace. The past had gone and was finished, what was to come hadn't happened yet. For the moment he was happy. Could you believe it? Happy. He could not suppress a chuckle that came bubbling up out of him. Helen heard him and still not turning her head mumbled, "What are you laughing at?"

He ruffled her hair with one hand. "Nothing," he said, "and everything." He kissed the back of her neck.

She made a small sound, and he could not tell if it was a laugh or a sob. "Are you ok, love?" he murmured, leaning his head against her back and wrapping his arms around her.

She nodded and squeezed his knee. "Yeah," she managed, "yeah, I'm fine."

In the shadows Annie peered at the pair and shook her head imperceptibly. This was not going to end well. People were going to get hurt. She gazed into the flames and sucked in the future that was so uncertain.

CHAPTER TEN

A week passed; the weather became more unsettled as late summer grudgingly gave way to the relentless approach of autumn. Rain swept in continually from the west blown by a persistent gusty wind that made a start on stripping the dying leaves from the trees and hedgerows.

The little town was gently waving hail and farewell to the balmy days of summer. The local council gardeners had arrived, digging up and carting away for storage the flowers from a dozen decorative town flowerbeds arranged as they were each year with eye catching patterns and colours. The town began slowly to take on a dowdier wintery appearance like an old lady who has put away her summer dresses and donned sensible winter tweeds. The hanging flower baskets that had swung gently from lampposts since late May were taken down and piled into little green trucks, also destined for storage until the sun came back next spring.

Many of the ice cream stalls and boat trip ticket huts that lined the waterfront were now closed and boarded up. Padlocks fastened to the door handles testifying that they

CHAPTER TEN

would not now be opened again for many months.

Ben's boat Esme was one of the few still vying for the depleted trade. Groups of fishermen who regularly came down to the southwest for a late season fishing break knew from past experience that old Ben's boat would be taking out fishing expeditions until early October. They knew that his experience and knowledge of the waters hereabouts would keep them safe, and for his own part Ben was content to do it, he needed the money.

For the locals life continued in its time-honoured way. They were aware of the change of the seasons and the effects on their lives, much more so than up country in landlocked towns and cities. Here on the coast and especially in a tourist town, each season had distinct differences from the season before and many of the locals had of necessity two or three jobs which changed with the time of year and helped to make life a little easier. It had always been so and would continue as part of the endless rhythm of their existence.

Sitting on one of the few remaining waterside benches that had not been packed up and taken away, Ben was repairing a worn mooring line from Esme. There was plenty of wear left in it yet once he had cut out the frayed end and repaired it. Such lines were expensive and there was, he judged, at least another season left in this one. The wind was keen today and he was glad of his blue seaman's knitted jersey to keep out the chill. His old sailing cap was pulled down firmly on to his white-haired head, keeping it warm. Grimly he acknowledged that as old age crept up on him, he was more susceptible to a chill wind.

He remembered an old friend of his, now long dead, always used to say, 'Age steals everything from us in the end'. He had scoffed at the time, naming his friend as an old dodderer, but now wholeheartedly but grudgingly agreed with him.

Looking up from his task, he watched a quartet of rooks probably from the big rookery that infested the stand of cedar trees on the headland march past his bench in Indian file like black clad judges on their way to court, arms folded neatly behind them hidden in the folds of their judicial gowns. He grinned at them and at the same time he noticed a tall, rather striking woman talking to a small group of local wives who had been gossiping a little way up the quay. As he watched he saw one of them point in his direction. Intrigued he straightened up and watched the woman walk hesitantly towards him. She was good-looking without being beautiful, he noted, with a fine head of auburn hair tied back now in a severe ponytail. She wore a no-nonsense trouser suit of dark rust, but with a heavier half-length fawn coat casually slung around her shoulders, as if she had suddenly noticed the cold and reached for whatever was available to keep herself warm.

She walked directly up to him and gave a sharp, nervous smile. "Mr Trelask, is it?"

Ben laid down the line onto the bench next to him and nodded. He suddenly had a premonition, a feeling of foreboding. "That's right. Can I help you?"

The woman nodded and looked out at the water. "I hope so." She seemed reluctant to continue and pulled the

CHAPTER TEN

coat more tightly around herself. Ben thought that she looked tired.

"My name's Mason," she said, "Pam Mason. I believe you know my husband David."

So, it had come. He and Annie had known it must, but he was surprised and disappointed that it was so soon. They had both hoped that the young people they liked and admired might have a little more time together before life caught up with them, but it seemed it was not to be.

He stood and tentatively held out his hand. She shook it quickly and withdrew her hand immediately. "Yes," he said. "Yes, Mrs Mason, I do know David. He works for me."

"Do you know where he is?"

"I do." He met her eyes, but she would not hold his gaze and stared out at the water again. "He's out with my boat. A party of fishermen."

"David? Steering a boat?" The scorn in her voice was palpable. "Really? Do you trust him?"

He was trying not to dislike this woman. He acknowledged that in many ways she was the injured party in this mess, but she was not making it easy for him with her combative attitude.

"Of course I trust him. He's done it many times. It's his job, young lady."

Pam stared at him and shrugged as if this was of no importance. "Very well."

She was thinking to herself that this old guy was like a caricature of the old man of the sea, but she would not like to cross him. 'David taking a boat out? What the hell?'

She peered up and down the quay, formulating her next question. "I'm also looking for a young woman that he's been living with. Do you know her?"

Ben nodded. "I do. She's a very close friend of my wife and I."

For the first time Pam turned and looked straight at Ben. "I see." They stared at one another, each trying to browbeat the other into submission. It was Pam who suddenly lost the battle and seemed to deflate before his eyes.

"Look," she mouthed, "I just want to speak with her, and with my husband. I don't know how much you know about what has happened, but I'm guessing not much."

Ben relented a little. After all, it was not this woman's fault and she looked very vulnerable now that she had stopped the pretence of self-righteous anger.

"On the contrary, I know everything," he replied. "Truth be told we, that is my wife and I, have been expecting you, although not so soon."

He indicated a small café just a few yards away. "Look, let me stand you a cup of coffee, Mrs Mason, it's a bit chilly here on the waterside and you look all in if you don't mind my saying. Just a cup then I'll take you to see Helen."

He gently took her elbow and Pam allowed herself to be chivvied across to the café. She had travelled down by train and then bus and had been on the move for over six hours. The anger and resentment churning over and over within her as she peered out of train and bus windows. But now

CHAPTER TEN

that she was here, she was not at all sure what to do. Maggie had wanted to take the day off from work and come with her as moral support, but Pam had shied away from that idea. This would be and should be a very private meeting with David, and she did not need her old friend, however well-intentioned, getting in the way.

Besides, she was assuming that somewhere hereabouts David would still have his car. What to say to him? What on earth to say? She had gone through a dozen scenarios during the trip down, in fact had thought of little else since Maggie dropped the bombshell news in the coffee shop. But even now at this late stage she was still not at all sure how the conversation with David would go.

"Helen," she said as they walked into the small coffee shop. "Is that her name, Helen?"

***

Van Morrison was nasally crooning through 'Into the Mystic' on the radio. She had not liked him for most of her life. She had always acknowledged that he was very good, and millions of people adored him, but Helen had never been able to see it. Dave had gradually changed her mind, playing him often they were alone, and now she grudgingly admitted that perhaps she had been wrong and that he had an appeal. She especially liked one of his newer offerings 'Every time I see a river' and hummed it often. For the moment she could only dimly hear the radio over the sound of the food processor.

Never a great cook, Helen had decided to take a stab at baking and was attempting to make scones. She knew Dave liked them with a passion, especially with thick cream and raspberry jam. So had decided to try. The large burgundy and white striped apron she was wearing over her jeans and t shirt was covered in flour as was much of the kitchen, the worksurfaces, and her face. Even her hair, tied back to keep it out of the way, was streaked with it. 'What the hell,' she thought dismissively 'It would all clean up, and she was enjoying herself'. It was Wednesday and because the museum was open on Saturdays, she had Wednesdays off, and although she liked to spend every minute that she could with Dave it was still nice to have a few hours to herself. She felt very grown up, domestic even. Baking in the kitchen, wearing an apron, and pregnant to boot. What on earth would her old friends back in the real world make of that? She chuckled and broke into song, joining in with Morrison as he crooned on.

She heard the door knocking and frowned. 'Who on earth was that?' Dave would not be back for an hour or so yet, and she wanted to finish the scones and have them ready to eat by then. She could picture his face as he came in and noticed a large plate of still warm scones nestled on the plate with a pot of cream and a pot of jam. She was smiling hugely at the thought as she turned off the processor and moved towards the door. On the way she lowered the volume on the radio. "Hang on," she called.

The door opened on the weather beaten, kindly old face of Ben. She grinned at him. "Hi Ben. I'm baking so you'll

CHAPTER TEN

have to excuse the mess. Come on in, I'll make us a coffee."

Strangely Ben did not move. His face was serious, careworn almost. "I won't, thanks, Helen," he said. "I won't stop, I just had to, that is I..." He looked at the young vulnerable face in front of him, flour on the end of the small, upturned nose and felt real concern.

Helen was puzzled. "What's the matter? Is it Dave?"

A tall woman in a trouser suit stepped out from behind Ben and fixed Helen with a cold stare. "I'm the matter."

Ben looked from one to the other and cleared his throat. "Helen, this is..."

Helen interrupted: "I know who this is." A cold feeling of dread had exploded in her stomach. Still that cold hostile stare.

"Good, then there's no need for introductions. Can I come in?"

Without waiting for an answer, Pam shoved her way past Helen and strode into the small lounge.

Helen gazed at her back and said "Erm yes, please go through". So, it had come, as she had known it must. Anxiety swept over her, and she had to take a deep breath to steady herself. Ben lowered his voice and rested his big, calloused hand on her shoulder. "I'm sorry girl, I had no choice. She knows all about you, and I wanted to be here when you met".

Helen rubbed her nose with the back of her floury hand and tried to smile. "That's OK Ben. It had to happen at some time". The smile did not quite work and made her look to Ben like a frightened apprehensive little girl. "How long will Dave be?"

Ben stroked his chin and looked towards the mouth of the estuary. "Mackerel fishing trip. He'll be a good half hour yet. I'm sorry. Do you want me to stay?"

Helen shook her head. "No, I'll be fine. You get off. Love to Annie." She shut the door in his face, which Ben thought was a sign of her confusion. He sighed and tramped off down the quay, shaking his head. He would wait near the water to alert Dave as soon as he came in.

Inside, Helen moved over and turned off the music before she went to the tiny kitchen and returned, wiping her hands and face with a tea towel.

"Sit down please," she said. "There's no need to stand."

"Quite the little housewife, aren't we?" Pam's voice was ice. "I'll stand."

The two women eyed each other warily like two boxers coming out from their corners. Helen thought Pam looked like the sort of woman who got things done, whilst Pam was in fact a little nonplussed. 'My God,' she thought, 'she's a child.'

"How old are you?"

Helen folded her arms in a defensive gesture. "I'm thirty but what's that got to do with anything?"

Pam shook her head in dismay, then shrugged off the coat around her shoulders and dropped it across the back of the sofa.

"Where's David?"

"Ben told you; I think. He's out on the boat with a fishing party. He'll be about an hour yet."

CHAPTER TEN

"He knows nothing about boats."

"Oh, but he does. He's very good. Ben says he's a natural."

"Is he? Is he really?" Sarcasm it seemed was the order of the day.

Helen decided not to be drawn. "Can I offer you some tea?"

"I hate tea."

"Coffee then?"

Pam's reserve fell away. "How the hell can you stand there and offer me coffee," she shouted, "when you are shagging my husband?"

Helen paled before the ferocity of Pam's voice. "I didn't, that is we didn't for a long time, it was all…"

"You didn't know he was married, is that it?" Pam's bellow must have been heard outside. "If that's what you're saying I don't frigging believe you, so you can save your breath, you little tart."

"I knew from the moment we met that he was married. Dave's never hidden anything from me." Helen felt a bit ridiculous, defending Dave from his wife.

"You must be broad minded, or did you just not care?" Pam's voice was still raised, and it occurred to Helen that the old couple who lived next door must be hearing every word. "He has two children who miss him terribly, did you know that?"

Helen nodded glumly. She could not really defend herself against such anger.

Pam's face was red with annoyance, her eyes glittered. "People like you make me sick. You just go through life doing what you want, taking what you want and the hell with anybody else. I hope you can sleep at night, I really do." She paused for breath, but a thought suddenly occurred to her, re-booting her anger. "But of course you sleep at night, don't you, you're sleeping with him." She almost spat the next words: "You little tripe hound".

For the first time Helen showed she had teeth. "Oh I've had enough of this," she screamed. "I'm trying to be civilized about this but if you just want to stand there and shriek at me then balls to you, lady. Your argument's with Dave, not me. If you hadn't done so much shouting in the first place, perhaps he would not have left."

Pam pumped more anger into her voice and took a step forward. "Don't lecture me, you little slag. How dare you instruct me on what I should or shouldn't have done."

Helen held up her hands in a calming gesture. "Look," she shouted and then taking a deep breath continued in a lower, calmer voice. "Look. This is getting us nowhere. I'm sorry for everything, OK? It's all my fault, everything's my fault. Isn't that what you want to hear." Her hands were trembling as she sat back on to the arm of the lounge chair. "Oh, why did you have to come?" A small sob escaped. "Why did you have to find him. Why now?"

Pam shook her head and some of the incandescent anger dissipated as quickly as it had flared. "Because I love my husband," she said. "Despite it all, I still love him."

CHAPTER TEN

Helen could not look at her. She stared down at the carpet and wiped her brow with the back of her hand and sniffed. "And he loves you."

Pam sat down heavily on to the settee. "He's got a funny way of showing it." She wanted to sound contemptuous, superior, the injured party, but the words did not come out quite like that. "Does he?"

Helen dragged her eyes from the floor and gazed at Pam noting the auburn hair, pulled back severely as some sort of signal. It was a nice trouser suit she was wearing – that too, she suspected, was meant to give an impression. She also noticed the lines around Pam's mouth. The marks of stress and anxiety on the brow. 'This woman must have been beautiful once,' she acknowledged and despite her own anguish she felt a surge of pity.

"Yes, he does," she sniffed. "Of course he does, and he thinks the world of his kids. If only you knew what he's gone through these last months."

"What *he's* gone through?"

Helen moved off the arm of the chair and sat down properly. "It must have been very hard for you."

Pam wanted to be angry. Wanted to scream and shout at this young woman, wanted to grab her hair and knock her head against the wall but she was just too damn tired. Exhausted both with the travelling and with the emotions of the last few days since Maggie had told her the news. And this girl was right. Her argument was with Dave. Not her, well not really. She closed her eyes. "Why couldn't he ring me?" Her voice was lower now. "Just once. Not one word in all this time, not one fucking word."

"He wanted to several times. Twice I was convinced he was going to."

Pam opened her eyes "Why didn't he then? Why?"

Helen shook her head and peered out of the window. "I don't know."

Some local youths were walking past the window talking and laughing, one of them was bouncing a football. It sounded loudly inside the room.

Pam opened her handbag and took out a packet of tissues "Do you know I'd begun to understand some of it. Some of the things I'd found out, I could see why he might feel like running away."

Helen looked up sharply. "What things?"

Pam snorted and her voice became more strident once again. "It doesn't matter, and anyway that was before I found out about you, missy."

Helen was anxious that Pam should not start shouting again so she stood abruptly. "I'll put the kettle on." She hurried past Pam before she could refuse and scuttled into the kitchen where she felt a little safer.

Pam took her first look around the room, noting the shabby but comfortable tiny suite with the patterned throw over it, the small occasional table topped with a few books, and realised how small everything was. It was like a doll's house. "Is this your place?" It was a brittle, inane comment, but she needed to know.

CHAPTER TEN

Helen replied from the kitchen over the sound of the kettle: "Comes with the job".

"Oh." Pam had assumed this young girl did not work. "What job's that then?" She could not bring herself to speak normally to this young woman. Was she the innocent in all this or was she a scheming ingénue? Who knew? Her voice remained harsh. She could hear the sound of cups clinking.

"Do you work as a barmaid or something?" She had adopted a superior tone. Her next comment would be sarcastic.

"I work at the museum cataloguing the exhibits and being a general dogsbody."

"Oh!" The museum? What the hell? "Oh, very arty." Pam could not keep the mild contempt from her voice.

Helen poked her head back into the lounge. "Sorry, what did you say?"

"Forget it. Are you local?" There were a million questions Pam wanted to ask, answers she needed to hear, but small inanities were all that she could think of at this moment. She should have bought Mags. Mags would know what to say, how to put this kid in her place.

"No. Only been here for six months or so."

Suddenly something occurred to Pam through her rage. A mind-blowing question that nagged at her and needed answering. "You said 'why now', what did you mean by that?"

Helen came back into the lounge and stood irresolutely in front of the fire clutching a tea towel, looking a little puzzled. "I don't know what you mean?"

Pam stood up again, flinging her handbag onto the sofa behind her. "Just now. You said why did I have to find you *now*." She narrowed her eyes as a ghastly thought raged in her mind. "What does that mean '*now*'?"

Helen hesitated and then decided that this conversation was for Dave to have. "Nothing at all. I meant nothing. It was just a figure of speech."

But it was no good, Pam had seen the fatal drop of guard, the small hesitation, the vulnerability, and although her whole being screamed at her to leave it alone, that it was too hideous to contemplate, she had to ask, she must know.

"You know for one moment it occurred to me that you might be pregnant, but then I thought that even someone as dim as you would not be *that* stupid." She gazed down quickly at Helen's stomach but could see nothing.

Helen folded her arms in a defensive gesture again and her chin lifted a little in defiance. "OK," she said, her voice quavering. "If you must know, yes, I'm pregnant. Satisfied?" She made to move back into the kitchen; the kettle had boiled.

"Oh no you don't!" Pam was shouting again. "What on fucking earth? Is it David's?" Her face was taut with anger and shock. She felt like crying and shouting at the same time. She must not shed a tear in front of this kid, but bloody fucking hell.

Helen took a step back from the blazing anger in Pam's face. "Of course it's Dave's," she said, her own voice rising. "What the hell do you think I am?"

Pam gave a harsh contemptuous laugh. "Oh you really don't want to know the answer to that one. Believe me."

CHAPTER TEN

It was suddenly all too much. The long tiring journey full of foreboding and doubt, this confrontation, the discovery of the truth, which was far worse than she had imagined, and now this. A small unwanted sob escaped. "You've ruined my life, you littler trollop, ruined it". Small bitter tears oozed from her eyes; she could not stop them. She must not show weakness, she must not. She lifted her hands to her face like a little girl who has been hurt.

Despite the situation that they both found themselves in, Helen found the time to have sympathy for the woman in front of her. After all, none of this was really her fault, was it? She had no idea what to say. Not a clue.

"Look," she said, her voice calmer. "Sit down please, you look all in. I'll make that coffee."

***

Dave could not help but laugh out loud. 'God, he loved this life'. His grin was an infectious thing. He lifted his head and laughed at the blue sky for the sheer pleasure of being alive on the earth and in this moment. Occasional white clouds drifted across the blue like ocean liners on a leisurely cruise.

The breeze chivvied his hair away from his face and he breathed in deeply the salty tang of it. He loved the sea, and the movement of boats. It always rejuvenated him and revived him in a way that nothing else had ever been able to do. True, it was quite chilly today, but he did not care. He was enjoying every moment of this day. Savouring it, loving it.

Esme felt alive under his hands, the small pirate style wheel kicking from side to side, needing his gentle reassuring touch to keep the old girl on course. She bobbed and rocked benignly as the incoming tide met the outgoing river current. Beneath his feet the old engine chugged on manfully vibrating the little craft and giving him a calming sense of its reliability and permanence.

Behind him lounging around the boat in various attitudes of relaxation the five fishermen, all part of the same party, all old friends from somewhere up north, chatted amiably and sipped beer from cans. All wore wet weather gear and seaboots of one type or another. It had been just before six on a fine but chilly morning when they had chugged out of the estuary. They had enjoyed a good morning's fishing and were now looking forward to getting back to their digs and changing before meandering down to one of the local watering holes to while away what was left of the day until dinner. Their talk was desultory and good natured, with the occasional burst of laughter as one of them made a witty remark. The atmosphere on the boat was relaxed and replete.

Concentration was needed here, as Dave made his way through the numerous pink painted marker buoys which were attached to lobster pots on the estuary floor. It was as well to be careful as each one had a line attached to it that snaked its way down to the pot on the seabed. Lines which could easily snag your propeller and bring the whole day to a grinding and expensive halt.

CHAPTER TEN

Many of the larger mooring buoys were now empty for the coming winter. The visitors' boats, which spent the summer moored to them bobbing gently on the water, were now safely ashore in the boat parks and would not see the open water again until next spring.

Dave glanced up at the estuary daymark, a large granite tower atop the sunlit green headland above him and to his right, before peering forward and left to the church tower in the middle of the town. Yes, he was on course and exactly where he should be. He noted the large bronze cockerel of the windvane atop the church was pointing to the northeast and nodded to himself – that was why the day, despite having a bright watery sunlight, was colder than of late.

A yellow painted and shabby crab fishing boat chugged past him, overtaking Esme and moving further upriver, a swarm of seagulls swooping and diving around its stern eager for anything that might be thrown to them. Dave raised his hand in greeting and the local fisherman at the wheel waved cheerily back then glanced at the 'lad' in overalls who worked for him and who was hard at work filling plastic bins with today's haul at the stern of the boat.

Once again Dave chuckled from sheer exuberance and 'joie de vie'. Here he was doing this, enjoying the sunshine, whilst he knew that many millions of people were slaving away at onerous and pointless tasks, locked away in some strip lighted office hidden from the sun and the fresh air.

He had been up since five o'clock this morning but had loved every minute of it. The boat, the fishermen, the water, the weather. This was what life should be like, surely. He remembered reading a saying by an old native American written many years ago which went something like 'When the last fish is caught, when the last animal is killed, when the last field is poisoned, we will realise that you can't eat money'. The verse crossed his mind now and he unconsciously nodded, aware of the inherent wisdom of those words. For a moment it dampened his mood, but then he looked around him again and his smile returned. A picture of Helen popped into his mind's eye, and he realised she would probably be cooking at this very moment. It was her day off and she had dropped heavy hints as he dressed this morning, watched by her as she crouched in the bed, that she was planning something special for him when he returned. She had meant cooking of course and not sex. It was rare for her to make a crude remark. He wondered what the culinary offering would be and thinking about it he realised he was hungry.

He was coming into the stone quayside now and was aiming for the steps. The same steps that he had staggered up exhausted just a short while ago. He had heard from the father of the boy that the child had been checked out and was fine, "thanks to you, my friend," the doctor had said. Dave had not known what to say, and just turned away the compliment and thanks with a chuckle and a "that's OK, no worries". He was not comfortable accepting such effusive praise and had quickly moved the conversation on. Now much later he was just glad the little boy was fine. He'd just done what anybody would have done, hadn't he? He needed to concentrate now,

CHAPTER TEN

it needed perfect timing here especially as a gusty little wind could catch the unwary and prevent you from touching the gunwale of the boat neatly against the quay. If the wind caught you unawares, forcing you to go around again there would be a chorus of good-natured chiding from the punters. Concentrating, he failed to notice until the last minute that Ben was standing atop the steps gazing down at him. 'What on earth is he doing here?' he thought. 'Checking up on me?' A flair of irritation soon passed as he realised that Ben would not do that. Something was wrong.

The old wooden sides of the boat gently nudged the stonework and with a practised hand he tied up to the iron ring set into the steps.

"Many thanks, gents," he called. "See you again soon I hope."

They clambered off, all thanking him in Midlands accents. The last one patted his back and handed him a fiver. "Have a beer on us, mate, and well done."

Dave grinned and pocketed the money. "Cheers. See you soon."

As they tramped away down the quay talking animatedly about beer and food, Ben plodded down the steps. His face was very serious. Dave turned off the engine and for a moment revelled in the comparative silence.

"Hi Ben," he greeted. "Everything OK?"

Ben stepped down onto the bobbing deck and stood in front of Dave. "No, son, it's not. Brace yourself, your wife's turned up."

CHAPTER ELEVEN

He ran. He ran as fast as the old seaboots that Ben had given him would allow. A million anxious thoughts went through his mind as he neared the purple door of the cottage. What would he walk into? What could he possibly say to these two women who had never met each other until today?

He was the guilty party here. He knew that, knew it with crystal clarity, with mind aching certainty he knew that everything was his fault. He had arrived in this place unthinking, in a fog of angst and chaos of mind. Instinct and blind panic had dictated his actions that day all those weeks ago. A mindset that had only recently begun to dissipate, allowing him some clarity of thought for the first time in months. Thought was the wrong word, for he still had not faced what the future might be. Not acknowledged that there would be consequences to his actions. Other people were involved, people he loved with a passion. His mind had rejected decision, turned away from reasoned deliberation. Even as late as yesterday he had still avoided the issue,

CHAPTER ELEVEN

choosing rather to submerge himself in trivia. The small events in any normal day that kept at bay pressing decisions that he knew must be faced and considered.

His legs pounded the cobbles as these thoughts swirled around in his head. His chest heaved with the exertion. He had never felt such apprehension of a confrontation before. Never realised he was at a total loss as to what to say.

Two or three people called out a greeting as he stumbled past them, but he did not hear and just kept running, eyes and mouth wide open, deaf to all but his own heartbeat and the voice in his head screaming at him to stop.

Arriving in front of the small and now all too familiar front door he skidded to a halt breathing heavily. He must regain some sort of composure before he went into the cottage. He knew Pam would be in there and cringed at the thought of meeting her dishevelled and out of breath as he was. What had occurred between her and Helen? He dreaded to think, shied away from the thought. No violence surely? 'No of course not, you bloody fool' he chided himself as the pounding in his chest slowed and returned to something like normality.

He leaned forward, resting his hands on his knees. A few deep breaths and he would be OK. Well, something near to OK anyway. He shook his head to clear it and felt slightly better, more in control.

"Take it easy, son," Ben had said. "Just be calm and listen to what she has to say."

He heard those words of reassurance again and almost convinced himself that all would be well. Somehow.

Although how on earth that would be he had no clue. For the first time he noticed that a slight drizzle was falling even though the September sun continued to shine.

He was glad of it, he needed to cool down, and raised his face to the sky, feeling the cooling drops on his forehead and eyelids. A seagull perched atop a bollard a little way down the quay tilted its head to one side and gazed at him with a liverish eye. 'What on earth had he done? What could he say? There was no excuse for his actions. No excuse at all.' It was only recently that he had started to think straight about anything, but how on earth could he tell Pam that?

His breathing was almost normal now and he knew he could delay no longer. He nodded at the seagull as if to wish it a good day and reached out to open the door.

Pam was standing at the small fireplace, her back to the door, peering at some of the photographs propped up on the mantlepiece, none of them in frames, just the photos themselves, each one beginning to fold over in the way photos do. Some were of an elderly couple, probably Helen's parents, Pam decided, two were of the man she had met earlier – Ben was his name, wasn't it? He was standing self-consciously with an elderly woman who must have been stunning in her prime, and both were smiling sheepishly at the camera, standing on the edge of the water with a boat behind them. The boat bore the legend 'Esme' on its stern. One or two of the pictures were of David, her David. In one he was standing with his arm around Helen, and both were laughing. They were leaning against an old white painted cottage wall. Hollyhocks grew

CHAPTER ELEVEN

up a trellis by the side of David and he looked happy, grinning hugely. A pang of anger and jealousy swept through her, and it was with a great effort that she kept her hands down and did not reach up and tear the picture to shreds.

The front door burst open and turning she watched David stumble in, but it was a David she hardly recognized. He was deeply tanned; his hair was much longer than she had ever seen it and it was bleached by the sun. He looked ten years younger than she remembered. He was dressed in an old pair of faded jeans, and a blue sailing jumper of some sort. Where on earth had he got those sea boots from? He looked like some sort of caricature of a seaside character.

"I'm sorry I wasn't here," he gasped. "I've run all the way...oh." Coming in from the sunlit day he was momentarily blinded in the gloom. Now he realised that it was Pam standing near the fireplace, and she appeared to be alone.

"Hello David." "Pam!"

"You remember my name."

He shook his head. The immediate rejoinder dying unsaid on his lips. This was too important.

"Where's Helen?"

"She's upstairs. Probably having a lie down."

"You haven't...?"

"Don't be ridiculous."

Dave shut the door and immediately the sounds of the ever-present seagulls and the purr of distant outboards disappeared. There was only the sound of the clock ticking.

"We exchanged pleasantries," continued Pam, the sarcasm in her voice obvious. "And she's gone to freshen up and change her clothes. Maybe she'll have a nap," she sneered. She was watching David like a snake, eyes unblinking, looking for his reaction. "After all," she continued. "You can't be too careful in her condition, can you?"

Dave closed his eyes briefly and nodded. "You know then." It was a statement rather than a question. He did not want to argue, did not want to shout. He had dreaded this meeting for so long now. Had known it must come, and been totally unsure of its outcome, of his reaction, of Pam's reaction, of Helen's reaction. 'God what a mess he'd made.'

Pam sat down in the small, battered armchair that he himself liked to slump into when he came in from a day at sea. "Oh yes." She gave an ugly chuckle. "I know. How on earth could you get that child pregnant, what the hell were you thinking?"

"She's not a child," Dave retorted, sounding petulant. "She's a grown woman and knows her own mind, thank you very much."

"Really." That sneer again from Pam. "And did she know she was bedding someone else's husband? Someone who has children of his own. They're fine by the way and thanks for asking."

Dave dismissed this latest barb with a shake of his hand and moving around the sofa sat down directly in front of Pam. "She's known everything all along, right from the start. And there was no 'bedding' for a long time. She took

CHAPTER ELEVEN

pity on me and was very kind the day I arrived, and I'll always be grateful to her for that. She has a good heart."

Pam laughed harshly. "I'll bet she does."

"Look." Dave's voice was raised but he checked himself and lowered it. "Look," he said. "Let's just cut out the recriminations, shall we? You're angry with me and I don't blame you, I've behaved very badly..."

"Nice of you to admit it."

"Will you let me finish?" For the first time Dave had raised his voice. With a conscious effort he controlled his voice and spoke softly again. "Let's agree that the fault is all mine. Leave Helen out of it."

Pam did not agree at all; in fact, she thought the little cow was at least fifty percent to blame, but for the moment decided to let it lie. She stared at her husband waiting for him to continue.

"How are the kids?"

"Darcy hates your guts and little Petey has started wetting the bed again, but what do you expect when 'Daddy' runs out on them?"

Dave looked into his own soul and knew that she spoke fairly. He was a jerk – what had he been thinking? For the moment all he could do was nod. He wasn't thinking that day, was he? That was the whole point. He had just needed to get away, to run. But how could he explain that when he didn't know the reasons himself?

"I need a drink," he said. "All we've got is a half bottle of wine, I'm afraid, do you want one?"

He stood and clumped into the kitchen. She glared after him – 'all *we've* got', had he really said that? As if they were an old married couple and she were the interloper. She could barely keep the rage and disdain out of her voice. "No thank you."

She looked out of the window at the day. Light rain was still falling in glistening golden ribbons illuminated by the sunshine. She should have brought Mags with her. Mags would know what to say, Mags would have put Dave and that little cow in their place in double quick time. Too late now.

Dave walked slowly back into the lounge, a small glass of wine in his hand and sat back down.

"How did you find me?"

"Does it matter?"

Dave slowly shook his head. "Probably not." He took a long swig of the wine and wiped his mouth with the back of his hand. Pam noticed that it was trembling.

"Maggie's friend Laura was down here on a dirty weekend with some bloke and saw your heroics when you saved that little boy."

Dave sighed; he was suddenly very tired. "Oh…Mags."

There was a creaking upstairs. It sounded as if Helen was getting up off the bed or maybe changing position. Their big old-fashioned wooden bed was terrible for creaking. They had laughed about it often. Both Pam and Dave looked at the ceiling and then back to each other.

"You haven't told me why yet?"

Dave was momentarily puzzled; he couldn't focus properly. "Why what?"

CHAPTER ELEVEN

"Why you did it, of course, you wanker, what do you think I mean?"

Dave shook his head and sighed again. "Lots of reasons. You... wouldn't understand."

Pam leaned forward; arms crossed on her knees; her eyes scornful. "Try me." She wanted to hit him so badly. To strike out at his face, to make him realise the enormity of what he had done, and the disdain she felt. But somehow, she couldn't, because there were other feelings involved. Relief that she had found him certainly, and gladness that he was still alive and had not done something stupid.

Dave shook his head slowly considering her question. He knew that if he tried to explain she would be scathing. "Never mind, leave it."

"Leave it? Leave it?" Pam's anger exploded again. "You turn our lives upside down, fuck off to live with some floozy on the coast and then tell me to 'leave it'. You've *got* to tell me something, *you owe me that much*." Her voice had risen to a shriek.

Dave drained the glass and stood up quickly. He moved to the window and peered out. This was not what he wanted at all. His wife was correct, in everything she said. He could not defend himself. If he tried to explain, anything he said would sound pathetic. He could sense her seething anger behind him; it filled the small room, dominated it.

"If it helps," he said, his tongue feeling huge in his mouth, "I've thought of you and the kids, often. I...nearly phoned you a dozen times. ...Nearly." His voice fizzled out.

"If it helps? Is that what you said – 'If it helps'? Do you think it does? Really? Really?"

She had stood up and was standing behind him, aggression in every line of her body.

He turned. "No," he said. "No, I don't, and will you back up a bit? What do you want to do, standing there with your fists bunched, hit me?"

"Oh yes," snarled Pam. "Very much." Nevertheless, she did back up and stood in front of the mantelshelf again, her arms folded defensively in front of her. They eyed each other like wrestlers looking for a weakness.

Dave looked at his wife and despite his need to respond felt a surge of compassion. This angry woman in front of him had been a good and faithful wife for many years, had borne his kids and brought them up, and put up with him. They had lots of good memories together. His latest deep and passionate feelings for Helen were new and an uncharted land, that was yet to be explored, but he remembered a thousand days of caring for this woman. "Look, for what it's worth, I repeat I'm sorry, I can't *keep* saying it." He felt tongue tied, struggling to get his words out, to formulate a sentence, it was as if he was drunk.

"Oh, that's all right then," bellowed Pam. "If you're sorry. That's great. Everything's fine."

Dave raised his own voice again. "Will you stop shouting?"

"I haven't started yet, you wanker." Her voice had gone up a further decibel, but suddenly it was as if the storm

CHAPTER ELEVEN

blew itself out and she felt drained and tired, so very tired. "Oh, what's the point?" she said and sat down again. Her eyes unbidden and expressly against her will were leaking tears. They were running down her cheeks and dripping on to her trousers. She rooted around in her handbag and extracted a packet of cigarettes, lit one and inhaled hugely. "You know," she said, "over the last months I've found out things... things that, well maybe, just maybe explained why. I began to understand a little of why you had done what you did." She took another drag and blew out a cloud of blue smoke in front of her. Her voice was rising again, finding new fuel, new energy. "But then Little Miss Muffet up there dropped it out that she was pregnant. I couldn't believe it. What the hell"? She was shouting again now as her rage caught new flame. "I mean, Christ on a scooter, David what have you done?"

Dave could only nod. She was right and he knew it. What the hell *had* he done? He'd run away and left his family behind to seek something else and live some sort of dream, but it wasn't real, was it? He'd been living a lie. God almighty.

Run away from his life, his responsibilities. Without knowing it he spoke out loud. "We can't ever run away, can we? Not really. We just create more mess, more complications. Whatever our problems are we take them with us, like barnacles on the hull of a boat, hidden beneath the waterline but there, nevertheless. Slowing us down, dragging on us. What a fucking idiot I am."

It was rare for David to swear, and Pam blinked with the shock of it. She realised the depth of his emotion. "What's this 'we' business?" she managed. "This mess is all your own making, matey." She took another drag of her cigarette. "So where do we go from here? Any ideas?"

Dave could not think of a thing to say, no defence that didn't sound banal. But as he was trying to formulate an answer the front door burst open, and an irate Annie stormed into the room, bringing with her a gust of rainy air.

"I won't apologize for barging into a private quarrel. You can both be heard halfway down the quay, and it seems half the town is standing listening."

Dave had never seen Annie angry before and despite the situation he was impressed. Her eyes blazed and her cheeks were crimson with rage. Her hair which he had only ever seen tied back in a bun was loose and flowing around her head like grey flames. She had a Barbour coat draped across her shoulders that he had seen Ben wear on occasion, and it was obvious to him that she had thrown it around herself as she exited her cottage in a rush.

She had been baking. Helen had told her she was going to bake today, and it had spurred on Annie to do likewise. She liked baking, the precision of it, the magical process that turned a collection of unrelated products into something that looked and tasted delicious. It had fascinated her since she was a little girl at her mother's elbow. Standing on a box watching with awe as her mom, flour-covered arms flying, kneaded the mixture and stirred in other ingredients in a

CHAPTER ELEVEN

large brown patterned crock bowl. The radio was always on, tuned to the 'home' service and big band music or ballads were the order of the day. Her mom enjoyed baking and she would encourage the infant Annie to sing along with her. They were treasured memories and Annie had smiled broadly as she remembered. The memories were so vivid she could smell the kitchen back then in the fifties. The flour, the butter, the milk. The aromatic cakes as they emerged hot from the old oven.

Despite owning an old but serviceable processor, Annie liked to do the mixing by hand as her mom had, vigorously stirring the wooden ladle. It was a small genuflexion to the past, to signify at least in her own mind that not everything had changed, was gone forever. Some things were ageless and would always be so. This philosophy was important to her as she assumed it was too many old people. Old people? Was she old now, really? She didn't feel old, didn't feel past it in any way. Her mind was still as sharp as a tack, and she still felt young. No different to how she had been in her twenties. It was as if she were an ageing person trapped inside a body that was slowing down, gradually collapsing in on itself. It really was most annoying and depressing if you thought about it. She had seen a film once in which during a scene from the actor's sixtieth birthday, he had said that he could not believe he was sixty already. "Don't it go by in a blink?" he had mourned. Well, she had found out the hard way as all old people do, the truth of that.

God had not seen fit to give her and Ben more than one child even though they had hoped and planned for more way back then. Mo had come along and from the start had been their treasure, their pride, their little ray of sunshine and laughter, and who would someday God willing give them the longed-for grandchildren. But it was not to be. Those horrible two years as she slowly faded away had been unimaginable, awful, and Mo had left them alone with just each other to carry on as best they could. The smile had momentarily disappeared from Annie's face as these thoughts flashed through her mind. She dismissed them with an effort and murmured to herself 'Come on, Annie girl, snap out of it'.

She spooned the mixture into the cake tin recesses and shoved it into the oven which had already been 'warmed up'. That was that done. She would make Benjamin a sandwich now and take it down to him on the quay. She had no idea why he had not come back yet; it must be almost lunchtime. 'Daft old bugger,' she thought, he must have met someone and be gassing down near the water.

There was a tentative tap on the kitchen door. She opened it onto a small boy of about ten. She had seen him around but did not know whose child he was. She smiled down at him. "Hello," she said. "What can I do for you?"

The boy grinned shyly. "Please missus," he piped in a shrill little voice, "Mr Trelask down near the quay asked me to give you a message." He held out a grubby hand and showed her the ten pence piece that nestled there. "He gave me some monies."

CHAPTER ELEVEN

Annie nodded. "Did he?" Odd thing for Ben to do, but what the hell. "That's nice. What's the message?"

With a deft movement the boy pocketed the money and looked up at the sky remembering. "Mr Trelask says to tell you that David's wife has turned up and has gone to see Helen." He nodded to himself wondering if he had said it correctly.

Annie had gone pale. "Oh my God," she groaned. "That's all we need." She turned and grabbed the nearest coat off the hooks behind the door. "Thank you, little man. Yes, you got the message right. Off you go now."

"Your boat had just come in as I left," the boy chirruped and then abruptly scampered off and was gone around the corner in an instant.

Annie had not the patience to manhandle her way inside Ben's big waterproof coat but merely shrugged it around her shoulders. 'Now what?' she thought. Helen was vulnerable now, for a number of reasons, and however justified David's wife might be, Annie was not going to allow someone from upcountry to turn up and shout at the young woman whilst she was alone, oh no. She thought David might beat her to the cottage but just in case. She slammed the door behind her and with a face set and determined strode off.

It was a relief somehow to realise that David had gotten there before her, but within yards of the cottage she heard the raised voices and saw the group of locals standing listening. She was not sure if her rage was directed more at them or the arguing couple inside.

Pam was taken aback by the sudden and unexpected entrance of this crazy, dishevelled old woman who was obviously angry about something.

"I'm sorry," she managed, her voice scornful, "but who the hell are you?"

Dave hurriedly stepped between the two women as if by accident. "Pam, this is a friend of mine and Helen's. This is Annie, she's Ben's wife."

There was a pause before Annie held out her hand. "Annie," she said, her voice quieter. "It's all right, David, you can move away. I don't think we're going to have a fight."

Pam took the proffered hand automatically, then stepped back to stand once more in front of the mantelshelf as if it were her place of refuge.

"OK. But I don't understand why you are here, Annie."

Annie shrugged the coat off her shoulders and draped it over the back of the sofa. Small droplets ran off it onto the flower-patterned fabric. "It's true I and my husband are friends of David's," she explained. "But young Helen is very dear and special to us, and I won't have her brow beaten by a stranger." She peered at Pam not unkindly. She could see that this woman was very tired, worn out almost, and obviously distressed. In normal circumstances, she thought, Pam would be a handsome woman. Lord knows what she had been through in the last months. She looked close to the edge. Having shown she had a temper of her own, Annie moderated her voice, seeking to calm the situation.

CHAPTER ELEVEN

"I don't want to interfere between you and David," she said. "You obviously have a lot to talk about, but I suggest you go for a walk, or to a pub or café – we have a lot of them hereabouts. Helen is… a little delicate at the moment." Annie had no way of knowing if Pam knew that Helen was pregnant and was not going to be the one to drop it out. "She is involved obviously and unwittingly has made the situation worse, I know, it would be idiotic to deny it, but sort yourselves out first."

She looked from one to the other and finally seeing the sense of it, Pam grudgingly nodded. "OK. David, let's go somewhere else. We don't need an audience."

She glared at Annie, but the older woman held her gaze and would not look away.

"Where *is* Helen anyway?" queried the older woman.

"She's upstairs, Annie, having a wash and brush up. I think this has all been a bit of a shock." Dave was anxious to hustle Pam out into the fresh air.

Pam looked at him and shook her head with disbelief. "She must have expected this, surely? She's not dim, is she?"

Dave didn't want to shout, didn't want to inflame the situation anew. "Of course, she knew it would come, but not without some warning, not out of the blue like this." He opened the front door. "Annie, you'll stop here?" His anxiety was plain.

Annie nodded. "Of course. I'll make a cup of tea." She started to move to the kitchen. "If you see Benjamin out there, will you tell him where I am?"

"Yes."

Dave ushered Pam through the door and slammed it behind him. The sudden silence was welcoming. Annie filled the kettle and put it on to boil. Tea. She would make herself and young Helen a cup of tea. This had all happened so suddenly, no one knew how to react. She would call the young woman down in a minute and they would have a chat. What could she say, what could any of them say? 'Lord what fools we all are,' she whispered to herself. 'What fools.'

CHAPTER TWELVE

David must go home. That was the inescapable truth. The unpalatable but remorseless truth. He was a married man with young children to bring up. He could not just abandon them, and neither did he want to. Helen knew that, of course she knew that. His wife appeared to be a decent woman, and David himself said that she was. A woman who had never let him down, who had borne, and reared his kids, who had kept house for him, who had done what work she could to help with the finances even though it probably left her feeling frustrated at a proper career that had long ago been put on hold.

He and Pam had spoken for almost two hours, nursing a succession of coffees in the little waterside bistro up the quay. The partially full little café meant that they could not shout and so had talked. Probably for the first time in many a long year they had conversed like two adults and not engaged in the almost monosyllabic conversation of the long-married. Pam's initial anger and disdain had partially burnt itself out and she listened to what he had to say with a glimmer of understanding and even sympathy, even though she was still seething inside to tell him what he had put her through.

He tried to explain to her his feelings and the desperation that had led him to behave in the manner he did all those weeks ago. She recognized that he was a man torn apart inside by forces beyond his control, and his flight had been the unconscious response of any creature that feel its life is threatened and turns to the basic instinct of running away. She could not forgive him, nor would she do so for many a long year, if ever. But she was intelligent enough to keep her silence on this matter and give this man whom she still loved despite everything a fair hearing. It was a testament to her overriding humanity, and he was overwhelmed by an upsurge of affection for her.

From the moment he had laid eyes on his wife in the cottage he knew with a devastating certainty that he must go home. Back to the financial problems, back to his real life with its drudgery and useless mind-numbing jobs and the broken dreams. Back to make peace with his young children whom he loved with a passion. But there was hope. He was a renewed man, wasn't he? He could face it all now, sort it out, be a loving father, and a dutiful husband? Yes, he could sort it. Give him a little time and all would be well. Surely, he could do that. They arrived at a sort of armed neutrality. Pam had not assuaged her anger, not by a long way, but she decided it would keep for the time being. She had found her man and he was coming home. Once more there would be two of them to face the world, and not she alone.

CHAPTER TWELVE

For his part he realised the reckoning would not end here, she had been hurt by him, was wounded, but for the moment appeared to be prepared to leave further recrimination for the future.

He was not sure of his own feelings; this latest cataclysmic eventuality had descended with stunning suddenness. Earlier this morning he was at peace with the world around him, nursing the trusty old boat 'Esme' back to a shore bathed in sunshine and just thirty minutes later everything had changed. He was going home, back to God alone knew what consequences. He smiled briefly as he realised that he would see his kids, tonight. Not at some time in the future, but today, before he went to sleep again. He ached to feel their hands on his face, to hear their voices in his ear.

But what of Helen? His smile was erased like a cloud blots out the sun. Helen. The new love of his life. Helen who had saved him from himself, who had shown him that it was OK to laugh again, to have fun. She was sunshine. Helen who now carried his new unborn child. What of Helen?

That had all been an hour ago. Showing amazing understanding and compassion for one who has been so wronged, Pam had said she would go with Ben to walk over to the boatyard and fire up their car, which the old man had stored behind the battered boatshed not long after Dave had first arrived. She told him she would fetch the car and have a chat with Ben and Annie. All in all, she reckoned she would be about two hours and was that time enough to pack his things and say his goodbyes? He had nodded and thanked her glumly. Yes, that would be enough time. He had reached over the small Formica tabletop in the bistro and laid his hand on top of hers. He could feel her wedding ring under his palm. She did not remove her hand but laid her other hand on top of his.

"We've come a long road, you and I, you bloody fool," she said. "And God willing we've got many more years to go yet. Promise me there will not be a repeat of this?"

He managed a weak smile and nodded. What had he done to deserve this woman? She was so strong. Many women would have folded long ago under the circumstances. He could see the new lines deeply etched under her eyes and down the side of her mouth. He had done that; he knew that for a fact, and he was ashamed of it. He would do whatever he could to bring her looks back. To put things right somehow. He silently vowed it.

Now he was sitting next to Helen side by side on the old sofa in the cottage. They were holding hands as they had done in the pub all those weeks ago. Her fingers were interlaced with his and she was gripping him with a strength he did not know she possessed as if she was afraid to let him go. There had been tears, a lot of tears earlier when he first arrived back at the cottage, from both him and her, but they were finished now. Her eyes were puffy and red, she did not think she could cry anymore if she wanted to, there were no more tears left in her.

CHAPTER TWELVE

"Helen," he said, his voice thick, "I am so sorry for all of this, so very sorry, but you know I have to go back, don't you?"

"Yes," she sniffed "Of course I know, I've always known. You've never lied to me, not ever." She sighed and leaned her head on his shoulder. "It's been magical though, hasn't it, love? I mean magical."

He leaned his head against hers. "Yes, it has." He couldn't think of anything else to say, not a damn thing. He loved this young woman with a passion. He had tried to explain to Pam that he had discovered that love was not finite. If you needed more, it was always there, multiplying as required. If you need more love to give to someone new it doesn't mean you have to take it away from someone else. He sounded pompously profound, he knew that, but Pam had smiled gently and nodded, allowing him to get away with the statement.

Dave sighed hugely and glanced up at the clock. "I'll have to be going soon." He felt her hand spasm in his as she realised the truth of his words. "My two hours are nearly up."

"I know," she said, her voice small and barely above a whisper. "Just a few more minutes."

He smiled weakly despite his pain. "OK," he said, "a few more minutes."

His clothes and meagre belongings such as they were were nestled in an old holdall by the door. She had asked him to leave a T-shirt and an old pair of jeans. "I'll leave them draped around the place," she had explained. "It will make it seem as if you are still here."

He peered up at the photographs on the mantelshelf and his eyes fell on the picture of Helen and himself, his arm across her shoulders, hers curled around his waist. They were on the quay laughing, the sunlight glittering on the water behind them. Big Saul had taken it. It was a picture he wanted to burn into his mind, carve it into his brain so that it never faded.

Finally, it was Helen who, letting go of his hand, stood up, breaking the spell. "Come on, you," she said, feigning briskness. "Enough of this, you've a long way to drive."

He stood up awkwardly realising the truth of those words. "Drive!" It had not occurred to him, it had been so long since he had driven, would he still be able to? Of course he would. What a bloody silly thing to say.

Like an automaton, not completely aware of what he was doing, he walked to the small front door and opened it. The sound of seagulls wafted in on the breeze. He would miss that sound; he would miss so much. He stepped outside into the twilight and turned to her for the last time.

"Well," he managed, trying vainly to smile but failing, "this is it."

Her fragile control broke then, and she clung to him, wrapping him with a desperate hug, sobbing into his chest.

"Take care of yourself, love," he heard her say through the tears. "Have a great life."

"I'll come back," he said, holding her arms and pushing her gently back until he could look into her eyes. "I'll come

CHAPTER TWELVE

back whenever I can to see you both."

She shook her head, tears flying off her face. "No," she said forcefully. "No, love, that's not a good idea. This is it, this moment, now, this must be the end."

"But why?"

"I think if you keep popping back into my life whenever you can, I think we may both go mad." Her eyes caressed his face, pleading. "Promise me you won't do that, promise."

He saw the sense of it but railed against it with every fibre of his being. He knew she was right. Of course, she was right. He nodded and laid his hand against the side of her face. "OK," he managed. "You take care of yourself too, and the little one."

She leaned her face into his hand and smiled.

He realised as he said it that he *must* come back to hold his unborn child, to see this woman again whatever he told her now. He had to come back. Had to. If he'd known the truth of it then, that in reality he would never see her again, his heart would have failed him.

They slowly wrapped their arms around each other one last time and he inhaled deeply the smell of her, the delicate scent she always wore, the smell of her freshly washed hair, he would remember it all forever.

Enough! He released her and turning swiftly heaved the holdall over his shoulder and strode away. He would not look back, dared not look back. He knew she would be standing there in the doorway watching him. He knew it, so he kept on walking even though a sudden rush of tears meant that he could not see where he was going.

Above him a raucous flock of seagulls swooped and dived on the air, crying, crying.

***

The car surprisingly started at the second time of asking. A quick splutter, a cough of blueish smoke from the exhaust and she was away, purring jauntily. Pam stepped out from behind the steering wheel and smiled at Ben. "Well, so far so good."

He returned her smile and nodded. He was finding he liked this woman. In different circumstances they might have been friends. On the walk over to the boatyard they had spoken in a sporadic and stilted fashion about her life, and her efforts to locate Dave during the last three months.

He was amazed at her resilience and strength. Many women he knew would have folded completely in similar circumstances and migrated straight to the parents' house for the duration. Spending their time in a sea of self-pity, bemoaning what the fates had dealt them and launching scathing attacks on the absent spouse. Pam had done neither and he admired her for it. She seemed to be an eminently sensible woman. He liked that. For the whole of his life he had disliked silliness, and more especially petulant behaviour. This woman displayed nothing like that.

He was not taking her side by any means. His feelings for Helen were as for a daughter and he would never

CHAPTER TWELVE

criticize his girl in any way. What she had done had been for the best of reasons. Initially for no better reason than the inherent goodness of her heart, she had offered shelter to a troubled and weakened stray who had turned up out of the blue. What had subsequently developed had not been a casual thing for Helen, not at all. That was a fact that he was acutely aware of and knew the fallout and aftermath of these latest developments would have to be faced and handled, not only by her but by Ben and Annie. They would do what they could to help. There was a storm to be weathered.

He sighed and tried to maintain his smile. Why did life have to be so complicated?

"There you go," said Pam, with an air of triumph. "I knew this old crate would not let me down." She patted the bonnet of the quietly burbling car.

She was feeling a great deal better. Nothing was settled, not by any means, but she had found David, and he was coming home. There was a lot to be decided, a lot to be faced, but the future was not as bleak as it had been for the last months. David was contrite and seemed to have gone through some sort of epiphany since she last saw him. Maybe she had been singularly unaware and dismissive of his struggles during the last year or so. She would need to have a think about that, but the kids took up a massive amount of time, and perhaps one neglected those closest to you in the hurly burly of modern life. Perhaps. For the moment she was just prepared to go with the flow and see what happened. Meeting David's pretty, young woman and discovering that she was pregnant had profoundly shocked Pam. God alone knew what Mags would say. Would she tell Mags? She was not sure – that would just give her best mate a big stick to hit David with, wouldn't it? And she was not sure she really wanted that. What went on between a married couple was private or should be. Mags would just complicate the situation if she knew too much. Well, that was for the future anyway.

She motioned for Ben to climb into the passenger seat. "I'll drop you back, Mr Trelask."

Ben smiled and did as she asked. "It's Ben," he said as he fastened his seatbelt. "No one calls me Mr Trelask."

She nodded and smiled briefly back at him. "OK, Ben."

"And when we get back, come on in for a cup of something before you set off." Ben was obeying instructions from his wife. "Annie wants to have a quick chat, and she has told David to meet up with you at our cottage anyway."

"Oh! OK." What did a quick chat mean? Pam was not in the mood to be lectured by someone she hardly knew and hoped it would not all turn sour, just when it appeared that things were looking a little calmer.

Ben must have seen the hesitancy in her face and smiled reassuringly. "Nothing heavy, Pam. Really. The old girl thinks the world of Helen as we both do, and she also likes your David a lot." His use of the term 'your David' was deliberate and he hoped it would assuage any doubts in Pam's mind. It did.

"She just wants to meet you properly instead of walking into a row as she did earlier."

CHAPTER TWELVE

Pam smiled and nodded. "Righto." She put the car into gear and shot off up the lane towards the town.

Annie was filling the kettle as they walked in. The cottage was warm and welcoming after the rather chilly twilight outside. It was going to rain again, and the temperature was dropping quite noticeably.

"Hello, you two," said Annie, a small smile of greeting on her face. The glow from the fire augmented the small lamps that she had turned on and gave the room a calm amber glow. "I'm just making a brew, tea or coffee, Pam?"

Pam sat tentatively on the pointed to chair and requested coffee. She was unsure of quite what to say. "Look, Mrs Trelask," she began, "I'm sorry if I was rude earlier on but you could not have come into that room at a worse time."

Annie stirred the coffee and held out the mug to her. "No need to apologise, Pam. Do you mind if I call you Pam?" Not waiting for an answer, she hurried on. "I blundered in on a private argument thinking that Helen was in the middle of it, which she wasn't, so the apology should be mine."

Both women smiled at each other, and Pam decided she quite liked this good-looking elderly woman and thought once again how beautiful she must have been years ago.

"So," said Annie sitting down opposite Pam. "You're taking David away from us?"

Pam bridled a little at this bland statement, but Annie hurried on. "Don't get me wrong, you have every right to do so. He's your husband, after all, and whatever else has occurred here he has responsibilities not to mention children elsewhere."

Sipping her deliciously hot coffee, Pam nodded and waited. Ben had clumped off up the stairs as if by arrangement, leaving the women to themselves.

"Ben and I only recently discovered the full story about David, and from that moment I have realised that he would have to go home. Before even he or young Helen knew, I knew." She took a long sip of her own tea and Pam realised she was using the pause to think about how she was going to say what she wanted to say.

"When David arrived here, he was a pathetic sight," she said. "Anxious, strained, pale, obviously not thinking straight at all. That much was obvious when I first set eyes on him. You could hardly get a coherent sentence out of him." She paused for Pam to react, but the younger woman said nothing, just sipped her drink, intent on watching Annie's face.

"Ben told me that young Helen had taken in a stray, that was the way he put it, and she wanted us to give him some work on the boat. Ben said he would meet him at least and when he did, he said there was something about David that he liked. Nothing he could put his finger on, but enough for him to give the chap a try."

This was hard for Annie. She wanted to explain a little why they had all acted the way they did way back then, but she did not want to alienate this wronged wife or irritate her before she left.

CHAPTER TWELVE

"Anyway, it all worked out well. David was good on the boat, and the punters liked him. Helen means a great deal to us for many reasons that I won't go into, but he made her smile, brightened up her young life. We had been worried about her before he came." She realised this might be making things worse, but she had to try to explain how it was. "What happened between them happened but not for some time, you have to believe that." The intensity of her gaze emphasised the truth of this statement and Pam found herself nodding. "For a while everything seemed as it appeared," continued Annie, "but we knew something was not right. Ben said that there was a darkness about David, some part of him that he kept private, never mentioned, some secret that was never spoken of. Helen obviously knew but she never said a word, and gradually David became better, looked more human, moved less jerkily if that makes sense. He became a local character; our old friends all liked him, and he began to laugh again." This was quite a speech for Annie, she was not averse to saying what she thought but this was garrulous for her, and she was a little embarrassed by it, but she *had* to try to make this woman understand.

"Helen has since told us that he was honest with her more or less from day one and in the following weeks and then months he spent long hours staring at nothing, unsure whether to telephone you or not. He talked about his kids a great deal, but felt ashamed, and guilty, too embarrassed to contact you." She took another long sip from her drink. "I suppose what I am trying to say before you disappear is that don't go imagining David running off for a prolonged dirty weekend with some floozy, I don't think he was thinking at all when he got here, let alone about any of that. Do you understand what I am saying?"

Pam finished her coffee and laid the empty mug down on the small coffee table. "Annie, this is very hard for me you must know that. I understand what you are saying, and I honour you for defending them both. I'm not sure if I agree with your take on it all but I *will* say is this, I'm not going to be screaming and shouting at Dave. We've got things to sort out, things to decide. I think, I hope, that we are staying together. We must make things better for the kids' sake if nothing else. But I'm not sure I can just forget it all happened and carry on as normal." Her eyes were watery again. 'God dammit,' she thought, angry at the way this kept happening. "But I will say that we'll give it a damn good go. We've been together too long to throw it all away." She wiped her eyes irritably, and reaching across, Annie offered her a hanky she had produced from the sleeve of her cardigan.

"I know you will," soothed Annie. "You're a good woman, Pamela, I can see that. Give it a chance. You've been through hell but so has he. We all do our best as we make our way through this vale of tears, isn't that what they say?"

Pam could not help but smile through her tears at this homespun but well-meant philosophy. But it was her final undoing and she sobbed gently into the handkerchief. Annie stood and moved quickly to hug her, and they stayed that way for some minutes, each taking comfort from the other.

CHAPTER TWELVE

***

The weather had changed for the worse as they left the well-wishing old couple and turned the car northwards. Annie had hugged David and murmured her farewells into his ear. It had touched him greatly, almost as much as the bear hug that Ben had given him and the gruff instruction to "just take things a step at a time, son. It will all be OK if you don't push too hard".

Now they were pounding northward along the dual carriageway that remorselessly took them away from the sea and back to real life. The rain was heavy enough to need the windscreen wipers, and the headlights of oncoming traffic starred and glared through the windscreen. David was intent on driving, and his necessary concentration after four months of not doing so kept other thoughts away.

Neither had spoken for the last twenty miles. The gently rhythmic swish of the wipers and the hiss of the tyres on the rain-soaked road were soporific and Pam almost dozed off but fought this as she realised it would certainly not be appropriate. Not at this moment. She needed to say something, she decided.

She wanted to break the silence.

"Was Helen OK?" was all she could manage, and she immediately felt a surge of anger at herself for so banal and even tactless a question.

Dave just nodded, keeping his eyes on the road. "Yeah," he said, "she was fine." She hadn't been fine at all but there was no sense in provoking a needless argument.

There was another silence. "She seems...nice," said Pam.

Dave did not want to talk about it, but he did not want to offend his wife either.

"Yes, she is." He nodded again. "She was brilliant to me the day I arrived." It seemed an age ago now, another life. It was all he could think of to say. He felt tongue tied, unsure of himself, like a teenager on his first date with a new girlfriend.

"I haven't seen you in that trouser suit before." His words felt forced, but it was the best he could do. "Is it new?"

Pam turned her head to look at him, a sarcastic rejoinder on her lips, but stayed the comment at the last minute as she realised he was struggling but was nevertheless making an effort. "Mags gave it to me," she said.

"Oh, Mags." Bloody Mags again, he thought, but then realised that Pam had probably leaned on her oldest friend a great deal lately. Woman needed confidantes, didn't they? And to be fair, Maggie was a good egg.

Pam knew that his mind was elsewhere and decided to broach the unmentionable. David was her husband, after all, and they had to talk about things.

"She'll be OK, Dave, really. She's a survivor."

"Is she?" Dave did not really want to go down this road but kept the impatience out of his voice.

"She's young, and resilient, and your friends Annie and Ben are going to keep an eye on her, you know that."

"Yes, I know that."

CHAPTER TWELVE

A thought suddenly occurred to Pam. "You're not going to keep in touch with her, are you? I wouldn't be keen on that at all."

Dave cut off a sharp rejoinder before he uttered it: "No I'm not". A car coming the other way obviously thought that he was too far over, and its loud horn shrieked at them as it passed.

"Are you sure you are OK to drive?"

For the first time Dave showed irritation. "Of course I bloody am." He would have said more but just shook his head and kept his mouth shut. There was a silence again for a couple of miles.

"Sorry," said Pam finally, "I just thought, you know, after so long not driving."

"It's OK, forget it. I shouldn't have snapped." He risked a quick look at her and gave an embarrassed small smile. "Anyway," he said, deciding to try to continue a conversation, any conversation, "whatever anyone thinks, I know I've made the right decision, the right choice."

It was her turn now to choke back an angry rejoinder, but she could still not quite keep the annoyance out of her voice. "What decision?" she said. "You never had a decision, not really."

Dave briefly thought about this and slowly nodded. "Yeah, I suppose you're right." He spoke almost to himself. "I never had a choice."

Pam decided to bring an element of practicality into this stilted conversation. "Look, we'll call at Mom's on the way home to pick up the kids. It'll be very late but what the hell, let's get it done. She'll have a few choice words to say to you, I'm sure, but you must be expecting that, right?"

"Yeah, oh yeah."

"Then tomorrow we'll sit down and make a plan."

Dave was confused. "A plan?"

Pam gave a harsh laugh. "Well we've got to find you a job for a start, what did you think? We can't survive on thin air."

Dave shook his head, old feelings of helplessness resurfacing. "No, of course we can't."

"The mortgage is well behind of course, and our credit card payments, you'll need to do some heavy phone work and try to gain some time." She held up her hand and started counting off on her fingers. "The car needs taxing in a few days, and you'd better check on its insurance. You'll need to get your hair cut; you'll never get a job with it like that. We'll have to lash out on a new suit. Faded jeans don't go in an office." She continued relentlessly, remorselessly itemizing his return to the world he had fled from.

Dave was aware she was talking continuously now, droning on piteously, summoning him back to modern life, his life, but her voice was fading as his mind took flight elsewhere. He was driving automatically, on auto pilot, whilst his thoughts were somewhere else on this rainy chilly evening. He was sitting on a sun-drenched hillside leaning against an old stone wall as he gazed out at the blue sea. Helen was leaning against him, he could feel the warmth

CHAPTER TWELVE

of her body through the thin summer dress and she was laughing as she spoke in his ear: "Go on, my love, say it, roll it around your mouth: Lovely, it's lovely, everything is lovely..."

With an effort he dismissed the scene from his mind. That way lay madness. He must listen to Pam, dare not let her know that he was not paying attention. But the windscreen wiper's rhythm summoned him back to that sun kissed day again. He could hear Helen's voice warm and caring: "Let's just enjoy today. The memory of it will last us into heaven". He winced and twisted his head as if he had been struck. This was no good, he must banish those thoughts, those memories.

"Let's have some music," he said. Knowing that in a not unkind way it would shut Pam up. He leaned over and deftly flicked the radio on. The car was suddenly filled with the professional mellifluous sounds of the night-time DJ.

'And now, my friends, on this rainy and chilly autumn night, let's relax to this oldie from the lovely voice of Randy Crawford as she sings the classic 'One day I'll fly away'...'

The gentle haunting introduction flooded the warm interior of the car and David and Pam sank into their own thoughts as the miles passed by.

CHAPTER THIRTEEN
EPILOGUE

In the end it was Annie who saved them all. Dear old practical, no-nonsense Annie, who had seen her own plans and hopes for an easier time with the man she loved, and a more fulfilling retirement shattered almost as soon as they were born.

To prevent David from doing anything rash, such as trying to contact Helen which she knew would lead to disaster, she telephoned him occasionally, assuring him that all was well, and he need not worry.

Because of these brief conversations she learnt that in the two months since he returned home, David had still been unable to find work and he and his family were surviving on some meagre savings and the dole. An idea occurred to her, and she contacted several of the local newspapers with a request. One of them was able to give her the contact details for the young surgeon whose son David had saved from drowning. Speaking with the medico on the telephone,

CHAPTER THIRTEEN EPILOGUE

she told him of their hero's predicament, and he was only too willing to speak with the hospital local to Dave and Pam and to secure him an administrative job. It was at a salary almost double that previously enjoyed by David and allowed him to buy the small luxuries he had longed to give his wife and children, and more importantly provided him with a solid career within which he was certain he was making a difference. Pam and David had come to a tentative understanding and their relationship was gently improving with every week that passed. If nothing else, they would never again take each other for granted, and David was forced to realise that he could not carry the world on his shoulders alone. He would always need the help and guidance of his wife who gave it willingly. He would be fine, and although he would never ever forget Helen, he abided by the advice given to him by both Annie and Helen herself that further contact would destroy the fragile repair job to his life and cast them all to the four winds of chaos. He could not, would not, do that to his (older) children. Annie had assured him that all was well, and he had to believe her.

Occasionally he would dream of Helen, and the brief life he had enjoyed with her, but he never mentioned it to anyone. What thoughts he had, he kept to himself behind his restless eyes that would sometimes stare to the far horizon as he remembered. Annie had assured him that all was well, and he had to believe her.

But all was not well. Annie and Ben watched in agony as Helen shrivelled up in front of them, looking like a flower that has been kept out of the sun. As her stomach grew, the rest of her body seemed to shrink. She looked ten years older, and Saul said to the group of friends as they sat discussing her in the pub one night that it was as if her inner light had been turned off. They were greatly perturbed and tried as best they could to bring her out of herself. Helen was never dismissive or unfriendly, but would just smile sadly and shake her head when invitations to gatherings at the pub, or small intimate meals at their cottage were offered.

One day Annie called around with a casserole for Helen to put in the oven and found her red eyed, tearful, and distraught, slumped on the small sofa in the lounge where she had clearly spent most of the day. Annie held the young woman throughout the evening as Helen sobbed into her shoulder. "Oh Annie," she heard through the tears, "I didn't know how much I needed him until I watched him walk away. It's as if life has ended for me."

"Now listen to me, my lover," said Annie. "You met a good man and now you've lost him. Do you think you are the only woman that this has happened to?" She took Helen's head between her hands and moved to within inches of the tear-stained troubled face. "You've got your whole life ahead of you, and now with a child coming to share it with you. You are so lucky." She needed to make sure this message went home. "Yes, he was a good man but here's some news for you: *there are others out there.* You hear me? It's time to get up off your arse and stop feeling sorry for yourself." She hated herself for adopting such a tone, but

CHAPTER THIRTEEN EPILOGUE

she was increasingly concerned at Helen's declining state of mind. All the vivacity, the humour, the zest for life had been washed away from the young woman.

Helen just nodded and said in a low voice that she would try, and yes that Annie was right. But it was unconvincing.

It was that evening that Annie decided on a radical course of action. Helen's mom and dad knew of course that their beloved daughter was pregnant by a married man and whilst not being entirely Victorian about it they had kept their chilly distance as they themselves vainly tried to assess what their own feelings were. Annie telephoned them and during a long conversation told them the full story of what had happened and what needed to be done to avoid an impending disaster. They could have bridled at her interference, but instead thanked her for her kindly intervention and did exactly what she had asked them to do. Which was to book and pay for a short holiday well away from southwest England, for their distraught daughter. Somewhere that Helen had always wanted to go: Venice. Annie and Ben were not destitute by any means, but there was no way they could afford to do this for Helen, it had to be her parents, and perhaps it would bring daughter and parents closer together, perhaps.

So it was that much against her will and after much cajoling and at one point stern speaking by Annie, that in early November Helen stepped off the plane at the airport that served Venice and decided to make the best of the next five days.

It was the third day of the short break and this morning when she awoke before she became fully aware and remembered, she had felt a young and carefree woman again and she smiled.

The sharp autumn sunlight streaming through the open balcony window was warm and the day already smelt of the sea. The pillow beneath her head was soft and the single sheet that covered her nakedness was sensuous and comforting.

She came fully awake then and remembered everything, and the world became cold. She rose and, putting on her thin wrap, stepped through the net curtains that billowed in the slight breeze onto her small cast iron balcony.

Venice in all its autumn splendour and sparkling colours lay beneath her. The canal that fronted the large hotel at which she was staying glittered in the early morning sunlight, its choppy waters already busy with small craft scurrying about their business.

Somewhere in the distance a bell chimed and as if it were a signal a flock of pigeons that had been self-importantly striding about on the small esplanade that fronted the hotel took to the air in unison, flew two circuits against the brilliant blue of the sky and were gone.

So far, despite the well-meaning generosity of her parents and the chivvying advice of dear old Annie, this break had been a failure. In fact, she felt more alone here than she had back home in her little cottage. "Get right away from everything that reminds you of him," Annie had counselled. "I know it's hard, my lover, but try to forget

CHAPTER THIRTEEN EPILOGUE

everything that's happened." That was easier said than done when every day that went by the child within her seemed to grow and become more restless. Well, here she was 'right away from it' and so far, the well-meant advice and best wishes of everybody had proven to be useless.

She had visited the usual tourist haunts during the last two days feeling her loneliness increase with every passing hour. With her interest in art and history she had always wanted to see this unique exquisite city, but not alone, not like this. A middle-aged couple from the hotel had coaxed her into joining them for the day yesterday and she had trailed along behind them through the Piazza San Marco, with its breath-taking gold mosaics, and had given only a passing glance at the Doges Palace. The soft rose colours and faded golds of the city had seemed too beautiful to be real and she ached for someone she loved, especially him, to be with her, to share her wonder.

This morning she could not face breakfast in the small, marbled dining room but called down on the house telephone for toast and coffee in her room. She planned her day as she nibbled the thin buttered slices and sipped at the coffee, strong and black just as she liked it. 'You'll soon be a caffeine addict if you carry on drinking that stuff,' he had chided her once and hearing his voice so clearly now she physically winced as if she had been struck.

The toast no longer seemed appetizing so, finishing her coffee, she dressed in a summer dress, and sandals. A cardigan around her shoulders as a genuflexion to the season completed the ensemble, and donning a pair of sunglasses she went out into the bright autumn sunlight.

She passed the morning ambling aimlessly through the streets and alleyways idly gazing at trinkets and gaudy cheap jewellery in small shop windows and peering without interest at the souvenir kiosks with their dried seahorses and small statues made of shells. As the morning wore on the air became clammy in the narrow still quite crowded streets and alleyways, and she sought out the small breezes near the water of the Grand Canal. Here pleasure boat captains vied for her attention with practised enticements: "A tour of the Grand Canal, lady? A trip across the lagoon madam?"

She crossed the Academia Bridge and paused briefly to stare down the canal at the famous church of Santa Maria della Salute lying like a basking cat bathed in the late morning sun. Moving on, she found herself outside a small café that boasted in green chalk script on a tiny blackboard a canal-side balcony at the rear. On impulse she decided to enter, the thought of another coffee was appealing, and her ankles were aching. Making her way through the dark, tiled interior she found herself on a large waterside terrace containing perhaps a dozen small round tables each covered with red and white gingham tablecloths. Most of the tables were taken even this late in the year so she turned to retrace her steps, but a smiling waiter dressed in spotless white shirt and black waistcoat chivvied her remorselessly to a table against the wrought iron fencing that fronted the canal three feet below. He pulled back the seat for her. "Coffee for madam, or perhaps iced tea?"

CHAPTER THIRTEEN EPILOGUE

She ordered coffee strong and black and tried to get comfortable. She could feel her baby this morning, and the heat and constant walking had added to her discomfort. Removing her sunglasses, she peered surreptitiously around her at the collection of tourists seated at the other tables. She was trying to decide what nationalities they were. It had been a game that she and David had played many times at local bistros or cafés, and she smiled at the memory. A fat couple at the next table with loud t-shirts and check Bermuda shorts were probably American, whilst the darkly tanned couple in tight designer jeans who held hands and peered lovingly into each other's eyes could not look more French.

"Lovely morning, isn't it?"

The deep friendly voice came from the man across the table from her. Mildly irritated that she had to reply, she glanced across at him. He was not looking at her but gazing down the canal. He was dressed in white jeans and a faded denim shirt. His dark hair was almost stylish but not quite, and his eyes she noticed were a most piercing China blue.

"Yes, it is," she answered.

"Hey, you're English." It was a statement rather than a question. "That makes two of us," he chuckled.

"Yes," she replied again, but feeling that so short an answer was rude added, "a tourist like all the others I'm afraid." She gave a small laugh of derision.

He had not looked at her. Was he embarrassed by her obvious pregnancy? Some men were odd about such things, especially when talking to young women they did not know.

Irritated, she immediately wanted to show this good-looking stranger that she did not care what he thought, so she half stood and smoothed her summer dress over her stomach, daring him to say something. But he didn't. He did not even look at her.

"And you?" she queried, sitting back down again. "Are you a tourist?"

He shook his head and finally turned to look at her. "No," he said, "I live here for the time being." His gaze had not moved away from her face at all. He must have noticed her condition, could not fail to do so, but had not uttered one of the usual banal enquiries she had gotten used to over the last months. She peered at him with a mixture of gratitude and suspicion. He grinned back at her showing a set of very white teeth against his tan.

She warmed to him a little. "You mean you work here, how marvellous."

A smile that was almost sad played at the corners of his mouth and she noticed for the first time how good looking he was.

"No, I don't work, I'm afraid. My sister's husband is renovating the wall paintings in one of the churches here. It's a long contract as you can imagine so a large house goes with the job. I'm staying with them for the time being."

'Why doesn't he work?' she wondered.

The waiter appeared with her coffee, and she leaned back in her seat as he placed it before her. "You want I should bring you another drink, Mr Andy?"

"Yes, please, Guido. Cappuccino, as I like it, please."

CHAPTER THIRTEEN EPILOGUE

The waiter mouthed OK and pirouetted away between the tightly packed tables. Helen sipped her coffee slowly, thinking of something interesting to say.

"If you're hungry you should try the Chicken La Burano," he said. "It's a house specialty here and very good."

She smiled and shook her head. "No, I'm not hungry thanks. Don't eat much anyway, comes with the condition." She laughed lightly to hide her embarrassment.

"Sorry?" he said. "What condition is that, if you don't mind me asking."

Was he being funny, or just stupid? She could not believe her ears. What the hell? She pointed at her stomach. "I'm pregnant," she mouthed. "Hadn't you noticed?"

"Oh, I'm sorry." He grinned, returning her look with those oh so blue eyes. "I'm blind. I thought you would have guessed."

It was fortunate, she thought later that he could not see her face. The shock of surprise, her open mouth, her annoyance at not having noticed.

"No," she managed to stutter. "You'd never know, really." How stupid did she sound?

His smile widened and she realised he was fully aware of what she was experiencing and was amused at her discomfort. She began to like this stranger.

He shared her own sense of humour. Leaning forward she rested her folded arms on the table. "Are you having a good time at my expense?"

He laughed out loud and nodded companionably. His denim shirt sleeves were rolled up above his elbows and she noticed the little black hairs that curled against his tanned muscles.

"So," he began. "How far along are you if you don't mind my asking? Any names yet? Is it you or your husband that gets to choose?"

She gave a small chuckle. "Four, nearly five months, and no names yet, and no husband either, sorry."

"Oh, I see." She could see now that it was his turn to be embarrassed. "Sorry if I'm being nosey. None of my business after all."

She leaned back in her chair again and took a sip of the delicious coffee. "No need to apologise. I don't mind at all. He, the father that is, didn't do anything wrong. I only knew him for a relatively short while; he was a good man, but it wasn't possible to take things further." That was all she was going to say. After all, it was no one's business but hers.

"He was...*is* a nice man," she continued, "but it's just one of those things that life throws at us. We just have to get on with it, don't we?" This was a long speech for Helen, especially when spoken in a rush to a complete stranger. Perhaps it was something she could say only to a stranger. With the increased perception that people with disabilities oftentimes display, he realized that she must have spoken these words to herself many times. It was some sort of litany. A comfort. She sounded nice, he thought.

CHAPTER THIRTEEN EPILOGUE

He nodded. "So why the holiday? Last time before you are tied down?"

"No," she laughed. "Nothing like that. One of my greatest friends, my surrogate mom, really thought it would be a good idea for me to get away for a few days and she cajoled my actual mom and dad into booking it and paying for it."

He grinned again and gave a low deep throated laugh that rumbled. "Very nice indeed, and why Venice?"

"I've always wanted to come here. I did archaeology at university, and I'm interested in all things historical. There's so much history here it was an obvious choice."

He looked suddenly attentive. "You're kidding me. History? Really?"

"Yes. Why?"

"Before I lost my sight–" he looked away obviously calculating something– "ten years ago now, I was a history teacher, local grammar school."

She just did not know what to say. This sounded like an improbable plot from a cheap romantic novel. Was he playing with her? She peered at him, watching for any sign of insincerity, of some kind of humour, but there was nothing. He meant it. How had he lost his sight? It could be any number of things; now was not the time to ask. 'Well, if not now than when, girl?' a little voice inside her said. She resisted and they moved on to talk of other things. He was easy to talk to, this stranger, and she needed the company. Needed the conversation with another person, anyone. She found the talk cathartic, soothing in the way nothing had since the departure of David. They both ordered more coffee and later still a third. Their conversation, easy, and uncomplicated covered a multitude of subjects and she found that he was genuinely interested in what she had to say. Much later she noticed with amazement that the shadows were lengthening, and the short autumn day was beginning to lose its light.

"I'm sorry," she said, "but I must be going." She pulled on her cardigan which had earlier been draped across the back of the chair. Even in Venice the evenings became chilly. "How are you getting home?"

He waved a dismissive hand. "My sister will be here to fetch me shortly. She has to wait for her husband to get home and take the kids. I hate being a burden to them, hate it, but they insisted I came." There was real sadness in his voice, and she realised what a tragedy losing his sight must have been to such a man.

He suddenly leaned forward and laid his hand on her bare arm. Strangely she did not mind.

"Look," he said. "This may be an awful cheek, I've only just met you, we don't know each other at all, but would you like to meet me here tomorrow morning and we can go on a boat ride on the ferry across the lagoon. To Murano, and Chioggia, and I can tell you the history of the place to thank you for taking me. I'll pay for the tickets of course and lunch will be my treat."

She did not say anything, nothing at all, and he hurried on, anxious for her to agree. "I can't go alone, you see, well

CHAPTER THIRTEEN EPILOGUE

not easily." His voice faltered as he waited.

A slow smile lifted the corners of her mouth and she realised with amazement that for the first time in too long she really meant what she was about to say.

"Yes," she breathed. "Yes I'd like that very much."

***

Two days later, on a typical grey November morning, Annie swathed in an old reefer jacket of Ben's and carrying a wicker basket that was full of small potted flowers and secateurs, pushed open the rickety lych gate to the small church graveyard and moved between the weathered headstones that leaned like so many drunkards.

She was glad of the wellingtons she was wearing as the long unkempt grass was wet from the light drizzle that had been falling relentlessly for some time and swished at her legs as she passed. She wished too that she had thought of wearing trousers rather than her tweed skirt, but it was too late to worry about that now.

The small squat little church built eight hundred years ago from granite squatted comfortably amongst the emerald-green rolling hills above the town like an old cat nestled amongst blankets near a fire. The lichen covered stones glistening in the dim autumn light. The main thirteenth century church that serviced the religious needs of the town was not the chosen resting place of locals. Rather, this shabby little building at the end of a small overgrown lane was preferred by generations of families born and bred here. She passed mildewed headstones naming centuries of Trelasks, and Pencarrows, and many other such notable local names. The men and women beneath them long since mouldered to dust. Their hopes and dreams, aspirations and fears all consigned to obscurity.

Despite the grey day, the persistent light rain, and her surroundings, Annie was feeling more positive than she had for some weeks. She was softly humming a little tune that only she could discern as music, but it pleased her. She felt that things were looking up a little. The last two months had been trying, and only her latent good sense and optimism had saved her from sinking into a deep despond. She and Ben had worked through times like this before, as had many old couples who have been together a long time. But she was glad that she could sense a possible end to it.

She had received a letter from David's wife Pam a few days ago thanking her profusely for intervening on their behalf with the medico who had secured her husband a good job at the local hospital. She had underlined several words to emphasize the depth of her gratitude and ended by hoping that all was well with Annie and Ben. There was also a veiled reference to the 'young woman' and hoped that she was also well. Annie had smiled grimly as she read that passage. It was obvious that Pam could not or would not write the name of the woman who had so nearly stolen her husband way for good. Well, that was all over now, thought Annie. For good or ill, everyone had made their choices.

CHAPTER THIRTEEN EPILOGUE

But what had lightened Annie's mood more was the telephone call from Helen herself that she had received only last night. Helen, her voice sounding different from the flat disinterested monotone in which she had spoken for too long now, had announced that she was enjoying Venice, finding it was rejuvenating her in mind and body, and after speaking with both the airline and her hotel to make new arrangements she was staying on for another week at least. Something had happened, that much was clear. Helen had sounded interested in life again, some positivity had returned, some echo of the old Helen. It was a start. The old lady grinned as she recalled snatches of the conversation. Helen was actively planning her future with her unborn child and looking forward to it.

Would Annie smooth over with Ben, who was a member of the town council, that she would not be back at the small museum for a few more days? Annie announced that yes of course she would.

"Call you again in a few days, Annie. Love you. Bye!" She had disappeared with a click of the connection.

A crow passed low overhead and its mournful caw brought Annie back to the present. Idly she stood and watched the bird swoop effortlessly to the branches of the large beech tree behind the church, which rustled and hissed in the rain. It was more than three months since she had been to this cemetery, and she felt guilty. Yes, she had been busy, but that was no excuse not to visit the grave of your only child, however morose such visits made you feel.

Mo's headstone was of black marble and in its immaculate condition despite the passing of ten years stood out amongst the surrounding much older edifices.

She noted that her visit was none too soon. A scattering of weeds had sprouted between the gravel that covered the small space in front of the little monument and bird droppings crowned the stone. Never mind, she had come prepared. She threw down a small waterproof cushion that she kept for this very job, and kneeling, began to work. It did not take long and presently the ground cleared, and several small freshly potted plants placed strategically, the plot looked much better. Her glance moved of its own volition up to the inscription:

> Maureen Violet Trelask.
> Beloved daughter of Annie and Ben
> Taken from us too early.
>
> *Reader pass by, there's nothing here to make you pause,*
> *What I am this enfolding clay ensures,*
> *Who I was is no concern of yours.*

As she read the old familiar lines once again Annie could not help but picture her daughter laughing her old infectious laugh, or sitting with her doting dad watching the TV, or running to her from the school gates when she was a small child. Living the million moments in time that stay fixed in every parent's mind for the whole of their lives. The inconsequential yet dear minutia of family life.

CHAPTER THIRTEEN EPILOGUE

Suddenly she felt sad again, her mood still mirrored by the day. She sighed deeply and started to replace the gloves and secateurs in the basket.

"Oh Mo," she said out loud, "I do miss you, my lover. So much."

"I know you do, Mom." The light, slightly accented voice that she remembered so well came from her right and she started and raised her head to look. Mo, dear old Mo, was sitting on the little weathered bench that nestled under the ageless yew tree. She was dressed as she always was before she died in her old jeans and a cornflower blue jumper with a ring of white daisies knitted into the neckline. She was smiling slightly, and her piecing blue eyes gazed at Annie through the gloom. She still looked the same as Annie had seen her that last day before she went to that bloody hospital for the final time. She looked calm and ageless.

Annie sat back on her haunches and smiled sadly to herself. This had happened before.

"Are you OK, Mo?" she managed, feeling despite the circumstances a little ridiculous. "Is it nice where you are?"

Mo smiled that old brilliant smile Annie remembered so well. "I'm fine, Mom, you know that. No need to worry about me."

Annie nodded and could not help her eyes filling with tears. "I know, my lover," she managed, "I know."

She straightened slowly, feeling her old bones creak as she did so and stood irresolutely in the rain, peering at her daughter. She could not move; she was rooted to the spot. If she took one step towards her, Mo would disappear, that she knew.

"Is Dad OK?" she heard Mo say. "You two have been going through a bit of a time, haven't you?"

Annie just nodded. She felt tears running down her old cheeks. "He'll do," she said. "He's a resilient old bugger, that's why I love him so. Nothing knocks him down."

Mo smiled a slow gentle smile full of compassion and sadness. "Yes," she said, "I remember. Dear old Dad. I loved you both so much, I'm so sorry I had to go and leave you both."

She was fading. Annie knew it would happen; it was ever like that. Precious moments with her daughter. She was not sure if it really was Mo come to see her or if it was just a silly old woman's imagination.

She'd watched on TV once a man explaining why he needed faith. The belief in something after death, that someone was watching over us. He'd said that when he was a little boy he would fall over and scrape his knee and run to his mother crying. His mom would rub his leg and kiss his head and say it was OK and that he would be fine. Off he would go back to play with his mates. His knee still hurt, but he could bear it now. His mom had told him it was fine and that everything would be OK. The man had said that he thought faith or religion, or whatever you wanted to call it, was someone for grown-ups to run to for reassurance.

Annie wondered if seeing or imagining Mo was her way of dealing with the world. She hoped not, she hoped it was

CHAPTER THIRTEEN EPILOGUE

real. She hoped she would somehow see Mo again someday.

Was Mo her someone to run to? She had no idea, but she loved these little exchanges. Brief moments of hope in a cold world. She shivered and drew the reefer coat more tightly around herself. The bench under the yew tree was quite empty now, perhaps it always had been.

"Who are you talking to, girl?"

She had not heard Ben come up behind her. He had told her that he had something to attend to on Esme, but would meet her here; she'd forgotten.

She turned and gave him a brief half-smile. "No one," she said "just talking to myself. I must be going doolally in my old age."

He looked down at her, this woman with whom he had spent his life, and he acknowledged that he still loved her with a passion. He smiled at the old saying that he knew she had inherited from her own mother and gently he reached out and took her basket from her.

"Have you finished with Mo's grave?" He peered down through the drizzle at the headstone. He was still unable to stay here for long, it was too upsetting even after all of this time.

"Yes." She leaned into his big rangy frame and gently patted his back. "Let's go and get a cup of tea. I suddenly feel a lot better as if everything is going to be fine."

He gave a small laugh.

"Of course it will be, girl. You know that." He glanced down once more at his daughter's grave and turned away. "We always come through it, don't we. We always have throughout the whole of our lives. Whatever life has thrown at us, we carry on. We have to. There isn't anything else to do, is there?"

She looked up into his craggy lined face and laughed out loud. "Yes, we always have, my lover. We always have."

Arm in arm they began to move toward the lych gate. "Now let's get that cuppa," said Annie.

The End